"Shouldn[...]
out of the jungle[?]

"What makes you think I'm not?" he asked
sarcastically. "I'm in a nice, clean hospital room
with no bugs and no germs, and I'm tied to this
traction stuff like a picnic ham waiting to be
smoked. Of course I'm glad!"

"You know, I'm not stupid. You want to go back
there, don't you?"

"I *have* to go back."

"I don't suppose there's any point in asking why." He
gave her a cold glance, and Mickie let it drop. "You
were a prisoner for a long time," she said after a
moment. "Was there anything you really missed,
anything you wanted?"

There was a taut moment of silence. "Of course
there was. I wanted a woman. Interested in
volunteering?"

Mickie felt her heart begin to pound. If what he
wanted were not just "a woman" but "this woman,"
if it were she…

Dear Reader,

When two people fall in love, the world is suddenly new and exciting, and it's that same excitement we bring to you in Silhouette Intimate Moments. These are stories with scope, with grandeur. These characters lead the lives we all dream of, and everything they do reflects the wonder of being in love.

Longer and more sensuous than most romances, Silhouette Intimate Moments novels take you away from everyday life and let you share the magic of love. Adventure, glamour, drama, even suspense— these are the passwords that let you into a world where love has a power beyond the ordinary, where the best authors in the field today create stories of love and commitment that will stay with you always.

In coming months look for novels by your favorite authors: Maura Seger, Parris Afton Bonds, Elizabeth Lowell and Erin St. Claire, to name just a few. And whenever you buy books, look for all the Silhouette Intimate Moments, love stories *for* today's women *by* today's women.

Leslie J. Wainger
Senior Editor
Silhouette Books

IMRL-7/85

Agent Provocateur

Lucy Hamilton

Silhouette Intimate Moments

Published by Silhouette Books New York

America's Publisher of Contemporary Romance

SILHOUETTE BOOKS
300 E. 42nd St., New York, N.Y. 10017

Copyright © 1986 by Julie Rhyne

Distributed by Pocket Books

ISBN: 0-373-07126-4

First Silhouette Books printing January 1986

10 9 8 7 6 5 4 3 2 1

America's Publisher of Contemporary Romance

Printed in the U.S.A.

Silhouette Books by Lucy Hamilton

Silhouette Special Edition

A Woman's Place #18
All's Fair #92
Shooting Star #172
The Bitter With the Sweet #206

Silhouette Intimate Moments

Agent Provocateur #126

LUCY HAMILTON

is happily married and the mother of a young daughter. She writes in her spare time and, she says, she looks forward to "translating a lifelong affection for books into a career."

Chapter 1

Michael Frances Blake, M.D., age thirty, board-certified orthopedic surgeon and lifelong resident of San Diego county, is sitting in a fancy hotel, at a fancy dinner, dying of boredom.

Mickie sighed. She could continue to recite her résumé, but she didn't think it would do any more to keep her awake than this abominably dull speech. Maybe she should start on vital statistics. *Height: five feet, seven inches. Weight: never quite enough. Hair: coppery red, short and curly. Eyes: cinnamon-brown...* No, that was as boring as the speech she was supposed to be listening to.

She glanced around the hotel ballroom. It was a huge room, now filled with tables for the banquet and speeches, but the tables would be removed to allow for dancing later in the evening. A full crowd was in attendance for the Stockbrokers' Association's annual gala dinner. They had dined on a meal of Beef Wellington with vegetables, followed by a very sweet chocolate mousse and rather weak coffee.

Mickie had toyed with the stupefyingly heavy meal, made numbingly polite conversation and tried to pay attention to the speeches, but she was nearing the end of her rope. Surely there was someone else in the room as bored as she? She risked another survey of the faces around her. It was amazing—she could barely stay awake, and everyone else was entranced.

She shifted restlessly in her seat. Beside her, Jonathan Caldwell, Jr., turned and frowned at her, annoyed by her fidgeting. The beading sprinkled across the bodice of Mickie's one-shouldered gown glittered as she shrugged her apology.

Jon's gaze moved over her bare shoulder and the hint of cleavage her dress revealed, and the censorious scowl softened into something approaching a leer. As he followed the movement of the shrug, his slightly blurred gaze traced the curve of her breasts beneath the black silk jersey. His face, ruddy by nature, was flushed scarlet from the martinis, wine and brandy he'd consumed during the course of the evening. He looked again, at her legs this time, and Mickie sighed, pulling the front slit of the narrow, ankle-length skirt closed over her knees.

Pointedly Mickie directed her attention to the speaker, who just happened to be Jon's boss at the brokerage. To her relief he did likewise.

This evening was turning out to be a disaster, even worse than she'd anticipated. The awards program was as dull as she'd feared, and all the alcohol Jon had consumed was having an unfortunate effect on him. Normally conventional, almost stiff, he had first become garrulous, then annoyingly amorous. Mickie was growing very tired of repeating that, no, she was not going home with him tonight. They were casual friends, little more than acquaintances. Mickie had no intention of taking their "relationship" any further than that.

She had an idea that even the superficial friendship they shared might not survive this night. They had met at a ten-

nis club and dated sporadically during the last three months.
Jon had been an entertaining companion at first, but lately
he had begun to make pointed remarks about the duties and
demeanor of a stockbroker's wife. He remained stubbornly
deaf to Mickie's assurances that she had no intention of ever
being any such thing.

He had also begun to show a peevish side, complaining
when her schedule at the hospital interfered with his social
plans. She wondered with some amusement what he really
expected of her. Did he actually expect that she would have
completed college, medical school, internship and residency training, only to throw all her diplomas and certifi-
cates and licenses away in an attempt to become his
conception of a quiet, submissive, terribly refined stockbroker's wife?

When pigs fly.

Mickie sighed again. She had realized well over an hour
ago that it had been a mistake to let Jon nag her into coming to this banquet. She was getting awfully tired of his
pushy attitude. She was also getting awfully tired of trying
to sit quietly like a proper little lady, with her hands folded
demurely in her lap, while she listened to Jon's boss dis-
coursing endlessly on the intricacies of mutual funds.

Mickie freely admitted that she had no idea what mutual
funds actually were. This speech hadn't clarified things for
her. After careful consideration, though, she had decided
that the short, plump man on stage, with his tight tuxedo
and his thinning hair combed carefully over a shining bald
pate, bore a remarkable resemblance to a penguin. Mickie
hid a yawn in her coffee cup and focused a blank smile on
the mutual funds penguin. Did he waddle when he walked?
She had to stifle a giggle.

Ten minutes later, when she had begun to worry that she
might actually keel over onto the heavy linen tablecloth from
sheer boredom, she was suddenly reprieved by a piercing
"beep-beep-beep" from her evening bag. The sound was
sweet music to Mickie's ears, but it brought Jon sharply

around in his seat, a scowl on his handsome, high-colored face.

"Damn it, Mick!" he snapped under his breath. "Why did you bring that thing?"

Mickie pressed the switch that silenced the pager and snapped her jet-beaded bag closed. "I'm on call tonight," she reminded him quietly. "I'm sorry to spoil your evening, but I have to find a phone."

She slid her chair back and began to rise. Jon caught her hand, holding her there. "Can't you at least wait until my award is presented, Mick?"

"I have to call the hospital, Jon," Mickie said softly, but very firmly. "Now." She freed her hand from his grasp and straightened. "If they don't need me to come in, I promise I'll be right back. In case I have to leave, though, I'll say goodnight now. Have a nice evening, Jon, and congratulations on your award."

She patted his hand and left him with a little wave and a smile that held more than a trace of relief. Head high, face impassive, she threaded her way between the crowded tables, oblivious to the glances that followed her. The bright light from the stage glowed on her short, copper-penny curls and glittered on the jet beads sprinkled over the bodice and the single long sleeve of her gown. She made a striking figure, tall and slender and dramatically dressed, moving with an unconsciously elegant grace through the room, but she wasn't really aware that people watched her. She certainly didn't expect it.

Mickie knew, better than anyone else, that not even the kindest observer would call her beautiful. There was a quicksilver energy in the heart-shaped face that just missed classic beauty, a gamine prettiness born of the combination of a narrow chin and a broad forehead, of large cinnamon eyes framed by thick lashes and dark brown brows that lifted with wry expressiveness when she was amused. Her mouth was too wide, she knew, and her cheekbones were high, but marred by a sprinkling of freckles. She considered her appearance about as far as one could get from sloe-eyed, sultry beauty.

No, she wasn't beautiful. Mickie was well aware of that. The best she could be labeled was cute, an obnoxious appellation to attach to someone who was thirty years old. When Mickie looked in her mirror she saw her individual features, but she failed to see the animation, the sparkle of life and interest and humor, which gave her something more compelling and attractive than simple surface beauty.

She slipped out of the ballroom at last, eased the ornate mahogany door closed behind her and heaved a heartfelt sigh of relief. Whether she was needed at the hospital or not, she wasn't going back in there! If she returned she'd either disgrace herself by dumping her coffee over Jon's head to dampen his alcoholic ardor, or she'd scream out loud from sheer boredom before the evening was over.

"No more stockbrokers' banquets for you, my girl," she muttered. "One is definitely enough!"

She was spared the need to wrestle with an ethical dilemma, though. Her presence was indeed required at the hospital, and she was needed, she was informed, "Stat!"

Traffic was light at that hour of the evening, and she drove her dusty red Jeep through the city of San Diego too fast. Not many minutes passed before she careened off the street into a driveway, past a sign that read "Doctors' Parking, San Diego Metropolitan Hospital" and swung into a parking stall, braking with a squeal of protest from her tires. She had been shifting mental gears in much the way she had shifted the Jeep's gears, and she was no longer Jon's reluctant date. Despite her evening gown and spiky sandals, the woman who hurried into the hospital was Dr. Michael Blake, an orthopedic surgeon with a patient to treat.

An unusual patient, she had surmised from the little she had been told. The charge nurse on the orthopedic floor hadn't been able to give her much information, but the little she'd been told was intriguing. Mickie knew the patient was a male in his thirties, that he had a fractured femur as a result of a gunshot wound several days old, and that he had been brought to the hospital by Naval ambulance. She didn't know why his wound hadn't been treated more promptly, nor did she know why the Navy had seen fit to bring him to San Diego Metro instead of the Naval hospital downtown.

Mickie strode through the automatic doors of the emergency entrance. The first greeting she received as she walked into the hospital was a long, low, wolf whistle. She grinned and waved at the perpetrator, an ancient gentleman operating a huge floor polisher.

"Thank you, Henry!" she called to him, and he bowed graciously over the handles of his machine.

Mickie knew perfectly well that an evening dress was not your everyday orthopedic surgeon's garb, but she hadn't stopped to think about just how much attention it would attract. It attracted a lot.

Ambulance drivers stared, nurses whispered behind their hands, orderlies wolf-whistled and called compliments, and a smitten intern, riding up in the elevator with her, kissed her hand and offered her a courtly proposal of marriage. She thanked him politely, regretfully declined, and escaped the elevator on the fifth floor.

"Hi, Connie." Mickie breezed into the head nurse's office with a smile and a cheerful greeting. "You're here late tonight, aren't you? Where's my patient with the bullet wound?"

"Hi, Mickie." Consuelo Ramirez's glossy black head was bent over a chart on the desk in front of her. "I know it's late, but I'm doing my monthly rotation on all the shifts. Your patient's in room 557, but—" She looked up and her jaw dropped. "Good grief, look at you!"

"Everyone in this hospital already has." Mickie tossed her beaded bag onto the desk. "Hector Delgado proposed to me."

Connie's dark eyes widened along with her grin. She got up and took Mickie's arm to turn her in a slow circle, examining every detail of the dress, the shoes, the makeup, the small diamond combs tucked into her hair.

"So Hector proposed, did he?" Mickie nodded. "Well, I can see what prompted him to take the plunge. He's had a crush on you ever since his Ortho rotation, and that was when he only saw you in greens! Have the two of you set the date?"

"I declined," Mickie told her dryly.

"Well, I hope you were gentle with the poor boy." Connie's grin was wicked. The suave and diminutive Hector had a well-established reputation as a lady-killer.

"He'll get over it." Mickie sat down in the office's one extra chair, crossing her legs. Connie raised an eloquent eyebrow as the slit skirt fell away from Mickie's knees, exposing a considerable length of leg. With a long-suffering sigh Mickie pulled the skirt closed. "I would have gone home to change into something a little more appropriate, but you did tell me to hurry right over here. Now what's all the mystery about this patient, anyway?"

"Exactly that—a mystery. We weren't told in advance that he was coming or anything. A military ambulance just drove up, they rolled him in, and the guy who's with him—who's wearing civvies, but says he's Navy—refuses to give the history to anyone but 'the doctor in charge.' He's uncooperative, to say the least. I told you everything that he told me: The patient—his name is Mark James, by the way—has a fractured femur secondary to a gunshot wound that occurred several days to a week ago. He didn't know exactly when."

"Did he say how Mr. James got the bullet wound?"

"Nope." Connie shook her head for emphasis. "He wouldn't say any more than that. Just kept insisting that he wouldn't talk to anyone but the doctor. The patient is in rough shape, though. He's debilitated and terribly thin. It looks like malnutrition, and maybe some tropical bugs, too."

"But this Navy person wouldn't say anything about that?"

"Not a word."

"Let's go see what he'll tell 'the doctor in charge,' then, shall we?"

They had no difficulty locating the "Navy person." He was standing in the middle of the corridor outside the patient's door, engaged in a noisy argument with the orthopedic resident on call that night. Stan Adams, the resident, was demanding to know how the bullet wound had occurred, and a short, stocky man whom Mickie didn't recognize was demanding to be allowed to talk to the doctor in charge.

"I'm not talking to you or any of the other flunkies around here!" he insisted in a loud, gravelly rumble. "I said I'm only talking to the doctor, and I'm gonna wait 'til he gets here!"

The man had the air of a pugnacious bulldog. An inch or so shorter than Mickie's five feet seven, he was powerfully built, and dressed, as Connie had said, in civilian clothes, rumpled from wear. His hair was iron-gray and cut very short, his face leathery and tanned. Lines of fatigue and bad temper scored his cheeks and brow, but he showed none of the anxiety Mickie had come to expect of a worried relative. His eyes were a watery blue. Cold and blank, they revealed nothing of his thoughts.

"You don't have to wait any longer." Mickie spoke from just behind him. He spun around and scowled at her. "I'm Dr. Blake, and I will be in charge of your—your associate. Or are you a family member? We'll need that information for the consent forms."

He didn't answer immediately, but looked her up and down in a slow, incredulous examination that missed no detail of her face, figure, dress and jewelry. His thoughts were regrettably easy to read. He assessed what he saw and dismissed her out-of-hand as too young, too dressed up and the wrong sex.

"Like I told them, I'm not talking to anyone but the doctor, lady. That's it."

"No, *I'm*, it," Mickie said coolly. "And it's not 'lady,' it's Dr. Blake. I'm the orthopedic surgeon who will be treating Mr. James, and I need some information from you."

His response was a fishy stare.

She sighed, exasperated. "You don't have to talk to me at all, you know, but if you want him to recover as quickly as possible, I'd advise you to cooperate."

He fixed her with another cold stare, which she returned without flinching. It was some kind of test, she knew, and she also knew she'd won when, after a long moment, he nodded. "Okay," he grunted at last. "Where can we talk?"

The staff lounge was comparatively private, and for a change it was unoccupied. Mickie seated herself behind a battered steel desk while the stocky man took the chair she indicated. She opened Mark James's chart and uncapped a pen.

"Can we begin with your name, Mister...?"

"Lewis. Commander Wilson Lewis."

She scribbled quickly on the chart. "Branch of the service?"

"Navy."

"And your relationship with Mr. James?"

"No relation."

Mickie read quickly through the list of questions regarding vital statistics. She learned that her patient's age was thirty-six, that he was six feet two inches tall, with black hair and brown eyes, that he had no known allergies and that his medical history was not remarkable. She did not learn his permanent address, or his next of kin. Commander Lewis's response to questions he declined to answer was a bland, "I couldn't say, ma'am."

"Can you tell me anything about Mr. James's condition and how he was injured?" she asked. If the man's injuries were a matter of national security, as Lewis's selective reticence suggested, this question seemed more sensitive than a request for an address. Mickie fully expected another evasion, but to her surprise Lewis answered without hesitation.

Mark James, she learned as she listened in growing shock, had been held prisoner for over a year by insurgent guerrillas in Central America. What his treatment at the hands of the guerrillas had been, Lewis either didn't know or wouldn't say, but Mr. James was suffering from malnutrition and possibly one or more tropical diseases.

He had escaped from the guerrilla encampment about a week ago, and had been shot in the leg as he fled. Despite his debilitated condition, a broken leg and a fever high enough to render him delirious much of the time, he had made his way through thirty miles of dense jungle to reach the coast, where he had been discovered by a local militia patrol. They had taken him to the American consulate, and he had been put aboard a US naval vessel on its way to San Diego.

"That was two days ago," Lewis concluded. "The ship's doctor did what he could to patch him up, but he said the leg needs an orthopedic surgeon." He inspected her suspiciously from beneath bushy, steel-colored eyebrows. "That's what you are?"

"That's what I am." Mickie had heard that question so many times that it no longer ruffled her feathers. She scanned the chart. "You didn't tell me what your relationship with Mr. James is."

"Like I said, no relation." Lewis's smile came easily, but it didn't reach his chilly blue eyes. They were opaque and unreadable, belying the cordiality of his smile. "I'm just acting on behalf of the government. Taking care of a US citizen, you know?"

"Um-hm." She noted that on the chart. "And you said he has no relatives we can contact?" She couldn't believe the man had no one. Even she, who had neither parents nor siblings, had distant cousins in other states.

Lewis shook his head and bared his teeth in another empty smile. "No relatives. I can sign whatever forms you've got."

"Okay. Start here." She handed him the chart and a consent to treatment form. "Sign at the 'X,' and then on the bottom, there." He grunted his assent, signed, and passed the chart back to her.

Mickie rose to take it, then moved across the room. She pushed the door open and paused before she left him, hoping to catch the commander off guard. "What was Mr. James doing in San Miguel, anyway? Why did the guerrillas hold him so long?"

"I couldn't say, ma'am." His face was set and closed, his cooperation at an end.

So she had once again ventured onto what the government considered sensitive ground. Mickie couldn't decide whether to be annoyed with the man for stonewalling her this way, or simply to be glad for the information he had given her. She had to wonder why there was a need for such secrecy, though. She was hardly likely to betray her country to an enemy agent. After a moment Mickie shrugged and walked from the room. The "whys" of this puzzling situation could wait; her patient could not.

"Hi, Stan," she said as she entered Mr. James's room. "How's our patient?"

Stan Adams had admitted Mark James to the hospital and had made the decision to call Mickie in on the case. She had completed her residency at San Diego Metro two years ago and, since she had established a private orthopedic practice in the city, she treated most of her private patients here.

A lanky, thin-faced, serious man, Stan was a few years younger than Mickie but looked older. He glanced over his shoulder as she entered, pushing the frizzy blond hair off his forehead. "He's in pretty rough shape, Mickie, but he may be coming around." His gaze slid past her and he scowled. Mickie looked around to see that Commander Lewis had followed her into the room.

"You'll have to leave, Commander."

"I'd like to stay." He began to protest, but she shook her head. If he wasn't going to be cooperative, then neither was she. He had no place in here.

"I can't allow that." Her reply was firm and flat. "If you want to wait, you can use the families' lounge. It's down the hall. Janet, you'll show him, won't you?"

The nursing assistant nodded and moved to shepherd Lewis from the room. "Come with me, Commander." Given no choice, he went reluctantly, looking back over his shoulder at the unconscious man lying on the bed.

Mickie closed the door behind him with a sharp jerk. "If he knows what's good for him, he'll stay out there."

Stan gave a smothered snort of laughter, and they turned to their patient.

He was, as Connie had said, very thin. He was also, despite the underlying pallor of illness, very darkly tanned, his skin burned by the tropical sun. His hair was jet-black and roughly cut, thick and wavy and crisp, with a spattering of white at the temples. His face was hard, with high cheekbones and a straight nose, complemented by a strong jawline. There was a sensual curve to his lips, and a hint of a cleft in the square chin. Black brows winged up at the outer ends over his eyes, which were still closed, his thick black lashes lying in a curve on his lean cheeks.

His wasn't a handsome face, Mickie thought, studying him. It would probably never be a handsome face, even when he had regained his weight and the drawn look of illness was gone. It was too hard to be handsome in the smooth, conventional mold of Jon's face. It was a more interesting face than Jon's, though. Stronger, with a masculinity that overrode the traditional standards of male beauty. She liked this face, Mickie decided. She wondered if she'd like the man behind it.

It would take some time to erase the marks of his suffering. The lines in his face were lines of pain and struggle, testimony to the cost of his long imprisonment and his escape. Mickie knew she had led a sheltered life; she found it difficult to comprehend the strength and determination and courage required for his trek through the jungle on a broken leg.

Mickie reached out to touch Mark James's face. She meant only to lift his eyelid and check his level of consciousness, but without deliberate intent her fingers moved to brush a wayward lock of hair off his forehead. The briskly clinical gesture became something gentle, almost tender, as she smoothed back his hair, finding it soft and thick beneath her hand. She traced her fingertips in a little caress down the hard line of his cheek, scored by a deep groove of pain. His skin was smooth; they must have shaved him on the ship. It was dry and warm, as well, much too warm. Though he was receiving medication, his fever was still too high. He would feel very ill. She smoothed her thumb over his lips, dry and cracked from fever.

"So much suffering," she breathed, unaware she'd spoken the words aloud.

"What?"

Mickie glanced up to see Stan looking at her very strangely. She pulled herself together with an effort. "I'm sorry, Stan, I was just mumbling. He's been through a lot, hasn't he?"

"More than most of us can imagine."

"Mm-hm." Mickie gently raised his eyelid, then lowered it again. "He's still unconscious. What's been done for his leg?"

Stan lifted the sheet away. "They dressed it on the ship and put on a transfer splint. They didn't try to do any more than that."

Mickie barely heard him speak. No one had bothered to tell her that they hadn't dressed Mr. James. His entire body was tanned as deeply as his face, and dusted with dark hair. The flat planes and curving lines of muscle were defined and emphasized by his thinness into a textbook model of the masculine form. She felt her breath catch in her throat as her gaze slid over his broad chest and flat stomach, past his narrow waist, then flicked skittishly over his loins and down to long, strong legs and a thick, bloodstained bandage which bound the injured thigh.

The wound was a desecration of such beauty, the white gauze stark and shocking against his skin. For a long moment she could only stare; then Stan moved forward beside her, saying something she didn't catch, breaking the spell. She shook her head, deliberately regaining her control.

"I'm sorry, Stan. What did you say?"

"I said I know the dressing needs to be changed, but I wanted to wait until you got here." Stan was frowning at her, and Mickie felt herself blushing. Poor Stan couldn't understand her strange behavior any more than she could.

Mickie twitched the sheet over Mark James's body again, baring only his injured leg, cursing herself for her stupid susceptibility. What was wrong with her? She was a doctor, a physician who had seen hundreds, maybe thousands, of men's bodies in the last ten years. And yet, tall or short, fat or thin, muscular or out of shape, none of her patients had ever prompted the almost physical jolt that this man, unconscious and unaware, had given her.

She didn't know what there was about him that affected her so powerfully. Perhaps it was his face, perhaps his body, or the bizarre circumstances which has brought him here.

It certainly isn't his personality, she thought with wry self-mockery. She couldn't tell very much about that so long as he was unconscious.

Perhaps it was nothing more than the late hour and her own fatigue. Or perhaps it was the contrast between this man, dark and hard and battered, and the blond, immaculate and slightly soft perfection of Jonathan Caldwell.

And maybe her imagination and hormones were getting the better of her.

"Pull up the dressing cart, Stan. We'll see just what we're dealing with here." She took bandage scissors from a tray atop the cart and carefully began to cut the soiled dressing away.

Chapter 2

He was drowning.

He was trapped at the center of a murky, choking whirl-pool that pulled at him, dragging him down. He fought it violently, struggling with all his strength toward the distant, unseen surface. Black water enveloped him, surrounded him, disoriented him until he couldn't even be certain where the surface lay, yet he could sense something, or someone, outside it. They were reaching for him, calling to him. He fought with everything he had, convulsively, reaching for the light and the air.

It was too much, though, too far. He couldn't get there, not quite. He could hear voices, sometimes clear, sometimes dimmed and garbled by distance. If he could only open his eyes, maybe he'd recognize his surroundings or the people who were speaking, maybe he'd recognize *something*. He tried, but his eyelids were too heavy to lift.

"He's still pretty far under."

Not that far under. He wanted to correct the unseen speaker, but he couldn't seem to utter the words. He could feel crisp linens and cool hands against his body, yet he could not move.

"...fracture's a mess," a woman's quiet voice said, "but at least the bullet's out."

"It did plenty of damage before it left, though." That was the first voice he'd heard, deeper, a man's voice.

"It didn't exit on its own."

He felt pressure against his leg. The pain that had been his constant companion was absent, leaving in its place a strange numbness. He was glad the pain was gone, but he was conditioned to wariness. He fought his own weakness as he struggled to concentrate. He had to think, needed to identify this man and woman, to determine whether they were friends or enemies. He needed to understand why he could hear them but couldn't see them. His weary brain refused to cooperate, and he let the effort go. It didn't matter. These were probably just more hallucinations, anyway, more of the persistent spectral voices of his delirium.

"See?" the female voice continued. "Right here. There is no exit wound. Someone cut that bullet out. He may have done it himself."

"Cut the bullet out himself? My God, that's..."

Cut the bullet out...

His exhausted brain retreated from a memory it refused to confront, and he slipped beneath the surface again.

Mickie drew the sheet carefully over Mark James's re-bandaged leg. Her professional detachment had been at least partly recaptured, but it was a fragile thing, and she wasn't yet ready to test it. She stepped away from the bed, shaking her head.

"He's gone again. I thought he was getting close to consciousness for a moment." She turned to the nurse who had joined them. "I want to continue the antibiotics they started on the ship, and I'll schedule him for surgery tomorrow morning. Would you see if there's an operating room free? I'd like to start early, because this may take a while."

"I'll check the schedule right away." The nurse was writing quickly on the patient's chart.

"I'd appreciate it. Thanks. Now, let's get him to Radiology, so we can see just what kind of problem we're dealing with."

Mark James didn't return to semiconsciousness, but remained quiescent and unaware while his X rays were taken and he was returned to his room in the care of the nursing staff. Mickie and Stan left him there and repaired to the ward office, where they clipped his films to the view box.

Mickie leaned close to study the record of his injuries. His leg was the worst, of course. The fracture of his femur was a bad one, but there were other injuries, as well, both old and new.

"There's a recent bullet wound to the soft tissue of the left deltoid," Mickie muttered as Stan scribbled on the chart. "In the lower lateral area a bullet entered and exited, but there's no damage to the bone. Multiple minor contusions and lacerations of the limbs and trunk. Badly healed fracture of the left distal radius, and a badly healed crush injury to the metacarpals of the right hand. The hand will need therapy, possibly surgery."

"No kidding." Stan squinted at the image on the film. "I'd be surprised if he can use it at all, the way it is. I've never seen an injury quite like that. How do you suppose it happened?"

"Look at the way the metacarpals and the knuckles were crushed." Mickie pointed to the film, keeping her voice level with an effort. "I hate to even say this, but it was probably torture. You can see that the injury is about as wide as a man's boot heel."

Stan sucked in a shocked breath, and Mickie had to clench her teeth against a wave of nausea. Her years of practicing medicine had inured her to many things, but not to this kind of deliberate viciousness.

She jerked the films off the view box and dropped them back into their large envelope. She'd study them carefully and at length before she operated on Mark James, but at the moment she felt better with them out of sight.

She sighed, running a hand through her hair and dislodging one of the diamond combs that held her curls off her face. She looked with surprise at the little bauble glittering in her palm, as if uncertain where it had come from. She jammed it haphazardly back into her hair with complete indifference to both the aesthetics of hairstyling and the value of the comb.

"Well, I guess we know what we have to do, Stan. Let's go see if we can wake Mr. James up and give him the news."

This time his return to consciousness was abrupt, complete and prompted by that female voice.

"Mr. James?" she was saying, her voice quiet, but firmly insistent. "Mark? Mark James? Can you hear me, Mark?" Cool fingers took his wrist and pressed firmly on the pulse point there. "Mark? Mark James? Can you hear me, Mark?"

His eyes still closed, he frowned. Who the hell was Mark James? Was there someone else in the room with him? He swam another degree closer to consciousness, and the memories began to return.

Mark James. Oh, yeah, *he* was Mark James. Silly damned games. Cloak and dagger. Silly name.

She repeated it yet again. Though she spoke quietly, even the soft sound of her voice was enough to make his head hurt. He'd better answer her, he realized, because she was evidently going to keep yammering at him until he did. Mark tried to look at her, vaguely surprised by the exertion required to lift his lids.

With a concerted effort he managed to open his eyes a fraction. The dim light of the room stabbed at him, sending hot waves of pain lancing through his skull. He squeezed his eyes shut and waited for the agony to subside. When he tried again, he forced himself through the pain, waited it out and managed to bring his immediate surroundings into a blurry focus.

"You're in the hospital, Mr. James," the woman said. She was speaking American English without an accent. "I'm your doctor, and you are going to be all right. You're in the hospital."

He could see that. He lay on a narrow, uncomfortable bed, with shiny steel safety rails on either side of him. The room smelled clean. People—a small mob of them, it seemed to him—stood around the bed, watching him. If he was indeed in a hospital, that made sense.

He blinked carefully at the faces hovering over him, seeking to sort them out, trying to identify the woman with the low, gentle voice. With some concentration he managed to resolve the mob into four individuals. There were two men and a woman, all dressed in green hospital clothing, and a second woman, wearing...

Mark closed his eyes again, unwilling to trust the message they had given him. He must be sicker than he thought. He was now hallucinating women in evening dresses in a hospital. Lately he had seen a lot of things that weren't really there, but this was bizarre, even for an hallucination.

He took a slow, careful breath and looked again. The woman was still there, and she was still wearing something black and glittery and one-shouldered. He'd been in the jungle a long time, he reminded himself, and he was in bad shape. That must be it.

"Mr. James?" The woman in the hallucinatory evening gown spoke again. Mark decided to ignore the phantom dress and struggled to focus on her face. It was a pretty face, concerned and compassionate beneath a froth of red curls. "Can you hear me?" Her voice was soft and firm. "Can you hear me, Mr. James? I'm your doctor."

"Yes," he replied, and was mildly surprised when no sound passed his stiff lips. He drew a painful breath. "Yes." It was a cracked whisper, but it was audible.

She smiled in satisfaction. "Good. I'm glad you're with us again. You are back in the United States, in San Diego, California. This is San Diego Metropolitan Hospital. You have a badly broken leg, as well as some other injuries, but those are mostly minor. I'm Dr. Blake, and I'm going to fix your leg tomorrow morning. Do you understand all this?"

"Yes," he whispered, struggling to absorb the information.

"Are you in pain?"

"No." That was an obvious lie, but she let it pass.

"Is there anyone you would like us to contact for you? Any family or friends?"

He almost laughed at that. Mark James had no family, no friends. "No," he whispered. "No one."

"All right. We're going to give you some medication to make you more comfortable and help you rest tonight. I'll see you again in the morning, before surgery. Do you have any questions?"

"Doc?" The word was a hoarse whisper.

"Yes?"

"What day?"

"Oh. It's Saturday, the fifteenth. Saturday night."

His reply to that was a terse epithet; then his eyes fell closed and he slipped away, back into the dark comfort of unconsciousness.

It was after two in the morning when Mickie finally braked her Jeep to a stop in front of her house, a sprawling, eighty-year-old adobe several miles outside the little town of Poway. She killed the engine and left the vehicle standing in the portico, too tired to drive around behind the house and park in the garage. She'd just have to get it back out again at six-thirty, so what was the point?

The night air was cold in the desert northeast of San Diego, raising goosebumps on Mickie's one bare arm. She hurried to turn her key in the recalcitrant front-door lock and shoulder the massive slab of oak open so she could slip inside. One dim light illuminated the tile-floored entry hall, and she paused to ease off her narrow-heeled sandals.

The cool tiles were as soothing to her tired feet as the quiet darkness was to her tired brain. It was a relief just to be alone.

Almost alone. There was a soft snuffling from the direction of the kitchen, and a huge, jet-black Labrador retriever padded around the corner, yawning groggily. "Hi, Sam." Mickie stroked the broad head, and the dog whined a greeting, his tail beating the air. She picked up her shoes and followed him back to the kitchen.

Her house was large, too large for one person, really, but it was the only home she had ever known. Even after her parents had been killed in an air accident, she had never considered living anywhere else. Built in the Mission style, the house had a cream-painted adobe exterior and was roofed in red Mexican tile. Its U-shaped plan enclosed a lushly landscaped courtyard, the eaves of the house forming a shaded gallery around a brick-paved patio. Flowering trees and shrubs of all kinds were planted in huge terra-cotta tubs that Mickie's grandmother had brought from Mexico. Beyond the two wings of the house, between the patio and a small orange grove, was a swimming pool Mickie's father had built.

The interior had the same southwest flavor, though Mickie's mother had wisely resisted a decor of heavy wood and dark velvet in favor of light colors and comfortable furnishings. The kitchen was spacious, with red tile for the floor and countertops, a big oak table in the center of the room, and copper pots and strings of dried peppers hanging from the ceiling beams. It was traditional, but with a difference. Arranged around the room was an impressive array of kitchen gadgets, at least one of every type available, from a commercial-quality electric mixer, to a food processor with all available attachments, to an electric knife sharpener to a pasta machine.

Mickie realized that she had a terrible weakness where such things were concerned, but she liked to cook, she was good at it, and she absolutely adored all these nifty little machines. Now she passed up both the electronic coffeemaker and the espresso machine in favor of a cold beer from the massive refrigerator. Sam whined eagerly beside her, anticipating his favorite treat, and she took an orange from a wooden bowl on the counter.

"Don't worry, boy, I won't forget you."

She took her beer and Sam's orange to the table, then peeled the orange while Sam watched intently. As she fed sections of fruit to the eager dog, she sipped her beer thoughtfully. It had been an eventful evening, and she had a lot to think about.

Mark James, for instance. He was an unusual patient, both because of the circumstances that had brought him to the hospital and the secrecy that surrounded him, but it was her own reaction to him that disturbed Mickie most. In her opinion she hadn't led a particularly cloistered life. She had known a lot of men, as friends, coworkers and colleagues, even as boyfriends, but she had never felt anything for any man like what she had felt tonight....

Mickie cut short her wandering thoughts. She must be more tired than she realized if she was fantasizing about a sexual attraction to a semiconscious patient! Not only was it ridiculous, it was inappropriate, and probably unethical, as well. She was a physician, this man was her patient. Her interest in him had to be professional, not personal.

And it isn't personal! Mickie told herself sharply. I've never taken an inappropriate interest in a patient, and I'm not starting now! What she'd felt was sympathy for a man who had suffered a great deal. Sympathy, that was all it was.

She drained her beer, dropped the empty can in the recycling bag and made her way to bed. Deep inside her a little voice pointed out that whatever she'd felt toward Mark James that night, sympathy was the wrong word for it.

She ignored the little voice.

Mickie arrived at the hospital very early the next morning. Despite the hour Commander Lewis was waiting in the nurses' station when she got there, and Mark James was already awake and establishing a reputation for himself.

"He's refusing all medication," the exasperated charge nurse informed her. "He says he won't take anything for pain, period. And he won't take his pre-op shot until he talks to 'the doctor in charge.'" She rolled her eyes. "He actually managed to make Stan mad!"

"*Stan* lost his temper?" Stan's placid temperament was well known.

"Did he ever! Oh, and Mr. James also made a student nurse cry."

"What on earth did he do? Throw something at her?"

"He said something to her. Something *colorful*." The nurse, a pretty girl named Ginger, rolled her eyes.

Mickie grinned. "He said something *colorful* last night, too, and he was barely conscious then." She turned to Commander Lewis, who stood to one side, placidly watching the exchange. "Can't you control your boy, Commander?"

"He's not my boy anymore. He's in your hospital now."

Mickie had the impression that Lewis was pleased to learn that Mark James was a disruptive influence, but she had no idea why he should be. She had already decided he was a strange man, but he didn't need to gloat over their problems.

"I just hope he quiets down once he's talked to you," Ginger told her. "We have enough going on around here without students crying in the rest rooms."

"Just give me a few minutes with him, Ginger. I'll quiet him down."

"If he's going to give you problems, I can come with you." Commander Lewis's offer was accompanied by a smug half smile that Mickie didn't like at all. He pulled a pack of cigarettes from his shirt pocket as he watched her face.

"If you want to smoke, Commander, there's a lounge at the end of the hall," she told him, saccharine-sweet. "And you don't need to bother coming with me. I can handle Mr. James without reinforcements." Mickie's ability to deal with difficult patients had been honed by experience and tempered by time. She had a lot of confidence in it.

Ginger had faith in her, too. "Sic 'em," she called, then grinned as Mickie walked away.

Mark James's injury was such that he hadn't been allowed to sit up, despite his repeated and vociferous demands to do so. In a major concession, and a vain attempt to quiet him down, the nursing staff had braced his injured leg, immobilizing it with sandbags and pillows, and then permitted him to have his head slightly raised. He had been watching the door to see who would be the next to beard him in his den, and he scowled at Mickie as she entered the room. Two steps inside she stopped, letting the door whisper closed behind her. For several seconds they simply studied each other.

His appearance this morning was much improved. Though still pale and obviously in pain, he was alert, in control. In spite of his illness he dominated the impersonally cheerful room, challenging anyone who might try to give him an order.

Though thunderous with bad temper, the face on the pillow was still the face she had lightly caressed last night. Looking at him now, though, Mickie had an idea he would not welcome such a gesture this morning. His lips were pressed firmly together, perhaps in suspicion or anger, perhaps because he was in pain, and the sensuous curve of his lower lip had become hard, even cruel. The black brows winged up and out over eyes so dark they were nearly black, as well, and those eyes impaled her where she stood. She could read nothing in them but hostility, and they made the lean, hawklike face threatening, saturnine, almost satanic.

Mickie shook her head to banish the image, cursing her over-active imagination. She wasn't going to let herself concoct any more idiotic fantasies about this man. In the cold light of morning Mr. Mark James was nothing more than a patient, sunburned and thin from his captivity in the jungle, and undoubtedly suspicious of strangers. It wasn't hard for her to understand how he had managed to make that student nurse cry, though. Mickie twitched her lab coat closed over her green scrub dress and crossed to his bedside.

"Congratulations, Mr. James," she greeted him with a hint of cool amusement. "I understand you've had a busy morning. They tell me that you've managed to offend just about everyone on this floor, and you even made a student nurse cry."

"Are you the reinforcements?"

"Trying for a clean sweep?" she asked with a little smile. "I warn you, I don't offend easily, and no patient has ever made me cry."

"Tough lady, huh?"

Mickie accepted the appellation with a shrug.

"So who are you?" he asked after a moment. "The supernurse, here to wash my mouth out with soap?"

"I'll admit the idea has a certain appeal." Mickie grinned. "But what I'm going to do to you will make washing your mouth out seem like a treat."

He digested that for a moment. "So who *are*...?" His gaze narrowed to the plastic nameplate pinned to her pocket. "Michael F. Blake, M.D.," he read aloud. "So what'd you do, lady? Steal the doc's coat?"

"I didn't steal a thing, Mr. James. It's my coat, and I'm your doctor."

"Michael?"

"My parents had a sense of humor. They said they were going to name the baby for my father, so they did. If you don't care for Michael, though, 'Doc' will do fine. That's what you called me last night."

He frowned, trying to remember, then looked sharply up at her, scrutinizing her face and hair. "You...last night?"

He shook his head and laughed. "So you *were* real! I thought you were a hallucination, red hair and all. What were you wearing, anyway?"

"An evening dress. I was called away from a dinner."

"Black? With something glittery on it?"

"That's it."

"I liked it better than this." He gave her scrub dress and white coat a disparaging survey, then looked her up and down again, more carefully this time. It was a blatantly male study, and it peeled away the unflattering clothing to assess the body it covered.

It also resurrected all the feelings Mickie thought she had managed to quell. He was stripping her naked with a look. As his gaze lingered on her small, high breasts and the slim curve of her hips, Mickie felt a purely feminine thrill rush through her, tingling in her breasts and settling low in her stomach. When he finally relaxed against the pillows she was painfully aware that her cheeks were flushed and her mouth unaccountably dry.

He glanced at the red-gold curls rioting around her face. "I guess I should have recognized you from the hair, but I thought the carrot-top was just part of the hallucination."

"Red hair has that effect on some people." Her reply was breathless; she could only hope he hadn't noticed.

She turned away to pull a chair up beside the bed, taking a deep breath to steady her oddly rapid pulse. It was just plain stupid to react this way. She would simply ignore it until it went away. She sat down and smiled at him in her best impersonal bedside manner. "So, how do you feel this morning? Besides crabby, that is?"

"You're really my doctor?"

"I really am."

He had to turn his head to look straight into her eyes, and he winced as the movement hurt him. "You any good?"

"I'm good," Mickie replied with simple honesty, and met his dark regard with a level, candid gaze. He was searching for something, judging her, evaluating her. Mickie waited quietly for his assessment to be completed, unable to read anything in his eyes.

It was unsettling, but she had the feeling that even in his debilitated state he was the stronger of the two of them, that he was in control. He seemed to look straight through her tough-lady-doctor facade to the not-so-tough woman inside. Mickie didn't like that sensation at all; she wasn't used to it. As a doctor she was accustomed to being in charge at all times. She had a growing suspicion that with this man she would be in charge only if he allowed her to be.

At length he completed his examination and nodded, apparently satisfied with what he saw.

"To answer your earlier question," he said, "I'm not hungry, I'm not dirty, and I'm not delirious. That's better off than I've been in quite a while. What're you gonna do to me, Doc?"

"I'm going to fix your broken leg."

"Gonna put it in a cast yourself? Are you qualified to do that?"

"I'm a board-certified orthopedic surgeon."

"That would probably reassure me if I knew what it was."

"A bone specialist. And I'm not going to put your leg in a cast, not right away, at least. It's badly broken, and it requires surgery. I plan to use an external fixation device and traction for a while."

His eyes narrowed. "Is all that necessary?"

"Your leg is in bad shape, Mr. James. It needs considerably more than a simple cast and crutches."

Though he was visibly tiring, he listened attentively to her explanation, asking several thoughtful questions as she described the type of surgery she would do and sketched a diagram for him on the back of a prescription pad. By the time she had finished and he had signed the forms for consent to surgery, a nurse was waiting at the door with a prep tray and the presurgical sedative injection.

"It's time to get you ready for surgery, Mr. James." Mickie pushed her chair back and rose. "I'll see you again in the operating room." She walked a couple of steps away, then paused and turned. "Can I trust you to cooperate with the nurses?"

"I'll be a regular little Boy Scout," he vowed.

Mickie choked on a bubble of laughter. She couldn't buy the idea of Mark James as a Boy Scout. "Don't promise anything you can't deliver, Mr. James. Just take your shots like a good boy, and I'll see you when the performance starts." She grinned and moved away.

"Break a leg, Doc."

Mickie laughed as she swung the door open. "I just fix 'em, Mr. James. Breaking them is your department."

Chapter 3

The room was quiet and shadowy as dusk faded into night. Mickie pulled the door closed behind her and walked softly over to the bed. He was awake, his eyes glittering like polished jet in the muted light.

"How do you feel?" She pulled the bedside chair around and sat facing him.

"Like hell," he replied hoarsely, and Mickie chuckled. "What is all this stuff, anyway?" He scowled at the ropes and pulleys and traction bars, the IV stand and cardiac monitor, which surrounded his bed like a high-tech hedge.

"I told you you were going to be in traction. That's what most of this hardware is. This," she touched the IV pole, "is your antibiotic, and that," indicating the quietly beeping monitor, "will only be here for the first twenty-four hours postop. It's strictly routine. Your heart's fine."

"That's nice to know."

"Don't be sarcastic, Mr. James. I'll have you know I worked damned hard on you today, and you're in great shape."

"Oh, right. I'm ready to go out and run a marathon!"

"Give it six months or so and you can." Mickie's voice was cool, and after a moment of hesitation he sighed heavily.

"Okay, Doc, I apologize. I'm sure you did a terrific job."

"As a matter of fact, I did, considering the shape your leg was in. I can't understand how you managed to walk through the jungle on it." She was watching his face in the dim glow from the cardiac monitor, and she saw a gleam of white as he smiled briefly.

"You couldn't exactly call it *walking*. I tried to use a fallen branch as a crutch. They do that in all the adventure stories, you know, but it's an overrated idea." He gave a rusty chuckle. "Mostly I crawled."

Mickie coughed to disguise a gasp, grateful for the dimness that hid her face from him. She didn't want her horror to show. "You must . . . you must have been awfully glad to see the last of the jungle," she finally said weakly.

He grunted, a nonanswer. "How long am I going to be here?"

"You'll be in traction for four to six weeks." She accepted the change of subject with relief. "Then we'll put a cast on your leg, and you'll be in the hospital another couple of weeks. If everything goes well I'll give you a walking cast at that point. That'll have to be on for a while, but we won't know exactly how long until we see how you're healing."

He swore harshly under his breath. "And after that?"

"You'll probably need a cane for a few weeks. How long you use it depends on how quickly you heal. You can help out, you know."

"I can? How?" His head turned on the pillow, and she could feel his gaze sharpen on her.

"By cooperating," she told him simply. "Do what we tell you to. Take your medication. Eat well, and eat as much as you comfortably can, because you need the nutrients and the calories to heal. Rest as much as you can. When we start therapy, do what's asked of you. It's all designed to help you recover as quickly and completely as possible.''

"Can that actually speed the process up?"

"To a certain extent yes, it can, but bones will only knit so fast. You are, if you'll forgive me for pointing it out, not as young as you used to be, Mr. James. You won't heal as quickly at thirty-six as you did at sixteen. You have to be patient.''

"Patient!" There was a wealth of angry disgust in the word. He dropped his head back onto the pillows, glaring at the ceiling. "I've already lost so much time, and now I have to be patient?''

Mickie shrugged. "I'm sorry, but that's all I can offer you." She hesitated a moment, then said, "Mr. James, I know it's none of my business, but shouldn't you be glad to be here, to be out of the jungle?''

"What makes you think I'm not glad?" he asked sarcastically. "I'm in a nice, clean hospital room with no bugs and no germs, and I'm tied to this traction stuff like a picnic ham waiting to be smoked. Of course I'm glad! Don't I look glad?" His teeth gleamed briefly in a smile that was closer to a snarl.

"You're just thrilled, I can tell. You know, Mr. James, I'm not stupid," she said tightly. "I let you get away with changing the subject to your recovery period because that's information you need, but nobody ever said the subject was dropped. You want to go back there, don't you?''

"No. I *have* to go back."

"Oh." Mickie considered that for a moment. "I don't suppose there's any point in my asking why?" He gave her a cold glance in reply, and Mickie let it drop. "You were a prisoner for a long time," she said after a moment. "Was there anything you really missed during that time, anything you wanted?''

There was a taut moment of silence; then he chuckled and the tension in the room eased. "Of course there was something I wanted. I wanted a woman." He rolled his head toward her on the pillow. "Interested in volunteering?" he asked in a low, caressing tone.

Tension of a different sort suddenly hummed in the air between them. Mickie felt her heart begin to pound at the vividness of the image that flashed into her mind. If what he wanted was not just "a woman," but "this woman," if it were her . . .

"I think you know the answer to that," she replied in a carefully bland voice.

He sighed heavily. "You asked me what I wanted." His voice was a plaintive whine, belied by the gleam of amusement in his eyes.

Mickie had trouble suppressing a grin at the mock-childish protest. "Yeah, well, what else did you want?"

He thought about it for a moment. "This is going to sound stupid."

Mickie could hear the smile in his voice, and she relaxed, a little. "Try me."

"I—"

He was interrupted by a knock at the door. "Mickie?" A unit clerk peered into the darkened room.

"Yes, Cathie?"

"I'm sorry to interrupt, but you have a phone call."

"Business?"

"No, it's Mr. Caldwell."

"Oh." Enthusiasm was noticeably absent from Mickie's voice. "Well, tell him I'll call him back tonight if I get a chance."

"He was really insistent. He's called several times already, but you were in surgery."

"Oh-oh. He wants to complain about my leaving him in the lurch at that dinner last night. Just tell him I'm with a patient and I'll call him when I get a chance, okay, Cathie? And if he yells at you, hang up on him."

The clerk giggled. "Anything you say, Mickie." She backed out, closing the door behind her.

When Mickie turned back, she found Mark James regarding her quizzically. "You left your boyfriend in the lurch last night?"

"In a manner of speaking." She shrugged. "I told you I was wearing that dress because I'd been at a dinner. He's not my boyfriend, either."

"Sounds like he thinks he is." Mark watched her face closely.

Mickie shrugged again, fervently wishing this whole embarrassing conversation weren't taking place. It wasn't doing her professional image any good at all to have Jon calling her at the hospital like an overly possessive maiden auntie. Damn him! Thanks to this childish attitude of his, she'd have to tell the staff to refuse all his calls. No doubt that would annoy him even more, he would take his annoyance out on the clerks who answered the telephone on the ward, and the clerks would be justifiably annoyed with Mickie for putting them in the middle of this stupid situation.

"I'm afraid I don't have much control over what he thinks." She dismissed the topic of Jon and his pique. "Now, what were you saying about what you missed?"

"It's going to sound dumb," he repeated.

"Don't worry about it. After all, there aren't any rules about what a prisoner ought to crave."

"Maybe not, but you'd think I'd want something like steak, or champagne, or ten-year-old Scotch, right?"

"I don't know." She shrugged. "I'd say it's up to you."

"Then how about fried chicken?"

"Huh?"

"Fried chicken. Southern-style. All that time, living on wormy beans and rotten bananas, I didn't think about steak or lobster or anything like that, just fried chicken. It seemed so American. It seemed like home."

Mickie thought about it for a moment. "I don't see why not. You'll be off the liquid diet after tomorrow, anyway.

How about if I cancel that diet one meal early and bring you some chicken for dinner tomorrow?''

"You'd do that?" He turned toward her again. The sudden movement rattled the traction weights and hurt his injured leg, and he swore sharply.

"Be careful!" She readjusted the weights. "Why shouldn't I do it? You're my patient, and if I want to prescribe fried chicken as part of your treatment, I can."

"Won't your boyfriend object?"

"I told you, he's not my boyfriend," she returned automatically, then silently cursed her defensive tone. She stood, gathering up her lab coat and a folder of notes. "I'll bring you that chicken tomorrow night."

"I'll believe it when I see it."

"You'll believe it when you taste it! See you tomorrow." Mickie laughed and left the room with a wave and a smile.

"Where have you been?" Connie Ramirez emerged from the medication room as Mickie passed, falling in step with her. "Or should I make a guess about your handsome new patient?"

Mickie glanced at her friend, who gave her a smile heavy with meaning. She rolled her eyes. "Connie, I went to check on him, that's all."

"Mm-hm." Connie's voice slid up and down the scale. "You couldn't just let the trusty and dedicated nursing staff check on him?"

"He's my patient!"

"And aren't you the lucky one?" Connie grinned as she opened the half door to the nurses' station. "All our patients should look like him!"

Mickie stopped, resting her elbow on the counter, forehead in hand, the picture of patient forbearance. "Might I remind you, Mrs. Ramirez, the man is my *patient*. I'm not planning to marry him!"

"We'll see, won't we?" Chuckling, Connie sashayed into the office. Mickie escaped before she could become the target of any more barbs.

Why on earth had she said something like that? She shook her head as she drove the Jeep out of the parking lot. Why in the world had she even mentioned the word "marriage"? That just gave Connie even more ammunition to tease her with. And why was she so bothered by the teasing, anyway? Connie teased her all the time; she ought to be used to it by now.

Maybe, she answered herself, this teasing bothered her more because it hit a little too close to home. She wasn't doing anything completely unheard of by bringing fried chicken to a patient; she had done similar favors for others.

But those other patients had all been under the age of fifteen. There was a big difference. Connie had been able to tell that Mickie had special feelings for Mark James, and it was too much to hope that she'd abandon the topic. Mickie sighed. She would have to smuggle that chicken past Connie tomorrow, or she'd never hear the end of it.

When she finally staggered into her kitchen that evening, her arms were full of bulging brown grocery bags. "I must be nuts!" she gasped to Sam, who followed close behind her, his liquid black eyes trained unwaveringly on the bag that smelled of chicken.

She reeled across the room to drop the bags on the counter with a sigh of relief. "Yeesh, that's heavy!" She turned from the bags to push the playback button on her answering machine. A burst of static resolved itself into the voice of her office secretary, giving a brief résumé of the business that had transpired since Mickie had last been in. The secretary completed her recital and there was a moment of silence, then the beep.

"Mickie, this is Jon," proclaimed the tape.

No fooling, she thought, rolling her eyes ceilingward. He'd probably filled the tape with his bad-tempered rantings.

"This is very childish, you know. I wouldn't have expected it of you. You can't keep ducking my phone calls forever, Mickie."

Oh, can't I?

"You know that I'll be leaving in a week, Mickie," he went on in an aggrieved tone. "I'll be in Switzerland for nearly three months, and before I go, I want to get some things settled between us. I want to know why you had to—"

"Save it!" Mickie punched the button, silencing Jon. If only he were that easy to silence in person. She knew she'd eventually have to face him and hear him out, but she didn't have to listen to him right now. And if she put him off for a week, she thought with a touch of cowardice, she wouldn't have to talk to him until he came back from Europe. Thank goodness.

Sam looked from her to the chicken bag and woofed softly.

"Don't worry, you'll get your treat. You know, Sam, I must be nuts. I got about three hours' sleep last night, spent most of today in the operating room, and now I'm gonna spend my evening frying chicken? What's wrong with me, anyway?"

Sam snuffled delicately at the bag resting on the counter, then nudged her thigh, whining. He wasn't interested in her reasons, he just wanted giblets. Mickie shoved his black bulk aside and opened a lower cupboard, searching for the state-of-the-art chicken fryer she'd been unable to resist at last winter's housewares sale.

Sam might not be interested in her reasons, but she was almost afraid to examine them. Not only was she going to spend her evening up to her elbows in chicken parts and hot oil, she had also bought potatoes, eggs, celery and a big jar of mayonnaise for potato salad. At this rate she'd be lucky to get to bed before midnight!

And why was she making herself a human sacrifice for that secretive, abrasive and utterly male man? You know why! she thought, and banged the fryer onto the tile counter. You know exactly why.

Mickie flattened her back against the cold green tile of the wall and peered cautiously around the corner. The corridor was empty, but she could hear voices from the medication room. If they'd stay in there for just a moment...

She slid around the corner with the stealth of a seasoned cat burglar, then had to dodge back into hiding as Connie and a student nurse emerged from the med room. Pressed against the wall again, heart pounding, Mickie listened as they moved away.

When she heard a door close behind them, cutting off the sound of voices, Mickie let her breath out in a long, silent sigh. That had been entirely too close for comfort, but at least it appeared that Connie would be occupied for a few seconds. Now, if she could only make it to Mark James's room in those few seconds...

She peeked again. The hall was clear, the door of Mark James's room only a few yards away. Mickie settled the heavy paper sack more securely in her arms, wincing as it rustled loudly in the late-afternoon quiet. She held her breath for a moment, listening, but heard nothing, so she slipped around the corner and scuttled toward her goal. She moved wraithlike along the wall, her rubber-soled shoes silent on the linoleum, and dodged into his room. She was pressing the self-closing door shut when Connie and the student nurse passed within three feet of her, returning to the med room.

She froze until they had passed, then shoved the door completely closed and wedged a chair under the handle. She heaved a sigh of relief, then turned to see Mark James watching her from amid his traction hardware, baffled by her antics.

"I've brought your chicken dinner." She set the bag on a chair and began unpacking it onto the nightstand.

"I can see that, but why did you sneak in here like you were smuggling contraband?"

"Because that's exactly what I am doing. If the head nurse catches me, she'll never let me hear the end of it!"

What she was telling him was the truth, but Mickie knew he would interpret her caution as fear of being caught breaking the rules, not fear of showing too personal a concern for him.

"Listen, I appreciate your doing this for me, but it wasn't necessary for you to get yourself in trouble." Mark James seemed disgruntled and a little uncomfortable to find himself the object of someone else's concern. Mickie had an idea he was accustomed to having sole responsibility for his situation. "When you said you'd bring chicken, I didn't know it would cause problems."

"Don't worry about it." Mickie set the last container on the table. "I'd just prefer to keep a low profile."

"Hmmm." Mark's murmur was noncommittal, but Mickie could read his mind. He wasn't particularly pleased to have her taking care of him this way, but he could smell the fried chicken, and his stomach was winning the contest with his pride. His next question gave him away. "You said chicken. What is all that stuff?"

"Chicken, of course." Mickie produced a paper plate from the bag. "Do you like white or dark meat?"

"Dark, please."

"You got it." She put two legs and a thigh on the plate. "And potato salad—I hope you like it with mustard."

"Mustard's fine." He couldn't lift his head far enough to see what she was doing, but it was obvious that the aromas were reaching him.

Mickie scooped a generous dollop onto the plate beside the chicken. "And sliced tomatoes. They're winter ones, but they were all I could get last night at the market. And finally biscuits, with butter and strawberry jam." She set his filled plate on the overbed table and rolled it carefully into position. "I'm going to raise your head a little so you can eat. I want you to tell me if you feel any movement in your leg, because I might have to adjust the ropes."

He nodded mute agreement, his eyes fixed on his plate as she raised the bed for him. Mickie helped him lift his head and slipped another pillow beneath it, then passed him a knife and fork.

"I hope you like it." She was a little unnerved by the rapt gaze he was directing at the plate. She had received plenty of compliments on her culinary skill, but she had never known anyone to gaze at her cooking as if it were a holy relic.

"I hope I don't wake up," he said, a self-mocking grin lifting one corner of his mouth. "If this is a dream, I don't want it to end until I've eaten." He took his knife and carefully split a biscuit. "Butter? Real butter?"

"I figure your arteries can stand the cholesterol just this once."

"I can hardly remember what it tastes like." He plastered the biscuit with butter and jam, and took a huge bite. Eyes closed, he chewed slowly, savoring the experience with all his senses.

Mickie was suddenly reminded of the theory that a man who completely enjoyed his food was also a man who would savor a sexual experience to the fullest. The sensuous curve of that mouth, with a little smear of jam on it, spoke volumes. Mickie could imagine, in another time or place, taking that smear of jam from his lips with her own, tasting the sweetness, tasting him.... She felt a blush scorching her cheeks and quickly turned away to fill her own plate and recover her composure.

"Fabulous," Mark sighed from behind her. "Ambrosial." He picked up a chicken leg and bit deeply into it, relishing it as he had the biscuit. He let his head drop back onto the pillows, eyes closed. "I have died and gone to heaven."

"You haven't died and gone anywhere," Mickie retorted. "I'll have you know I took very good care of you in that operating room yesterday, and I have no intention of letting you die."

"Well, if I'm not dreaming, and I'm not dead, then you have to thank the person who cooked all this." He tasted the potato salad and kissed his fingertips. "It's fantastic. If I had dreamed a meal when they were feeding me rotten bananas, this is the meal I'd have dreamed of. My compliments to the chef."

"Thank you, kind sir." Mickie grinned, and inclined her head in a little bow.

He jerked around to look directly at her. "You? You cooked this?"

"Well, sure, I did. Who did you think?"

"I don't know. A caterer, or your cook or somebody."

"My *cook*?" Mickie stared at him, dumbfounded. "What on earth would I do with a cook?"

"Have your meals fixed, I guess."

"But why?"

"Because you're a woman doctor. You're obviously busy with your profession. You don't seem like the type to slave over a hot stove."

"I like to cook," she informed him with asperity. "If I've had a hard day I'm not likely to make a crown roast of beef for dinner, but I can't imagine hiring someone to cook for me."

"Your boyfriend must appreciate that decision. It isn't every man who eats like a king."

Mickie sent him a quick glance from beneath her lashes. "He's *not* my boyfriend," she told him, carefully keeping her voice expressionless.

"Mmm." He seemed considerably more concerned with the chicken than her statement. "This chicken really is great. And I'm not just saying that because it's been a long time. You put something in it—"

"I appreciate the compliment, but you're embarrassing me. I'm just glad you like it." She searched for a change of subject. "Did the volunteer bring the book cart in today? I left a message for them. I thought you'd be interested in something to read."

"Mmmph," he mumbled around a mouthful. He swallowed. "Over there."

She hadn't noticed before, but the nightstand on the far side of his bed was piled high with newspapers, news magazines, a couple of nonfiction paperbacks on political themes and, to her surprise, several fiction bestsellers. He must have emptied the volunteer's cart completely. She told him so.

"I did, if the 'volunteer' is a little old guy in a pink jacket."

"It's salmon, actually, but that's him, all right. Was he pleased?"

"Seemed to be. He said he'd see what else he could find for me tomorrow. Said he didn't want me to be bored."

"I don't think there's much danger of that." Mickie eyed the small alp of literature. "I guess you missed reading, didn't you?"

"Wouldn't you?"

"I'd go crazy," she admitted. "I always have a book or a magazine, or maybe both, in my purse or briefcase, just for empty moments."

"Briefcase? I thought you docs all carried those little black bags."

"We do. There's a murder mystery in mine right now, tucked between the stethoscope and the tongue depressors."

"What is the title? Who's the author?"

She told him. "Do you read his books?"

"I read a lot of fiction, and I like his stuff. I like the way he handles the exposition, working it in without making it intrusive. You learn the facts you need to know, but you're never really aware of having been 'told' those things."

"You sound like a writer or something, analyzing his technique. I just read mysteries for fun."

"I read for enjoyment, too, but it's interesting to see how different writers handle different problems."

"If you say so." Mickie frowned doubtfully at the bite of potato salad on her fork. "I never thought much about analyzing mystery stories before."

"You were too busy with biology and chemistry and all that scientific stuff."

She laughed. "That's truer than you know. I didn't really read fiction at all while I was in college and med school, just textbooks and professional journals. It's still a treat for me."

"So what else do you like? Other mystery writers? Or maybe science fiction, or something else?"

"All kinds of things, really." Mickie sat back in her chair, counting off a list of her favorite books on her fingers. Mark responded with a list of his own, and Mickie managed to relax again. They shared opinions easily, sometimes agreeing, sometimes arguing, enjoying the contest of intellect and will. Mickie didn't glance at her watch until the meal was over and she was replacing the lid on the potato salad. She was startled to see that more than an hour had passed.

"Oh, my gosh, look at the time!" She stood and began stuffing the debris of their dinner back into the sack. "They'll be bringing your P.M. meds in here anytime, and I've got to get the evidence out of here before they show up!"

"Aren't you making an awfully big deal out of this rules and regulations business?"

"Have you met the head nurse?" He looked blank. "Mrs. Ramirez?" Mickie prompted, and recognition dawned.

"Oh, yeah, I've met her. You're right; you'd better get rid of that before she finds out about it. I don't want to get on her wrong side again!"

"Again? What happened?"

"She informed me that if I made another student nurse cry I would definitely regret it, traction or no traction. I had the feeling she meant it."

"Oh, she meant it all right. And that's why I'm getting this mess out of here right now." Mickie gathered up the bag and a stray paper napkin. "Shhh." She pushed the barricading chair away from the door and eased it open a crack to peer outside. "All clear," she whispered to Mark. He gave her a thumbs-up and she slipped out the door and down the hall to the trash chute.

With the incriminating evidence disposed of, she took a few minutes to check her messages and freshen her lipstick in the ladies' room. When she caught herself grinning at her reflection in the mirror she paused, lowering the hand that had been poised to color her lips. She hardly needed cosmetics; her dinner with Mark James had done more for her looks than all the paints and powders in the drugstore could. Her cheeks were pink, her eyes sparkling, even her lips seemed more rosy than usual, and she just couldn't suppress a smile.

It wasn't difficult to figure out the reason, either. She had enjoyed that meal more than she wanted to admit. She *enjoyed* Mark James in a way she couldn't imagine enjoying someone like Jon. She enjoyed his humor, his intelligence, his sometimes unexpected ideas. They were as appealing as his sexiness, and that sexiness was awfully appealing.

Suddenly warm, Mickie ran cold water over her wrists and hands. She'd heard of animal magnetism, but she'd never expected to feel its pull. She'd thought herself immune to such phenomena, but the last two days had proven just how wrong that assumption had been. What sort of lover would he be, a man who could make an ecstatic experience out of eating a homemade biscuit? Feeling her cheeks heat up again, she stuck out her tongue at herself in the mirror and left for Mark's room.

She could hear the angry voices as soon as she entered the corridor. Raised in argument, they were coming from Mark's room. Staff members were already looking toward the source of the noise, and as Mickie ran toward the room she could hear questioning murmurs from the doorways she passed.

She flung the door open and whipped into the room to see Commander Lewis leaning over Mark's bed, shaking his fist and shouting, "You can't go back there, you can't do *anything* without official approval, and I'm going to guarantee that you never have that approval! You may think you're hot stuff, Ca—"

"Stop it!" Mickie shrieked, shaking with anger. "Stop it!"

Chapter 4

Stop it!'' Mickie shouted again. She shoved her way in front of Lewis and pushed him away from the bed. ''Stop it! For heaven's sake, don't you know where you are? Stop it now, or I'll call Security!''

Lewis backed reluctantly away, scowling at Mark, who glared back, his lean face a forbidding mask. At another time Mickie might have been frightened by such naked rage, but right now she was too furious herself to be intimidated by their anger. Her hand was still planted in the middle of Lewis's chest, so she gave him a last little shove for good measure. She looked from one man to the other, her expression somewhere between frosty and arctic.

''Just what the hell is going on here?'' she demanded. Though her voice was low, her fury was not in the least muted. ''This is a *hospital*, in case either of you has forgotten. There are sick people on this floor, but they certainly aren't getting any rest with you two providing the floor show!''

Lewis had the grace to look uncomfortable. Mark just looked stonily angry.

"Would either of you *gentlemen*," Mickie went on with stinging sarcasm, "care to tell me just why you felt the need to bellow at each other? What you," she looked at Mark, "need official approval for? And what you," she turned to Lewis, "will see that he doesn't get that approval for?"

Neither man replied, and after a moment Mickie realized what had happened. Though bitter antagonists, they had formed a united front in their refusal to tell her anything about the argument. That conspirators' silence was somehow more infuriating than their noisy argument. She endured it for a few seconds, then decided to put an end to the whole scene.

"You!" she snapped at Lewis. "Get out of this room! And if you can't remember that this is a hospital and conduct yourself accordingly, I'll have you barred from this unit. Now go!" Her tone brooked no argument. With a last scowl at Mark James, he went.

"Thanks for getting rid of—"

"You be quiet!" She rounded on Mark as he began to speak. "I'm tempted to throw you out, too, traction and all! I don't know what that was all about, official approval, or whatever. It doesn't matter. And I don't care if you want to go back to San Miguel and get yourself captured and tortured again. That's your business. I would like to suggest, though, that you at least wait until you've recovered from this time!"

She pinned him with a last icy glare, then spun on her heel and stalked out of the room. All her myriad emotions, including simple fury at Mark James, were tangled in a confusing knot. She couldn't decide if she'd rather kiss him or smack him, but a combination of the two held a certain appeal for her. Especially if she were to smack him first. Hard.

"What's got you so steamed?"

"What?" Mickie looked up to see Connie standing squarely in front of her, grinning like the Cheshire cat.

"As if I didn't know. Your hunky Mr. James and his weird friend were making plenty of noise in there. What was it all about?"

"I don't have the foggiest idea. Would you believe neither of them would say a word to me about it?" The outrage was clear in Mickie's voice.

"But they didn't really have to tell you, did they?" Connie's grin widened as she added a little fat to the fire. "All they really had to do was knock off the yelling when you told them to."

Mickie shot her a fulminating glance. Connie was right, but she didn't have to be so smug about it. "Maybe they didn't, but after all that uproar they could at least have told me what it was all about, couldn't they?"

"Don't you mean, 'couldn't *he*?'" You've dealt with difficult patients before, Mick, and you haven't lost your cool. You're just upset this time because it's this particular patient. You wouldn't be so mad if you weren't more than a little interested in him."

"Thank you very much, Dr. Freud," Mickie retorted sarcastically. Connie had hit far too close to the truth. "I'm going home!"

With a very satisfied smile Connie watched her go.

The moon scattered a trail of light across the gently rippling surface of the pool. It was nearly midnight. Mickie sat on the poolside, one leg drawn up, her arms wrapped around it and her chin resting on her knee. Her other foot dangled just above the surface of the water. She watched that band of moonlight for a moment, then kicked her dangling foot in the water, shattering the light into a million glittering shards. Sprawled on the decking beside her, Sam jerked his head up and woofed softly, startled from sleep.

Connie was right, of course. That was the problem. In the face of Connie's questions Mickie might deny any interest in Mark James, but she couldn't deny it to herself. There was something about him—no, she corrected herself, there were lots of things about him that intrigued and attracted her. His sexy body and face, his mysterious situation, his alternately captivating and infuriating personality, all were as impossible to ignore as they were to resist.

It was more than a little unnerving for Mickie to realize that she could be so fascinated by a man she had known less than three days, a man, moreover, who was her patient. She wasn't supposed to get personally involved with her patients in any way, especially her male patients. But here she was, unable to resist Mark James.

She thought about that for a minute. "Well, so what?" she asked the night around her.

What she was doing wasn't really so terrible. There was no valid reason why she shouldn't care a little more for Mark James, why she shouldn't be more involved with him than with most patients. The involvement would only be unethical if it were to adversely affect his care.

It wasn't so terrible, nor was it so surprising, she decided. Mark James was an unusual man in many ways; it was only natural that he should evoke an unusual response in her. He had been through an ordeal that would have destroyed most people; he seemed utterly alone, with no family or friends to care about him and provide him with companionship. In fact, the only advocate he seemed to have was Commander Lewis. Advocate, perhaps, fellow conspirator, certainly, but Mickie would never call Lewis a friend. Perhaps that was what drew her to Mark James, the feeling that he needed a friend.

Or maybe it's hormones, she thought wryly. Mark James might need a friend, and she might be responding to that need, but her first impression of him, unconscious and magnificent, had not been based on anything as pallid and bland as a possible friendship. No, that first impression had been much more personal than a charitable impulse, and much more powerful, and it was all the more shocking for the short time she'd known him.

It was difficult for her to remember that her first meeting with Mark James had taken place only forty-eight hours ago. Forty-eight hours. In a strange, almost eerie way, she felt, and felt strongly, that she'd known him for years, maybe forever.

Call it what she would, charitable impulse or simple lust, Mickie knew her feelings for Mark James would not simply fade away. Not only couldn't she ignore them, she had no intention of trying. She would continue to do what she could to make his hospitalization more comfortable, easier to bear. She wouldn't feel guilty about it, either.

She rose to her feet in one smooth motion and stood poised on tiptoe for a moment. She raised her arms to shoulder level, bobbed on her toes and dived in a graceful arc, cleaving the warm water with hardly a splash.

"Well?" Connie had been away for a week and was eager for news. She waited for an answer while Mickie struggled with a too-large bite of her hamburger.

"Well, what?" Mickie shook her head and took a gulp of iced tea to wash down the dessicated meat. "That hamburger must be older than I am. I wish the cafeteria didn't feel they have to keep them on the grill until they have the tender texture of old gym shoes."

"If you managed to get here before the cafeteria closed, Dr. Blake, you might get something a little more edible and a little less overcooked."

"Believe me, I want to give this food every chance I can. I got held up this afternoon, though. I was taking Robbie Bates's cast off."

"How is Roaring Robbie?" The highly active, tow-headed nine-year-old had come into the hospital two months earlier. He had broken his leg falling out of a tree. In spite of his phenomenal energy level and penchant for messy pranks, he had become a favorite of the staff during his two-week stay, and they still remembered him six weeks after he'd gone home.

"He's still a doll, and he's still a pistol. His leg's done really well. I took a couple of extra films to make sure, and that bone has healed better than I ever expected. I just hope he can keep from breaking it again for a couple of years. That kid's got more energy than I can cope with."

"He's a firecracker, all right," Connie agreed. "I don't know how his mother keeps her sanity." She sipped her coffee. "I'm still waiting for an answer, remember?"

"Oh, that." Mickie nibbled a french fry. "These fries aren't bad, you know. At least *they* aren't petrified yet."

"Mickie..." Connie's voice rose warningly. "I already know what your supper tastes like. I had the same thing an hour ago, and it was terrible then, too. I want to know what's happened since I went on vacation!"

"You've only been gone a week, Connie. What could have happened in a week?"

"That's what I'd like to know. Plenty has happened on *General Hospital* this week. Now I want to know what's happening in the soap opera here."

"There's no soap opera here, Connie." Mickie's manner was one of exaggerated patience.

"Just the romance of the century, that's all."

"Try to control yourself, Connie," Mickie advised dryly. "It isn't very appetizing to watch you drool on the table. As to what's going on with Mr. James, more often than not he's somewhere between surly and obnoxious. It's hard to get mad at him, though; I can understand how he feels. After all, being tied to that bed by a traction apparatus bigger than he is has to seem like being a prisoner all over again."

"Yeah, I can see that it might. So what are you and the staff doing to keep him entertained and cooperative?"

"You name it," Mickie laughed, "and we've tried it! He has a lot of physical therapy. You know the routine—weights and exercises to keep his strength up while he's immobile, therapy for his leg, and special exercises for the hand that was injured so badly. If you give him a challenge, he works himself hard to meet it. As a matter of fact,

I'm thinking of prescribing extra exercises just to keep him occupied.''

"Are you going to do surgery on his hand?"

"Believe it or not, I don't think it will be necessary. He really has done a lot of work with the therapist; and it's been even more effective than I expected.''

"How about treatment for boredom? He must have missed a lot of things while he was a prisoner.''

"A million of them, at least! He has cravings like a pregnant woman, hamburgers one day, chocolate the next, and a *mignonettes de boeuf* dinner from *Chez Louis* last Monday. I had them deliver that for two." Mickie grinned, remembering. "It was delicious." Suddenly she realized how much she was giving away. She definitely felt more comfortable with her feelings—whatever they were—for Mark, but that didn't mean she was ready to share them. She quickly changed the subject. "He's catching up on his reading, too.''

"What kinds of things does he read?" Connie leaned forward eagerly, chin on hand. "That must tell you a lot about him.''

"All it's told me is that he's interested in absolutely everything. Detective stories, bestsellers, newspapers, news magazines, business magazines, a book on global economic policy. Oh, and the soap opera synopsis mags for the past year.''

"The soap magazines?"

"Absolutely. He had to catch up on his favorites so he could follow what's happening now. He watches several of them every day, and the housekeepers have started doing his room from eleven to three, so they can watch with him. They have a pool going on what will happen on *The Young and the Restless*.''

"I can't believe it! A man who reads about global economic policy and watches the soaps!''

"A man of eclectic interests.''

"No kidding. What else does he like?''

"Let me think." Mickie propped her chin on her hand gazed up at the ceiling while she considered. "Cards."

"He plays cards?"

"Sure."

"Who does he play with?"

"Me, usually. So far he's won about thirteen dollars off me. We watch TV, too, and talk."

"What do you talk about? Does he tell you about his adventures in the jungle?"

The innocent eagerness in Connie's voice made Mickie laugh. "If I didn't know you better, Connie, I'd think you were after him yourself! Besides that, you read too many adventure stories. He doesn't talk about himself at all."

"Not even a little bit? Like his childhood or something?"

"Not even a little bit. He has defenses up against anything personal. He uses anger, or confrontation, or humor—even charm—to deflect the questions he doesn't want to answer. We just talk about general things, like world events, even philosophy, if you can believe that I'm capable of discussing *that*.

"Nothing personal, though?'

"Hm-mm. Not even anything that's kind of personal." Mickie pushed her plate away. "If I were starving, I couldn't choke down any more of that." She stirred a packet of powdered creamer into her coffee. "In a strange way I feel I understand him better than I would if we'd just talked about facts, like what his family does and where he went to school. In spite of all his defenses, I feel I know the way he thinks, and not just the statistics. Does that make sense?"

"Of course it does. Look how easy it is to let a job or a title get in the way of knowing the real person behind it. You and Mark don't have any of those things cluttering up the picture." Connie sipped her own coffee, then glanced at Mickie from beneath the screen of her thick black lashes. "Has he kissed you yet?"

"Connie!" Mickie's head jerked up, her color rising. "He's my patient!"

"I know he is." Connie's voice lost her teasing tone. "But I also know there's more to it than that. I've seen you with him, Mickie."

"I know." She sighed. "I hate to think my feelings are that obvious. And to answer your question, no, he hasn't kissed me."

"But you wish he had?"

Mickie shrugged helplessly. "I can't answer that, Connie!"

"Well, can you tell me how you feel about him?"

Mickie grinned ruefully. "I wish I knew!" She shook her head. "I find him interesting . . . fascinating, and yet there are so many things I don't know about him."

"How does he compare to the other men you know? To Jon Caldwell, for instance?"

"To Jon? That's different, Connie. Mark James is my patient, and Jon is—"

"John Caldwell is a pain!"

"Connie!" Mickie felt she ought to protest on Jon's behalf, but her voice lacked conviction.

"You know exactly what I mean, Mickie; don't deny it. Is he still calling the unit for you three times a day?"

"Not since he went to Switzerland."

"He's gone, then?"

"He left last Thursday, for several months."

"That must be a relief," Connie said dryly.

"I hate to admit it, but it is." Mickie grinned. "I'm hoping that I'll get lucky and he'll meet a nice *fraulein* over there who'll take his mind off me."

"Don't get your hopes up. It's his ego, you know; you've become a challenge to him. He can't believe you don't want someone as wonderful as he is."

"Well, I've certainly been trying to tell him. I figure if I keep saying no, eventually he'll get the message."

"Don't hold your breath. Jon's type can be pretty dense." Connie sipped her coffee and studied her friend for a moment. "You can't compare Mark James to Jon, huh?"

"It isn't a fair comparison." In spite of his annoying persistence, Mickie was feeling a twinge of guilt at picking Jon apart when he wasn't there to defend himself. "Jon can be fun, you know."

"For about fifteen seconds."

Mickie ignored that. "Jon can be fun, and he's a good stockbroker and all, but Mark..." Her voice trailed away.

"But Mark?" Connie prompted.

"He's a mystery—in a lot of ways."

"He's an awfully sexy mystery, if you ask me."

"I didn't."

"And speaking of mysteries..." Connie's voice dropped, heavy with implication.

"Oh, please! Not the spy theory again!" Mickie dropped her bright head into her hands in mock despair.

"I don't understand why you think it's such a far-fetched idea. It all fits perfectly."

"Like two left shoes, it fits perfectly," Mickie muttered.

Connie ignored her sarcasm. "Take that Commander Lewis, for instance. I don't care what he calls himself, he's not in the Navy."

"Why shouldn't he be in the Navy? Lots of people in San Diego are in the Navy."

Connie scowled, exasperated. "I know that, but Lewis doesn't *look* Navy. Take Miguel, for instance; just picture him." Mickie could easily picture Connie's younger brother, the image of military spit and polish. She nodded. "He *looks* Navy. This Lewis person is too sloppy."

"Could it be that he's just a slob by nature?"

"Miguel was a slob by nature until he enlisted. The Navy made him a changed man. And that's not all. Mark James was brought back to the US on a Naval vessel, but they only did that because that ship happened to be handy. He doesn't seem to have any connection with the Navy except Lewis, and I've already told you what I think about him. There are other things, too. There's all this secrecy surrounding Mr. James. Doesn't that seem strange to you? He was a prisoner in a country that American citizens have been advised not to travel to, and he and Lewis argue all the time. You know, I've even heard Lewis call him by some other name."

"I've heard him call Mark by another name, too, for what that's worth," Mickie said. "It's probably some kind of sailors' insult or something. Come on, Connie! You can't assume the man's a spy on the basis of that!"

"But it all makes sense! Lewis, the arguments, the alias, all the secrecy. It adds up."

"It only makes sense if you've been reading too many thrillers. Anyway, I argue with Lewis, too. The man's obnoxious. Does that mean I'm a spy?"

"No, it doesn't mean you're a spy, silly. And I know Lewis is obnoxious. Interesting, isn't it, that he should be the only visitor Mark James has?" Mickie shot her friend a dark look, and Connie grinned. "Ah, but he isn't the only visitor, is he? There's a certain doctor who visits Mr. James faithfully every evening."

Mickie decided not to press the issue. She drained her coffee and began gathering her dishes onto the tray. "A certain doctor who had better get going. I'll see you in the morning, Connie."

"Just think about what I said, okay? Think about Mark James."

She had thought of little *but* Mark James since the night he had arrived at the hospital, Mickie reflected as she hurried through the hospital corridors. The effect he had on her was so unexpected, so profound, that she found herself constantly surprised by it.

She'd never thought of herself as leading a sheltered life, but Mickie was realizing that in many ways she had. Her social life had been severely circumscribed by the demands of her education. When medical school and her residency were at last behind her, she had found she had no taste for the desperate artificiality of singles' bars or the forced conviviality of blind dates.

She hadn't lived like a hermit, though. She had dated casually, men she'd met at the hospital or through friends. But those dates had never amounted to even a small romance, much less a great one. For a time Jon had been an entertaining escort, but since the Stockbrokers' Dinner fiasco, she wasn't eager to commit herself to another evening of his company. She had been granted a reprieve while he was out of the country. She could only hope that by the time he returned, he would have forgotten about her deserting him at the dinner.

Not that Jon, at his most charming, had ever made her feel anything remotely like what she felt when she was near Mark James. Jon had tried, certainly; he seemed to consider himself quite the ladies' man, and Mickie's persistent indifference to his kisses and caresses had frustrated him intensely.

And Mark didn't even have to try. Good grief, Mickie thought in amazement, he didn't even have to be awake! He had made her heart pound and her knees weaken that first night when he was unconscious! Familiarity had failed to breed contempt, and the more time she spent with Mark, the more powerful was the attraction she felt to the man with the hard, sardonic face.

They were still physician and patient, though. This wasn't supposed to be happening. She had tried to conceal the way she felt, and certainly Mark James had never showed by word or deed that he returned her feelings. It was a doomed attraction, but that knowledge wasn't enough to alter Mickie's feelings.

She increased her pace eagerly as she neared his room, ignoring the quickening beat of her foolishly smitten heart. Outside his door she paused, breathless and giddy as a teenager waiting for a date. She knew she was being really silly, but she supposed she was entitled to a foolish crush once in her life, even if she'd had to turn thirty before it finally happened to her.

"You're a nut, Michael Blake," she muttered to herself and shouldered the door open.

"Where the hell have you been?" snarled the object of her romantic dreams.

Mickie froze, her hand falling limply away from the door handle. "I beg your pardon?"

"Where the hell have you been?" he demanded again. "Why are you so late, and what have you been doing all this time?" He levered himself up on one elbow and glared at her. "I'm damned sick and tired of this, you know that? I'm sick of being tied up in this Rube Goldberg mess of ropes and weights and sandbags! I'm sick of this room, of this bed, of being flat on my back, and as a matter of fact, I'm getting pretty sick of *you*! I can't stand the sight of this room, and—"

"Would you like to get out?" Mickie interrupted the tirade as she walked over to his bedside. She was fighting back the beginnings of a grin. She'd mentioned his defenses to Connie; now she was seeing them in action. He'd missed her that evening and didn't want to admit it, so he was snarling at her instead.

Mark stared at her. "Get out of what?"

Mickie leaned against the bed and folded her arms across her chest. "Out of traction, out of bed, out of this room. Take your pick." She paused until she was satisfied that she had his attention. "I spent a long time looking at those films we took this afternoon. That's part of the reason I'm so late. It's a judgment call, but I think you're ready to graduate from twenty-four-hour traction. I'll put a cast-brace on your leg so you can go to the PT department for your therapy, and you can be taken around the hospital and grounds in a wheelchair." She gave a little shrug. "I know it's not much," she apologized, "but at least it'll be a change from this room."

Mark stared at her for an instant; then with a deep laugh he threw his arms around her. He caught her completely off balance, pulling her off her feet and down onto him. Before Mickie could absorb more than the warmth and strength of the broad chest beneath her and the hard arms around her, he cupped the back of her head in one big hand and found her mouth with his. Mickie's reaction to the kiss was instinctive and unguarded, her body melting, her lips softening against his in a sweet invitation. Their lips clung hotly as his fingers tightened against the soft skin at her nape, holding her tightly for one mad instant until sanity washed back in.

With a sinking sensation Mickie remembered where she was and what she was doing. Mark James's chest was solid and warm, her breasts were flattened against him, and her hands were clutching his shoulders, the warmth of his skin burning through the thin hospital shirt he wore.

In that moment of comprehension her acquiescence became the beginnings of resistance. Mark's arms loosened about her as the same realization came to him. Very carefully Mickie took her hands from his shoulders and pushed herself upright, aware that her face was very red, but striving to achieve at least a surface calm. She took a deep breath and forced herself to look at him, forced herself to pretend that the earth had not just shaken beneath her.

It seemed as if a lifetime had passed in a blink of time, and yet the kiss had happened too quickly to be of any great significance. As she straightened, Mark let his arms fall away from her. Their gazes locked, and for the briefest instant Mickie wondered if she saw a question in his eyes. Then he grinned up at her and the moment was gone.

"Thank you!" he shouted, laughing happily. "Thank you, thank you, thank you! If I could dance with you, I would, but for now the kiss will have to do. Thank you!"

Mickie shook her head, laughing with him, a little flushed, a little flustered. She wished she could conceal both reactions.

"I've just been doing my job," she told him. "Nothing special. It's nice to be thanked, though."

Casual, she reminded herself, keep it very casual. If he wanted to call that kiss a thank-you, who was she to argue, though it had been so much more. That had been a kiss of passion between a man and a woman.

"When will this happen?" Mark was asking. "When can I get out?" Mickie pulled a chair up beside the bed, trying to recapture her professional manner. Her gaze fell on the deep vee of smooth skin and crisp hair revealed by his loose shirt. She had lain there; she could have pressed her cheek to that warm skin.... Mickie pulled herself together. She couldn't think about that, not now.

"I've scheduled everything for tomorrow," she said briskly. "We'll put your leg in a cast-brace that can be attached to the traction apparatus, but you can be out of traction for up to four hours a day at first. You have to realize that this isn't total freedom. I'm trying to reach a balance between the need for immobility so the bones can heal, and the need for some stress so they won't lose too much of their strength."

"And here I thought you were just concerned about my going crazy tied up here!"

"I'm an orthopedic surgeon, not a psychiatrist. Anyway, I think your mental status is pretty good. It's the status of your femur that concerns me."

"You always know how to take me down a peg or two, don't you?"

"Somebody has to," she observed dryly. "And I don't want you to get too carried away with this. I don't want you to expect too much, at least not right away. Keep in mind that you aren't going to feel like running a marathon on Thursday."

Mark refused to be cautioned. "I don't care how much gloom and doom you preach to me," he teased, "I refuse to let you rain on my parade!"

Chapter 5

"You're the one who told me not to rain on your parade,"
Mickie reminded him late the next day.

"You could have forced me to listen."

"How? By hitting you over the head? That's not considered standard medical practice."

Mark rolled his eyes at the ceiling. "I thought I was going to get out of this bed," he grumbled, "not be tied to it again with the addition of seven thousand pounds of wet plaster!" He scowled at the offending leg, suspended once again from the traction frame, but now encased in plaster from hip to knee and from knee to ankle, with a steel brace between the two casts.

Applying the cast-brace and taking repeated X rays to determine that the bones were in correct alignment had taken most of the morning. Mark had been returned to his room shortly after noon, but the thick plaster of the cast had still been wet. The bed was protected from drips by plastic sheeting and towels, and two electric fans were trained on the cast to speed drying, but the process was going to take at least twenty-four hours. Mark was less than thrilled.

Mickie strongly suspected that his mock-serious protests and complaints were a cover for deeper feelings of frustration and helplessness. She went along with the charade, aware of his need to ventilate his feelings and also aware that she was simply the most available target. She had a pretty tough hide; she could take it.

"If you will recall," she pointed out, playing the game, "I explained all this to you last night. This is a big cast—"

"No kidding!"

"This is a big cast," she repeated carefully, "and a big cast takes a long time to dry. If you'd managed to get yourself shot in the little finger, you'd have a little cast that would dry quickly, wouldn't you?"

"Very funny lady, my doctor," he commented to the ceiling. "She ought to be on TV, not in the operating room."

"Behave yourself, Mark. If you're a good boy, you and your seven-thousand-pound friend there can have a big treat tomorrow."

"And what might that big treat be?" he asked with heavy sarcasm.

Mickie moved toward the door, smiling sweetly. "If you're very good, I might—I just might—let you sit up on the side of your bed tomorrow."

Grinning, she slipped out the door, closing it quietly on the volley of angry curses that followed her announcement.

Mark hadn't taken her seriously when she warned him that he would feel weak. The next morning he found that simply sitting erect on the side of his bed presented more of a challenge than he had anticipated.

"The body adjusts to prolonged periods in a supine position—"

"What's supine?" Mark muttered, leaning heavily on the supporting arm Mickie held around him.

"Lying down. Lying on your back, actually. Anyway, the body adjusts by lowering your blood pressure to compensate for the absence of the pull of gravity. As a result, when you assume an upright position again, you become dizzy. It's called postural hypotension.''

"Is that so?" Mark's tone was dry.

"Just sit still and don't close your eyes. That can make the room go around."

"How did you know the room was going around?"

"I'm a doctor; we know all that stuff."

He laughed softly, the broad muscles of his back flexing beneath Mickie's hand.

She was standing close to Mark, facing him, one arm around his shoulders, the other resting lightly across his chest to keep him from falling forward. So close to him, holding his lightly clad body in her arms, her leg pressed against his naked leg, Mickie marveled at her ability to make coherent conversation. Mark was troubled by a sense of vertigo that was much more severe than he had expected, but Mickie was dealing with a certain amount of dizziness herself.

She could think of nothing but him. A good diet and strenuous therapy had done remarkable things for him. He had regained much of the weight he'd lost, but more striking was the strength he had regained. His arms and chest were lean but powerful, his back broad and strong. Mickie's supporting hand rested, by lucky—or perhaps dangerous—chance, on the warm strip of skin bared by the loose back of his hospital gown. She fought a wanton urge to caress the length of his back and kept her hand perfectly still.

She was afraid to even consider what, if anything, he might be wearing under that gown. She wasn't sure she could stand it. Beneath her hand the muscles flexed as he sat straighter. He took a deep breath and shook his head.

"I take it this gets better with time."

"The dizziness will go away faster than you think. Is the room still spinning?"

He looked up, then dropped his head again. "Yes, damn it, it is!" Suddenly he flared into anger, swearing under his breath. "This is ridiculous! You'd think I could at least sit up, for God's sake!"

"Mark, I told you that—"

"I know what you told me, damn it!" he snarled. "All you ever seem to do is tell me things; I'm getting a little bit sick of it, too!"

His frustration was easily understood, but Mickie's feelings for him were so confused that this time his anger hurt. She bit her lip, controlling her feelings; then quietly, carefully, she said, "I know you are. I don't mean to be too bossy, but you have to remember that your quick recovery depends on following the directions we give you."

He sighed heavily. "I know that, and I know you mean well, and you're a real saint, but right now I'm not in the mood, okay?"

"Sure," she replied without expression. "The nurses can stay with you until you're ready to lie down again. I'll see you tomorrow." A nurse responded quickly to the buzzer, and Mickie left with the briefest of goodbyes.

She was smarting from Mark's sarcastic words, and surprised that her understanding of the basis for his anger did nothing to mitigate the hurt. It frightened her that his casually thoughtless words could do that to her. She was becoming more and more involved with him, and there seemed to be nothing she could do about it.

On the other hand, she wasn't entirely sure she wanted to do something about it. It was too easy to remember what she'd felt with her arms around him, the warmth of his thigh against hers as she stood so close. He made her melt without even realizing what he did to her. What would happen to her if he were ever to try?

She took no chances, though. When she went to Mark's room the next afternoon she took reinforcements with her, in the form of a strapping young physical therapist named Keith. Mark was going to stand for the first time, and if he lost his balance, Mickie would need help to prevent him from falling. That was the objective reason for bringing

Keith, but Mickie hoped he would also provide a nice, impersonal buffer against her emotions.

Keith lowered the bed, parked a wheelchair beside it, locked the wheels and helped Mark to sit up. Then he and Mickie positioned themselves on either side of Mark, their arms linked around his back, ready to steady him.

"I don't want you to put your weight on the cast yet, Mark," Mickie cautioned him. "But if you need to touch your foot down for balance, that's okay."

"Mr. James, if you'd slide forward enough to touch your feet to the floor..." Keith helped Mark move until his feet were firmly on the floor. "Now stand upright as quickly as you feel comfortable doing, and—" His instructions were interrupted by the piercing demand of his beeper.

"Keith, if you need to go, I can stay here." Mickie's tone was calm, but inside she was shaking. The best laid plans...

"Thanks, Mickie, I'd appreciate it. I'm running behind this morning anyway. I have a treatment to do, and I told them to beep me when the patient got there. Ready to stand up, Mr. James?"

"More than ready."

Carefully, keeping his weight on his good leg as instructed, Mark rose to his feet. Keith stood by Mark's side, and Mickie moved in front of him, bracing his body with hers, her arms securely around him.

"Do you feel dizzy, Mark?"

He shook his head, surprised. "No, actually I don't."

"Good. Put your hands on my shoulders, and we'll stand here for a while before we put you in the chair. We'll be all right now, Keith. You can go to your patient. Thanks for the help."

"Anytime, Mickie. Good luck, Mr. James."

Keith went off with a breezy wave, leaving them standing in each other's arms. There was a long, rather uncomfortable silence.

"How do you feel?" Mickie asked after several moments of gazing at his jaw. She could see the shadow of his beard, the hard, exciting line of his lips, firmed now in concentration. Something had to be said, if only to break that silence.

"A little light-headed, but better than I expected after yesterday."

"Are you having any pain in your leg?"

"It aches a little, but it's been doing that all along."

"Nothing new?"

"Nope."

"Good."

The awkward silence returned. Mickie could think of nothing more to say, could think of nothing at all but Mark James. He was a taller man than she'd realized, and they were standing locked together in a parody of an embrace. His arms were around her shoulders, her hands clasped behind his back, the warmth and strength of him surrounding her.

She dropped her gaze from his jaw, only to find a more disturbing vista. He wore a scrub shirt and pants today, with a hospital bathrobe over them. The neck of the loose shirt revealed a vee of deeply tanned chest, hard and muscular and dusted with dark hair. Thinking to steady her rapid pulse, she drew a deep breath, but that only filled her senses with the scent of him, warm skin and hospital soap and something else elusive and male.

He moved his hands from her shoulders to her back, and Mickie leaned closer, thinking he was off-balance. Her own hands slipped over his back in a subtle caress, sensing the play of muscle there, then moved again, unable to resist temptation. The impact of his closeness was like a blow, stealing Mickie's breath, weakening her knees. And she wasn't the only one.

She could feel the tensing of Mark's muscles, sense the slight catch in his breathing as his hands began to move, gliding over her back, shaping the line of her ribs. His fingertips pressed gently at her waist, finding spots that sent little thrills of delight through her. Mickie's bones seemed to soften, and instinctively she leaned into the curve of his body, wanting more of this drugging closeness.

Her greed was her undoing. However much Mark might have wanted to take her weight against him, he was still far too wobbly. Wearing a heavy, full-leg cast that he was not yet accustomed to, with only one foot securely on the floor, he couldn't balance them both. He swayed, then grabbed Mickie's shoulders, leaning heavily against her. Mickie clutched his back, struggling to brace him, but his weight fell onto his injured leg.

"Ah—" He bit off the exclamation, struggling to balance himself again. Mickie moved quickly, wedging her shoulder under his arm, taking as much of his weight as she could.

"Can you get to the chair?" she gasped. "On your good leg?"

"Yeah, I think so."

"I'll turn you around, if you can just come with me..." Mickie moved carefully, helping Mark to turn with her, bracing his legs with hers until he could carefully lower himself into the wheelchair. As soon as he was seated she moved away, ending the dangerous contact between them.

"Is your leg okay?" She knelt to lower the footrests and position his cast, trying to hide her embarrassment behind a briskly professional manner. "Are you feeling any pain?"

"I'm fine. Don't worry about it." Mark reached down to take her chin in his fingers and lift her face. "Don't try to hide it, Mickie," he said softly.

"Hide what?" For one idiotic moment she imagined he was referring to his cast. Then she understood. "Oh." Her color rose, but she met his searching gaze bravely. "There really isn't anything to hide, is there?"

After a moment's scrutiny of her face, Mark laughed softly. "Okay, if that's the way you want to play it, *Dr. Blake*. You and I will know the truth, though, won't we?"

Mickie said nothing. With an effort she hid her feelings.

He laughed again and released her chin, leaning back in the chair. "So where are you taking me on my first tour?"

"What would you like to see?" Mickie took the brakes off and moved behind the chair, relieved to be out of his line of sight. He had already seen far too much.

"You're the tour guide," he told her. "What are the attractions?"

Back on safe ground again, Mickie began to smile. "Well, sir," she said in her best officious-tour-guide manner, "we have the hospital cafeteria, a particularly exciting stop for the discriminating gourmet, or there is the main lobby. The gift shop, perhaps? And, not to be missed, the solarium."

He shook his head, laughing, the tension between them easing at last. "It all sounds too good to pass up! Why don't you just show me everything, taking the most scenic route, please."

She snorted in derision. "If you think there's a 'scenic' route in this hospital, you've led a very sheltered life." She turned the chair to back out the door, and Mark smiled to himself.

He couldn't see her, but he didn't need to. The light whisper of her fragrance surrounded him, mingling with the woman-warmth of her skin in a powerfully erotic perfume. The warmth of her body still lingered on him, the feel of her in his arms. He smiled again. For such a brisk and bossy thing, she was quite a woman. He wouldn't have expected the red-haired spitfire that was Dr. Blake to melt against him in such sweet surrender, wouldn't have expected the sudden clinging heat of her body.

He wouldn't have expected the shyness, either, the blush that had pinkened her cheeks when he had mentioned their attraction. An unusual mixture, the tough doctor, the sweetly responsive woman and the shy girl. He felt his body respond to his thoughts and willed the response away. This was not the time or the place.

"For the first stop on your tour, we have the fifth-floor solarium," she began in a tour-guide's monotone patter.

"This lovely room was redecorated as recently as 1957, in institutional green and bland beige, calming colors which I'm sure you will enjoy."

"You're really going to show me everything, aren't you?"

"As promised, sir," He could hear the smile in her voice. She did her best, wheeling him through the maze of corridors from one wing of the vast hospital to another, keeping up her guide's patter all the while. When she had exhausted the hospital's entertainment possibilities, she made for the large courtyard in the center of the complex. It was a grassy expanse, sunny and protected from the breeze, dotted with hibiscus and palm tress, with park benches and picnic tables. Mickie found a shady corner and parked the chair by an unoccupied bench.

"So, was the tour worth the money?"

Mark frowned, considering. He 'considered' so long that Mickie finally poked his arm.

"Come on, you can hardly expect Cook's Tour service from a poor overworked orthopedist!"

"Very nice, actually," he said with a finicky tourist's air of qualified enthusiasm. "A bit short on excitement, perhaps, but restful."

"Keep it up and you'll find yourself back in traction before your four hours of freedom are over, buster."

"Great tour!" was the hasty response. "Absolutely fantastic. I'll never forget it! And you know—" he turned to gaze intently into her eyes "—I think the *most* fascinating part was the main lobby. There's just something so...moving about those marvelous 1950's stainless-steel light fixtures. It choked me up; it really did."

Mickie shook her head in admiring wonder. "If you ever decide to go on stage you'll have a great career waiting for you. That was one of the most impressive, albeit nauseating, pieces of acting I've ever seen."

"That good, huh?"

"Very convincing."

"To tell you the truth, it's great just to be out. Do you realize that this is the first time I've left my room except to go for X rays or surgery? Actually, this is the first time I've been free to move around since I was captured." He looked at the brilliantly blue sky, at the people around them, walking, talking, laughing. "It feels good."

"I'm glad," Mickie said softly. She looked out at the other afternoon strollers. "I'm glad you—" She stopped short when Mark seized the wheels of his chair and turned himself awkwardly around so that his back was to the sunwashed center of the courtyard. Mickie stared at him. "What are you doing?" She turned on the bench to see his face, closed and impassive. "Is something wrong?"

He shrugged. "The sun was in my eyes. It's really bright, isn't it?"

"This is San Diego," she reminded him dryly. "Sunny is a fact of life. Now, what's wrong?"

"Nothing," was his terse reply. He was studying his hands, which were lying loosely on his knees, with intent concentration. "Nothing's wrong. It just seems like there are an awful lot of people out here, kind of a crowd."

"Oh." She looked around again. There were quite a few people in the courtyard, but it didn't seem especially crowded to her. He had been held prisoner for a long time, though, she reminded herself. Perhaps he felt a sort of claustrophobia here.

"That's no problem," she said, standing and taking the chair handles. "We don't have to stay here. Just tell me where you'd like to go next."

"No!" His voice was low and harsh. He grabbed the wheels, holding the chair still. "Stay here!"

"What in the wor—"

"Miss?" Mickie was interrupted by someone behind her. She turned to see a small, dark man standing very close. He was dressed in a cheap gray suit, tight and shiny, and his face was screened by dark sunglasses. "Miss?" he repeated in heavily accented English. "Can you direct me to the main desk? I wish to visit my sister, but I do not know where to find her."

He took a step closer, coming so near that Mickie involuntarily backed a step away, bumping into Mark's wheelchair. She was sandwiched between the side of the chair and the small man, practically sitting on Mark's lap, and she had to grab one of the handles to keep her balance.

The man in the shiny suit tipped his head to the side, waiting for an answer. Mickie couldn't see his eyes behind the nearly opaque glasses, but he didn't seem to be looking at her. She thought he was looking around her, at Mark, who sat with his head bent, rummaging in the pocket of his robe.

"Certainly I can," she began. "The main desk is through that door." Mark blew his nose noisily, and she glanced down in surprise. His face was buried in a handkerchief. "That door," she repeated, pointing across the courtyard, wishing the little man would move away and stop invading her personal space. "Go through there and turn left at the first corner. That corridor will lead you to the information desk. They can tell you how to get to your sister's room."

"*Sí.* Yes, thank you. Thank you, miss. Good day, miss—sir." He bobbed a little bow, nodding around Mickie at Mark, who blew gustily into the handkerchief, which still covered his face.

"Good day," Mickie said firmly. The little man took the hint and moved away at last. He walked slowly toward the door, looking back to wave and bow to them before he finally vanished from sight.

With a last sniffle Mark finally emerged from the depths of his handkerchief. Mickie looked from him to the door through which the man in the sunglasses had disappeared, then back.

"What on earth was that all about?"

"Hmm?" His look of innocence was masterfully done. Mickie didn't buy it for a minute.

"Blowing your nose, that's what! You don't have a cold, and you know it."

"Hay fever, I guess," he said, and sniffed again. "All the flowers out here must be aggravating it."

Mickie raised her eyebrows skeptically. "Funny that you haven't had any hay fever until today, isn't it?"

"I haven't been outside until today," he pointed out blandly. "You know, I'm getting kind of tired. Do you think we could go back inside?"

"You're the boss." Mickie rolled the chair toward his wing of the hospital. "It's odd," she reflected after a few minutes, "but you were tested for the most common allergies before we gave you medications. We didn't find that you had any."

"There must be something uncommon out there."

"Sure."

She wheeled him on through the hospital, her unspoken opinion hanging in the air between them. He hadn't sniffled or sneezed once until the man in the shiny suit and sunglasses showed up. There was a connection there, but until he chose to tell her what it was, she had to remain in ignorance. Mickie didn't like being left in the dark; she didn't like it one little bit.

When she did her evening rounds she found herself presented with another situation she didn't like. As was her habit, she had visited her other patients first, leaving Mark for last. She wasn't sure exactly what she wanted to say to him, but after that afternoon's weird incident, she knew they needed to talk.

"Well, Mark, are you ready to tell me what all that nonsense was about this afternoon?" Mickie breezed into his room, received a subdued greeting, and went on the offensive.

"I was just sneezing, I—"

"I need to talk to you, Miss Blake." The interruption came from the doorway behind her, and Mickie spun around to see Commander Lewis enter.

"It's Doctor Blake," she told him coolly.

"Uh, yeah." Lewis crossed to the bedside and dropped his burly bulk into the chair. "Mark, you all right?"

"Yeah, I'm fine."

The two men seemed to be getting along awfully well, certainly better than they had up to now, she thought. Mickie knew she was probably paranoid, but their uncharacteristic accord somehow seemed more an ominous sign than a positive one.

"I'm a little surprised to see you here so late, Commander. Is there some problem?"

"Yes, there is," he replied, and Mickie dragged up the other chair. She might as well sit down to hear the bad news.

"So," she said, when she was comfortable, "What's wrong?"

"Mark has to be moved to another room, preferably a room on another floor."

"Why?" The question seemed a reasonable one to Mickie, but neither man would even meet her eyes, let alone answer her.

"It's necessary that he be moved," said Lewis after several seconds.

That was no answer at all, she thought, so she repeated her question, ignoring Lewis this time.

"Why do you need another room, Mark?"

He shrugged. "Let's just leave it at the fact that I do. Unless I could be discharged now?"

Mickie shook her head firmly, her annoyance growing at this unexplained demand. "No way. It's too early to discharge you." She looked from one man to the other. "You know, I don't appreciate the two of you insulting my intelligence this way. Just why do you need another room, Mark? And why," she looked from him to Lewis, "are you two getting along so well? That in itself is enough to make me uneasy."

Mark stifled a laugh, and even Lewis's stony face showed a rare twitch of humor, but it was obvious that Mickie wasn't mollified.

"Miss Bla—" Lewis stopped."Doctor Blake," he rephrased himself carefully, "I can only tell you that it is imperative that Mark be moved to another part of the hospital. And that it should be done as soon as possible."

"I'm sorry, Commander, but that isn't good enough. I'm perfectly well aware that there are a lot of unusual aspects to Mark's case, and that you haven't seen fit to apprise me of many of them. If I'm going to be forced to operate in ignorance I see no reason to be blindly cooperative." She sat back and folded her arms across her chest, waiting.

Lewis shifted uncomfortably in his chair, annoyed by her stubbornness. He shot her a furious glance, his heavy-featured face reddening with irritation.

Mickie met his eyes with a bland half smile. She knew that she was a particularly irritating thorn in his side. Lewis was the type to like women who knew their place and kept quiet. Mickie suspected that he also felt a reluctant respect for a woman who would stand up to him. She had no intention of doing anything less.

She was thinking hard while she waited, trying to work out the solution to this puzzle on her own. After a moment understanding began to dawn. Connie would have guessed the reason right away. It was too obvious, and too ominous, and she knew immediately why she hadn't been willing to see the truth before.

Chapter 6

You want to move him because you want to hide him!" If she had been at all uncertain, the flicker of dismay that crossed Lewis's face would have confirmed her assumption. Now that she was on the right track, everything was beginning to add up. "You want to hide him," she repeated triumphantly, "and you want to do it right away because of that little guy who asked for directions today! That's it, isn't it?"

Neither of the men said no, and that was as good as a yes.

She turned to Mark. "You should have known I'd see through all that nonsense about colds and hay fever. I've been looking at your lab results and blood tests, remember? Your white count is good, and everything else is absolutely normal. You don't have a cold *or* hay fever."

"I had to hide my face. That was the only thing I could think of."

"It worked." Mickie almost grinned. "All I could see was your ears."

"How much do you think he saw?"

"About the same, I imagine. Did you recognize him? Was that why you hid your face?"

"I didn't recognize him, not specifically. I've never seen him before. He was in the wrong place at the wrong time, though. He came all the way across the courtyard to us, past several people who could have told him where the desk was, just to ask you that question. That doesn't make sense, and I have to be suspicious of things that don't make sense."

Mickie regarded him with disbelief for a moment. "This is silly!" she said, and shook her head. "This is nuts! You two sound like a spy story!"

"That may be true, but it isn't silly, Miss—Dr. Blake." Lewis leaned forward in his chair to make his point. "It's—"

"*I* think it's silly as hell," Mark growled. "And I agree with Mickie. This resembles nothing so much as a spy novel. A bad one. I hope you know I'm only going along with this damned room-change business because I can't be certain that you government guys can keep these people away from me."

"It was being too casual about security that got you in this position in the first place," Lewis retorted, earning a dark look for his reminder. "You really ought to be in a military hospital, where those 'government guys' can look out for you. I know this is only one small group of fanatics that we're dealing with, but you can't take them lightly. They may think you know too much about their operation, and they won't stop trying to silence you."

"Well, it's your job to see that they don't succeed, isn't it, Will? I'm not going to a military hospital, though, and that's final. They'd see that as an admission that I know something. I may be in some danger here, but I'd be a sitting duck there!" They were nearly shouting at each other again, and there was something both reassuring and sobering about that.

Mickie interrupted the escalating argument. "I can't believe this is actually happening! You're really serious about this, aren't you? You two are actually serious."

"Of course we're serious!" Mark snarled at her. "You don't think I'd be going along with this nonsense otherwise do you?"

"Look," Mickie said placatingly, "if you want to change your room, we can change your room. That's no problem. We can't move you to another floor, though."

"Why the hell not?" Lewis demanded.

"You know, I wish you would both quit yelling at me. Why the hell not is because his traction setup would call too much attention to him. On any floor but Orthopedics that would be as good as a printed announcement of where he is."

"Terrific! So where does that leave us?"

Mickie glared at Lewis. "Will you be quiet for a minute and let me think?" He subsided into his chair, and after a moment's thought she turned to Mark. "There's one place that might work. The isolation room on this floor is empty right now. It's down at the end of the hall, and it has an alarm system on the door. Whenever anyone goes in or out a signal lights up at the nurses' station. The door can be locked, too."

They looked at each other, then at her. Mark nodded.

"That sounds like it will do okay," Lewis said. "When can we move him?"

"Tonight, if the room doesn't need to be cleaned. We just roll the bed and the traction setup down the hall."

"Right," Lewis said," I want only the minimum number of staff to know about this. As far as everyone else is concerned, that room is empty."

Mickie squelched an urge to snap, "Aye-aye, sir."

Apparently unaware of her reaction, he continued, "The hospital records will show that Mark was discharged today, and if asked, you and the staff taking care of him will have no knowledge of his whereabouts."

Mickie managed to hold her tongue as Lewis rapped out his final instructions, but turned to Mark with an incredulous chuckle when he finally departed.

"Whew!" She was standing by the bed, and she looked down at him. "He's used to giving orders, isn't he?"

"Too used to it, if you ask me. It bugs the hell out of him when he doesn't have the final word."

"I could tell," she said dryly.

"Let me apologize for him. He can't help it, you know. I'm sorry for all the trouble, too. I don't want to make waves and upset the system around here, but as much as I hate to admit it, he may be right. What really worries me is that you could be in danger, too, because of me."

"Me? Oh, come on, that's silly! No one is going to be interested in me."

"You're my physician of record. They'll figure I may have talked to you, and they won't want to take any chances. They'd kill you without even giving it a second thought."

"Oh, please!" Mickie scoffed. "Now you really do sound like something out of a spy story." Mark reached out to seize her wrist in a painful grip before she could move away from the bedside.

"It doesn't matter if this all sounds stupid to you; it isn't. If you don't feel like you can go along with the precautions we ask for, I'll do what Will wants and check into a military hospital!"

"I thought you said you'd be a sitting duck at a military hospital."

"I would be. Will is being naive to think I'd be safer there. These guys are convinced I'm military myself, so that's where they'd expect to find me."

Mickie studied him soberly for a long moment. His face showed no flicker of uncertainty. "I still think this is all too bizarre for words, you know. You're obviously convinced, though, and I can't discount that. I'll do what you ask." She tried to pull her wrist free, unsuccessfully.

"And you'll be careful?" His fingers tightened.

"I'll be careful."

"Good."

Mickie waited a moment, then asked, "Can I please have my hand back now?"

He looked at their hands in surprise. "My God, I'm sorry!" He released her, staring in horror at the imprints of his fingers. There would be bruises later. "God, I'm sorry, Mickie! I didn't realize I was doing that."

Gently, tenderly, he took her hand lightly in his. Carefully he smoothed his fingertips over the reddened blotches. "I'm sorry," he whispered. "I didn't realize..." He cupped his hand around her arm and brought it to his lips, to press one kiss, then another and another, to the bruised skin of her inner wrist.

Those kisses jolted through Mickie like bolts of lightning, running hot along her veins, electrifying her. The pain of her bruised wrist vanished as if it had never been, supplanted by a different sort of pain. His lips moved softly over her skin, seeking the injured places, heating, healing. The delicate pressure of his touch drew her toward him, but whether his pull was physical or something less tangible, yet more powerful, she couldn't have said.

Her fingers moved, curving around his hand as her body curved over his, a captive on his narrow bed. She was drawn to him, impelled by a force she didn't fully understand, a force she couldn't have fought if she'd wanted to. And she didn't want to.

In slow motion she went down to him, her hands sliding up his arms to curve beneath his head, her fingertips tangling in the hair that waved crisply onto his neck. She bent slowly to him, savoring the anticipation as the scent of his skin, the strength and warmth of his body below her, filled her senses.

She met his eyes, gazed into fathomless dark depths, then looked down at the exciting curve of his lips. Her mouth was dry, and she moistened her lips with the tip of her tongue, sensing the sudden acceleration of his heartbeat beneath her.

She had only to lower her lips a fraction and they would meet his, only the merest fraction....

Their mouths touched, brushed, a whisper of contact, brushed again, then came together with a need that could no longer be denied, clinging greedily, hungrily.

For just a moment Mickie gave herself up to the sheer delight of it, ignoring all the reasons why this was crazy, wrong, a hopelessly stupid thing to do. How could it be wrong when it felt so utterly right?

And yet it wasn't right. It *was* wrong, and she forced herself to pull away from him, slowly, reluctantly. He resisted for an instant, his hands tightening on her arms until he, too, understood and let her go.

Mickie could feel a blush scorching her cheeks when she realized that she was sprawled halfway across the bed—half across Mark. She shoved herself hastily upright and backed apprehensively away from the bed. She couldn't even meet Mark's gaze, but turned quickly to the traction setup, checking the adjustment of the weights. She fiddled with them as long as she could, but eventually she had to face him.

He was lying back against the pillows, watching her, when she turned to him. She could read nothing in his eyes; dark and opaque, they gave no hint of what he was thinking. Mickie wasn't sure she really wanted to know his feelings. Her own were too confused to be sorted out.

"I have to go," she blurted after an awkward pause. "Is there—is there anything you need?" He lifted one eloquent eyebrow and, too late, Mickie realized what she'd said. She flushed painfully and turned away. "Good night, Mark. I'll see you tomorrow."

"Mickie—"

She stopped with her hand on the door and looked back at him. "Yes?"

"Don't beat yourself over the head about a kiss, Mickie. It was only a kiss, after all, not a catastrophe."

"Yeah," she agreed quietly. "Good night, Mark."

She walked out. So the kiss hadn't been a catastrophe? Or perhaps it just wasn't important? The latter was right, she was sure. That kiss had no doubt been born of little more than propinquity and hormones, but what did that say about the uproar within Mickie herself? That kiss might not have meant anything to Mark, but what it was doing to her was practically cataclysmic.

And how on earth, Mickie wondered, was she going to deal with this?

The answer to that question eluded her over the next several days, though she actually had little time to consider it. She was too preoccupied with the mechanics of keeping Mark James hidden to think about much else.

Try as she might, Mickie found it difficult to take all the subterfuge and secrecy seriously. It felt like a child's game of cops and robbers to her. Granted, it was being taken to a startling extreme, but it still felt like a game. The cloak and dagger elements, the carefully—but discreetly—guarded door of the ostensibly unoccupied isolation room, the sneaking along hallways, the double entendres in which those who shared the secret had to speak, all seemed just on the edge of silliness.

She really did try, Mickie thought, but it was just so difficult to keep a properly serious attitude. Connie didn't help, exercising such an exaggerated degree of caution that Mickie fully expected her to come to work in a disguise one day. A battered trench coat and fedora, perhaps.

Despite her personal reservations, Mickie supervised the arrangement of Mark's room as a complete treatment center, moving in all the equipment he would need. There were numerous administrative details to be attended to, from arranging a nursing schedule and smuggling in his meals to writing up false but plausible discharge papers and placing them on file in the records room. Only one or two nurses on each shift knew of Mark's presence on the floor; to all others, the isolation room was off limits until it was "renovated."

Since Mark was officially discharged, Mickie had to take over the duties of the ancillary personnel who had been participating in his care. She became, by default, his dietitian, his nursing assistant, his physical therapist and, on one memorable occasion when his temper got the better of him and he heaved his water pitcher at the wall, even his housekeeper, scrubbing the floor in his room with mop and bucket.

She found that by concentrating on each task she could use constant busyness to keep the intimacy from recurring between them. It appeared, on the surface at least, to be a highly effective tactic. Their conversations seemed to revolve almost exclusively around medical matters.

Piece by piece, with the cooperation of the hospital administrator, who had agreed to the deception, she and Connie had smuggled exercise equipment into Mark's room. Having taken over as Mark's therapist, Mickie prescribed exercises for him and helped him through them for the first several days after his move into hiding. He didn't seem particulary enthusiastic, but he dutifully followed the daily routine, prompted by her reminder that his recovery depended on his cooperation and hard work.

He needed to be motivated, though, needed a challenge to keep him interested and working hard. Mickie considered the problem for a few days, then put a plan into action. A week after his entry into seclusion, Mickie brought her own exercise clothes when she came to his room for their session.

Mark sat in his wheelchair, waiting for her. "I'll be right with you," she told him, and vanished into the room's tiny bath to change.

"What are you doing, dressed like that?" Mark demanded when she emerged. He looked her up and down, frowning at her outfit of pink tights, lavender leotard, and an ancient and faded University of California at San Diego T-shirt. Like her, Mark was dressed in exercise clothes, but his were more restrained: blue gym shorts and a plain white T-shirt.

"I'm going to exercise with you." She grinned. "A little competition will do you good, you know."

"Yeah, I guess it would." Mark spun his wheelchair around and rolled toward the multi-function exercise machine. "So who's going to be the competition here?"

"You're looking at her." Mickie flexed a slim but strong arm. "Orthopedics is a physically demanding specialty, you know. That's why there aren't very many women in the field. It takes a lot of pushing and pulling to get bones back into line. Just plain brute force. Actually," she laughed at the memory, "at one of my interviews for my orthopedic residency, the professor who was interviewing me insisted on arm wrestling, just to see if I was strong enough for the work!"

Mark was frankly skeptical. "Brute force, huh? Did you have to use brute force on my leg?"

"Did I ever!" Mickie looked up from adjusting the tension cylinders on the machine and rolled her eyes. "Your trip through the jungle on that leg did nothing to make my job any easier. I had a resident and a couple of medical students in surgery with me that day, and I put them all to work."

"What did they do?"

"They pulled, I pushed, and we finally managed to line your bones up." She stepped back and gestured toward the machine. "You go first. We'll start with curls."

"And you?"

"I'll do my sets after you. You want to keep score?"

"You got a deal, lady doctor." With a confident smile he moved himself from the chair to the machine.

That smile was fraying by the time they'd done several sets of exercises. Mickie's idea of challenging him to push his performance to new limits was a rousing success, but another challenge hung unspoken between them, a challenge of a different sort.

Dressed in her body-hugging exercise clothes, Mickie looked very little like a doctor and very much a woman. She knew Mark was aware of that, as acutely as she was aware of him as a man. She watched his body surreptitiously, fascinated by the strong lines of bone and muscle, by the flex and stretch as he moved. She tried to keep her ogling discreet, but when she surprised Mark watching her, she knew her efforts had failed. She looked hastily away, but the knowledge in his eyes sent a warm glow through her.

There was more than one issue being contested, but for the time being they both concentrated on the tangible challenge of athletic performance. Mickie used slightly lighter weights than Mark, in deference to her slighter build, but she surprised him with her strength and stamina. Especially her stamina.

"You weren't kidding, were you?" he asked as he finished a set. He was slightly breathless.

"Kidding about what?" Mickie helped him off the machine.

"About needing strength for orthopedics."

"Nope. It's the truth. I'm not using as much weight as you are right now, because I need the repetitions. When I'm pulling on a bone, though, I'd better be able to pull as hard as a man."

"How much weight can you press? Just one press."

"I don't know. I never tried just one press. What's it set on now?"

"Number four. I don't know how many pounds that is, but it's pretty stiff. I have to push myself to do a full set of repetitions."

"Okay, let's see." Mickie slid onto the vinyl seat and squirmed into place, reaching up for the hand grips just above her shoulders. She pushed experimentally and grimaced. "I didn't realize how stiff this was. You're making better progress than I expected."

"Quit trying to avoid the issue, Doc. Let's see how strong you are."

"Nag, nag, nag." She settled herself and pushed. Her face reddened with the effort, but the cylinders hissed softly and the handles slowly lifted as her arms and back strained. With the last of her strength she reached full extension and dropped her hands with a gusty sigh. The handles drifted back down with a gentle whisper as the air was forced from the cylinders. "Whew! I wouldn't like to try for a full set of those!"

"That's not bad, though for—"

"Don't you dare say, 'for a girl!'"

"I was going to say, 'for a woman,'" he retorted with an offended glare. "But if you want to be that way about it, I won't say anything."

"Well, excu-u-use me!" She fought to keep a straight face. "Now I have a surprise for you."

"Uh-oh. Do I dare ask what it is?"

"It's your leg."

"My leg?" He studied the long, sturdy limb below his shorts.

"Not that leg, the other one. The one in the cast!"

"Really?" He clumsily extended the injured leg. "What can I do with this leg besides drag it around in the wheelchair?"

"You can do leg-presses with it, that's what."

"No kidding?"

"I won't let you use any resistance at first, but you can do them, all right. It's time to start moving that leg to prevent damage to the joint. I'm hoping to start reversing the atrophy of the muscles and strengthen the bone, too."

"Well, let's get to it!" Mark started to lift himself out of the chair, but Mickie moved quickly to forestall him.

"No, wait." She pushed him back into the chair. "I'll help you get onto the machine. That's what the presses are for—to get you ready to stand up on your own. You have to take this one step at a time."

"So let's get to the first step!"

With her help he maneuvered himself into position. Mickie released the tension from the cylinders, positioned his leg and bent over him to steady it as he moved. She stood facing him, her head almost touching his chest as she held the lower-leg cast lightly between her hands.

"The knee brace will move freely front to back," she told him, "but keep in mind that you have no mediolateral rotation with it."

"What's that mean?"

"You can't turn your lower leg in or out. Try to avoid that kind of movement so you don't put extra stress on the leg."

"Okay. What now?"

"Now push on the pedal, slowly, and stop if you feel any pain, anything at all. If you feel you can't control the motion, don't try to go any further."

"Right." He pushed slowly, following her instructions, concentrating intently. His movements grew more confident as he repeated them, smoother and more sure.

Too soon for Mark, she called a halt. "Okay, that's enough." She held his cast steady as the pedal stilled. "I don't want you to overdo it."

"You're a spoilsport, you know that?" He took his hands from the braces and dropped them to her shoulders. Mickie looked up from her crouched position, her hands still clasping his plastered ankle, her face on a level with his lean midriff.

"Spoilsport, am I?" She grinned up at him, then the grin faded. He was watching her face intently, a gleam in his dark eyes.

"No, maybe I spoke too soon." He smiled. "Not a spoilsport at all," he said softly, "but a miracle worker."

"Hmmm?" She didn't understand.

His hands moved to stroke her hair. "A miracle worker. When I was crawling through the jungle I was convinced that even if I got out of there alive, the first doctor I saw would take one look at my leg and amputate it. I knew—I was *certain*—that I was going to lose my leg. And until today, until now, when I actually moved it, I don't think I really believed that it would ever be useful again." He stroked her neck, his fingers curving around her nape, toying with the coppery curls there as he lifted her face. "You did that for me, Mickie. I know I'll walk again . . . because of you."

Mickie meant to protest, but the only sound that escaped her lips was a little sigh as he captured them with his own, captured them in a kiss. Sitting on the exercise machine, with Mickie crouched at his feet, he might have been as able-bodied as she, big and strong and very, very male. It began as a kiss of triumph and thanks, but blossomed rapidly into a kiss of passion, searching and sweet.

Mickie pretended no coyness but sank into that passion, reveling in it as Mark's hands moved over her shoulders and down the length of her spine to pull her into his arms. Drawn up against him, she melted into the curve of his body, her breasts pressed against his chest as her arms twined around his neck. Striving for even more closeness, she pushed herself up on her knees—and nearly knocked Mark off the machine.

He lurched to the side, grunting an oath as their lips were jerked apart. Mickie grabbed at him, clutching his waist, his arm, struggling to keep him from falling. She hooked one leg around an upright to brace herself and pulled Mark back until he was safely seated again.

"Are you okay?" she gasped. "Is your leg okay?"

"I'm fine, I'm fine." He waved her hands away irritably. "I'm *okay*! I just feel kind of insecure up here. Can I get back into the wheelchair now?"

"Oh! Oh, yes, of course!" She helped him back into the relative security of the chair. "I've got to get this stuff picked up. It's all over the floor and—" She would have turned away, but he caught her hand and held her there.

"I should probably say I'm sorry for that kiss," he told her, smiling lopsidedly up at her, "but I won't. I'm not sorry. I've been wanting that for days now."

Mickie tipped her head to the side, a tiny smile on her lips. "I wouldn't want you to apologize," she said softly. "There's no need. I've wanted it, too."

Mark's face went still, whether in surprise or shock Mickie wasn't sure. Apparently he'd expected some sort of maidenly protest from her rather than an honest answer. Mickie bent over him in the wheelchair, winding her arms around his neck again.

"You must have realized." She smiled.

He reached up to remove her hands.

Mickie saw the change, felt the coldness in him. "Mark, you know I care a lot about you." She tried awkwardly to explain. She could tell she wasn't making herself clear to him. "I'm glad you're recovering so well."

He pushed her away almost roughly. "Is that what you're doing? 'Caring' about me? Is this how you care about *all* your patients?" Mickie straightened to stand silently before him, confusion and hurt welling up in her. His voice grew angrier. "I can see what you're trying to do, lady," he said harshly, "and it won't work with me! You aren't going to manipulate me into anything I don't want!"

Mickie drew herself up, tall and proud. "Is that what you think?" she asked quietly. "That I'm trying to manipulate you?"

"What else?"

"I'm just telling you the truth."

He said nothing, and she shook her head, a little rueful, a little sad. Mickie pulled her lab coat over her exercise clothes and stuffed everything else into her gym bag. "I'll have the nurse come in to help you to bed," she said over her shoulder as she crossed to the door. With her hand on the knob she paused, looking back at him.

"Mark?"

"What?"

"Why should the truth bother you so much?" she asked quietly, and left him staring at the door.

Chapter 7

Mickie didn't have much appetite for lunch as she stood in the cafeteria line an hour later. She was too preoccupied with thoughts of Mark, that kiss and his oddly hostile reaction. It didn't make a lot of sense. He'd been perfectly free with his admission that he wanted to kiss her; why should he be so upset when she was equally honest?

He should be flattered, she thought indignantly. He should be pleased that she felt confident enough to reveal her feelings to him. But no, he expected the sort of silly-little-woman, handkerchief-fluttering playacting that had gone out in the Victorian Age. Talk about the old double standard, it was alive and well in the person of one Mark James!

It didn't make sense, and yet it did. He didn't hesitate to admit to simple lust for her, but he was extremely uncomfortable when she admitted that she felt something for him. Maybe it was another defense mechanism. His feelings for her included simple lust, that much was obvious, but they had to go beyond that. He wouldn't feel he had to fight so hard against simple lust. Interesting thought.

She wasn't in the mood for company, so after blindly choosing several dishes, she took a free table in an isolated corner of the room, slid her tray onto it and looked with dismayed surprise at the ill-assorted meal she had selected. Potato salad, a taco, and a piece of rhubarb pie looked back at her. She shuddered. If she ate this combination she'd pay for it all day.

"Yuck! And half the night, too," she muttered. "I can't eat this stuff." And she wouldn't. She wasn't hungry anyway, so she'd just get rid of it and go back to work.

"Excuse me?" asked a heavily-accented voice before she could move. A tray slid onto the table beside hers.

Mickie looked up—and froze.

She managed to show no overt reaction, but her eyes widened fractionally as alarms and sirens went off inside her head. Unless she was very much mistaken, she was being joined for lunch by the same little man who had asked her for directions in the courtyard.

He was dressed differently today, in the clothes of a working man, and he no longer wore dark sunglasses, but he was the same little man. No, she reminded herself, he wasn't just a little man who asked directions, he was very likely an agent of the guerrilla group that had held Mark captive. Suddenly all the cloak-and-dagger secrecy seemed horribly appropriate.

Mickie didn't know if she had the sangfroid to maintain that secrecy in a face-to-face encounter, but she was about to find out. It was obvious that this was not a chance meeting. She had chosen a table tucked away in an inconspicuous corner; he had followed her. So, she deduced, thinking fast, he knew who she was and had sought her out. Presumably he wanted information about Mark, information she would not give him.

He behaved as though they had never met, so he evidently didn't expect her to recognize him. If he didn't think she recognized him, Mickie decided, it would be in her best interest not to reveal that she did. He might already be suspicious of her. She had to give the appearance of complete innocence.

"Excuse me?" he repeated, and indicated the empty chair opposite hers. "May I take this seat? The room is crowded."

Mickie glanced around them and saw several free tables. She decided not to point that out.

"Of course," she agreed with bland politeness. She moved a folder of notes out of his way, and he pushed his tray into place.

"Enjoy your lunch, please, Miss" he said.

Mickie smothered a groan. She was going to have to do more than give the performance of her life. In order to keep up the appearance of normality and throw this man off Mark's trail, she was going to have to eat the weird combination of food she had chosen. The only thing that could possibly make this lunch worse than it already was, was having to eat it. And thanks to this creepy little spy or assassin, or whatever he was, she would have to do just that. She looked down at her tray and winced. If he turned out to be responsible for her having indigestion all afternoon, she would see that he paid for it. She took a first reluctant bite of the potato salad and opened her folder of notes again. "What is that, miss? That you are reading?" "What—?" Mickie looked up to find the man watching her intently, too intently. She laughed lightly, easily. "These?" He nodded, his eyes cold and unwavering on her face. "They're notes for the Grand Rounds this afternoon. I'm giving a presentation to a group of doctors and medical students. We have a very interesting patient on the Orthopedics ward right now." She could see the quick flare of interest in his eyes and smiled cheerfully. "We've been working on developing a new technique for treating a certain type of hip injury. There's a nine-year-old girl on the unit now who has shown very satisfying progress." She had seen the interest die from his eyes are soon as she mentioned a nine-year-old, but

Mickie took a perverse satisfaction in chattering brightly on
and on about the little girl and her treatment plan, liberally
lacing her monologue with medical jargon he couldn't possibly understand. She tried her best to make her discourse
unbearably boring and considered herself successful when
he suddenly stood.

"Excuse me," he said abruptly, interrupting the bur-
bling flow of Mickie's words. He glanced at his watch. "I must
go now. I am late."

"Oh, that's too bad," Mickie cooed sympathetically.
There was a quick flash of anger in his face, but she wasn't
cowed. "I was enjoying our talk so much."

"I must . . . I must go." He stood and picked up his tray.
Mickie made polite protesting noises, but he escaped with
another muttered, "Excuse me." That seemed, Mickie
thought nastily, to be his favorite phrase.

She watched him until he left the cafeteria. When he had
been gone for several minutes she walked to the house phone
on the wall nearby and dialed Connie's office. Her stomach rumbled in protest, and she patted it comfortingly.
There were antacids for sale in the gift shop. Her call was
put through to the isolation room, and she waited for Mark
to answer

"Yes?"

"I've just been talking to your friend."

"Huh?"

"You remember him. The one with the dark glasses and
the shiny suit? Needed directions to his 'sister's' room?"

There was an explosion of swearing. Mickie held the receiver away from her ear until it abated. "What the hell
happened?" Mark demanded.

"He must have followed me to the cafeteria. I was sitting
at a table way back in the corner, and he came up and asked
if he could sit with me. He was awfully interested when I
told him we had an unusual patient on Ortho."

"I'll bet he was interested! What did you tell him?"

"I told him I was doing Grand Rounds for the residents and med students on this real interesting patient. Then I told him *all* about Marcie Wilkins, a little girl who's had hip surgery. I told him absolutely everything there was to tell about her, using as much medical jargon as I could."

"I hope you bored him to death." She could hear the smile in his voice.

"I'm darned sure I bored him. It made him mad."

"Not too mad, I hope." Mark's voice was suddenly serious.

"He left in disgust," Mickie replied. "I think he gave up on me as a source of information."

"Be careful," Mark warned her. "For God's sake, be careful! If they realize that you've been helping me, they could decide to dispose of you, too."

"*Dispose* of you?"

"Those were his exact words."

It was evening now. On Mark's advice, Mickie had gone through her day as if nothing untoward had happened.

"Well, *now* will you take this seriously?" Connie leaned back in her chair and folded her arms across her chest, frowning severely at Mickie. They were in Connie's office, the door securely locked against intruders and eavesdroppers.

"I have to admit I didn't like the sound of the phrase, 'dispose of,' but I don't think there's any real threat to me." She grinned. "Unless that guy decides he wants to get even with me for boring him to death today."

"This isn't funny, Mickie!"

"I know it's not funny, Connie." Mickie sobered. "And I am worried, you know—for Mark. There really are people out there trying to find him, and it isn't hard to figure out what they want to do to him. I just wish he weren't tied to a bed and a wheelchair, unable to protect himself."

"*We'll* protect him," Connie said firmly. "If that guy thinks he can come on my floor, threatening a patient, he can just . . ." She dropped into Spanish, muttering something ominous about the spy's fate if she got her hands on him. She poured coffee for them both from the carafe on her desk.

"Thank you." Mickie added powdered creamer to her cup. "You won't have to rip him limb from limb, Connie. We won't let him get anywhere near here, okay?"

"You've got that right!" Connie's determination was plain. She peered inquiringly at Mickie. "So how are you and the mystery man getting along these days?"

"I'm in love with him," Mickie replied casually.

Connie gasped, and choked on her coffee. "Wha—?" Her voice was a strangled squeak, and Mickie came around the desk to thump her on the back. "What?" Connie repeated. "What did you say?"

"I said I'm in love with him."

"Oh, are you now? And when did this happen?"

"I don't know." Mickie considered for a moment. "I just now realized it, though. I guess I've been falling in love with him all along."

"I knew something was happening between you two. I was all for it, too, if you'll recall."

"No kidding. You'd do a land-office business as a matchmaker."

"I think a little romance would be good for you; you could use a little spice in your life." Mickie shot her a dark glance. "But this has happened awfully fast, hasn't it, Mick? After all, how much do you really know about the man?"

"I love him. I know enough for that." There was a sort of irrefutable feminine logic in that statement, but Connie was unconvinced.

"You do realize that's crazy, don't you?"

"Mm-hm." Mickie smiled at her, unperturbed. "I also realize that it's ridiculous, amazing and probably very dumb. It was inevitable, though, and it's true. I don't understand why it happened, Connie, but it did. It's too late to worry about it now." She sipped her coffee, then looked across the desk at Connie, her face thoughtful. "You know, looking back at all that's happened, I can't imagine *not* having fallen in love with him."

"You're not the least bit bothered by it, are you?"

"I'm not, not anymore. That's odd, isn't it? I mean, I should be all upset because I've fallen in love with a patient."

"Why should that matter?" Connie demanded loyally. "The fact that he's your patient isn't the problem. It hasn't affected his care."

"It may have made me more careful, but that's all."

"So if anything he's getting even better care than usual. There's nothing wrong with that. Doctors aren't supposed to fall in love with their patients, but as long as it doesn't affect your professional judgment, what's the harm?"

"There isn't any, I guess," Mickie shrugged.

"Are you happy about it?"

"I am, you know." Mickie seemed almost surprised.

"How does Mark feel about it?"

"He doesn't know."

"Are you going to tell him?"

"I don't know. Maybe I'll wait until he falls in love with me."

"Will he?" Connie was skeptical.

Mickie shrugged, a little embarrassed. "This is going to sound awfully egotistical, but I can't believe that something that feels so right could simply fade away. It just seems like it *has* to be, like he has to love me eventually."

"That's what I'm worried about. I don't want you to be unhappy, Mickie, but don't you think you're setting yourself up for a fall?"

Mickie shook her head. "He's going to love me, Connie. He doesn't want to feel anything for me, but he will."

"I hope you aren't ever sorry you said that."

"I told you you'd be sorry," Connie reminded her a week later.

"I'm not sorry, I'm mad!" Mickie was fuming after a heated exchange with Mark during her morning rounds that day. His attitude had not improved in the seven days since their kiss, and her patience with him was wearing thin.

"Forgive me the error," Connie drawled, fighting to hide a smile. "You know, you don't look like someone who's basking in the glow of love's young dream."

"I never," Mickie replied with great dignity, "said one single word about love's young dream, *or* its glow. And that man could extinguish love's young dream with one," her voice began to rise, "nasty, surly, bad-tempered, egocentric, insulting, disagreeable temper tantrum!"

"Boy, whatever he said to you this morning must have been good!" Connie tried unsuccessfully not to smile. "He's had you steamed all week, but this is the worst."

"He's just impossible! I mean, I ask a few simple questions about his physical condition, and he accuses me of voyeuristic sexual aberrations! I'm his physician, for Pete's sake!" Connie's lips twitched, and Mickie glared at her.

"You're cute when your professional dignity is offended, Mickie."

"I swear to God, Connie, if you so much as chuckle..."

"I'm trying, I really am." Connie clapped a hand across her mouth, but half-smothered giggles escaped.

"Thanks a lot, Connie. I knew I could count on you to understand." Glowering, Mickie picked up an armful of charts and went to finish her rounds.

Mickie wasn't sure if she'd been seeking condolences or a blunt instrument when she had stalked into Connie's office. So, okay, Mark wasn't in love with her, and he was clearly uncomfortable with the possibility of a relationship between them. That was still no excuse for the kind of outburst she'd been subjected to that morning.

Maybe she should have lied when he said he'd wanted that kiss. Maybe she should never have admitted that she had wanted it, too. Maybe she should have blushed and stammered and protested in maidenly confusion, but she really didn't see what that would have accomplished.

Mark had accused her unfairly of manipulating him, yet if she'd reacted in the manner he had evidently expected, her behavior would indeed have been manipulative. It was ironic that by declining to use feminine wiles she had managed to get herself accused of being a scheming female.

"Damned if I do and damned if I don't," she muttered in frustration.

"I beg your pardon, Dr. Blake?" A staff nurse was eyeing her curiously. Talking to oneself was not approved conduct when walking along the corridors.

"Nothing. It's nothing." Mickie forced a smile, aware that she was reddening. "I should learn not to talk to myself."

"Uh, yeah. Sure." With a curious glance over her shoulder the nurse left. Mickie shook her head and walked on, exasperated with herself. In love with him or not, she should know better than to let Mark James get to her this way. Even if he was the most thoroughly obnoxious man she'd ever met, she should know better.

She didn't know better, though, because she loved him. She didn't regret loving him, and despite her frustrated anger she wanted to help him to heal, both physically and mentally. No matter how tense things got between them personally, she would not take herself off his case. She was too confident of her ability to heal his leg. His suspicious hostility was a different matter. His reaction to her frankness had been far too violent to have been directed at her alone. Mickie had no idea what had created his cynical attitude toward women; she could only hope that her love would be enough to break through the wall he'd built around himself and overcome that cynicism.

She had left his room so suddenly, she realized that she had neglected to check the reflexes in his foot, looking for symptoms of the nerve damage that the prolonged wearing of a cast could cause. She wasn't particularly anxious to face him again so soon, but it had to be done. Maybe his mood had improved. She finished her other visits and slipped back into his room. The door closed quietly behind her, and she turned to see Mark glaring at her.

"What the hell do you want *now*?"

"So much for love's young dream!" Mickie muttered. She would send Connie in to check his reflexes.

"He's doing better than I expected." Connie turned a page in Mark's chart and read on. After another week, during which Mark's manner toward Mickie had become civil, if not warm and friendly, she and Connie were reviewing his progress.

"He's doing better than anyone expected. Look at this." Mickie pointed to a graph of Mark's strength tests. "I guess I really got through to him when I told him that eating well and following his exercise program would make a difference."

Connie skimmed the last pages and flipped the metal cover closed. "He could be discharged in a week or so, you know."

"He'd have to have a new cast."

"I know, but you've seen the films. His femur is healing really well. With a new cast he could be ready for discharge."

"In the right circumstances, yes. If he were an ordinary patient he could go home and his family would take care of him until the cast came off."

"But he's not an ordinary patient."

"And I won't discharge him into anything but the right circumstances." Mickie leaned back in her chair. "That's the bottom line, Connie. I could discharge him, but I won't do it unless I'm sure he'll be in an appropriate situation."

"What would you consider an 'appropriate situation'?"

The question came from behind Mickie, and she twisted in her chair to see Commander Lewis standing in the doorway. "Don't you ever knock?" she demanded.

"Sorry." He shrugged, not sorry at all. "What would you call an appropriate situation?"

"If you were eavesdropping long enough you should be able to figure that out for yourself." Mickie spoke with angry sarcasm, but Connie just rolled her eyes. He was a spy and she expected spies to eavesdrop, after all.

"I can arrange to have the Navy take care of him. A Naval ambulance can pick him up." Lewis ignored her words. "When should I schedule—"

"Just a minute!" Mickie cut him off. "Nothing is going to be arranged until Mark has agreed to it and I approve of it."

"There's no need for all that. I'll just call the San Diego commander and—"

"I said *wait*! I don't like your eavesdropping, Commander, and I don't like your pushiness, and I'm not too crazy about you! This isn't your decision; it's Mark's. I'd appreciate it if you'd remember that."

Lewis's thin lips tightened, but he made no reply. Mickie knew her bluntness had angered him, but she really didn't care. He had infuriated her again and again with his high-handed interference in Mark's care. This time he wouldn't interfere, though. This decision was Mark's, and his reponse to the suggestion was predictable.

"I'd rather rot here in this damned hospital!"

"Well, thank you very much. I'm sure the damned hospital would appreciate hearing that. You know," Mickie went on, playing devil's advocate, "the commander says he can get you set up somewhere, and have the Navy take care of you."

"I don't care what he says! I'm not going to be locked up in some on-base apartment with a bunch of MPs standing guard."

"I'd have thought you'd be anxious to get out of here."

"Of course I am!" Mark turned as far onto his side as his traction would allow. The weights clanked in protest, and he waved angrily at them. "Don't you think I want to get out of this?"

"I know you do." Mickie pulled a chair up beside the bed. "I know, but I can't just put a new cast on you and boot you out the door. You will have to be followed as an outpatient, and you won't be able to stay entirely by yourself until the cast is off."

"Do you know how long that will be yet?"

"Six to eight weeks."

He swore under his breath. "I'll be able to walk with this new cast, won't I?"

"With crutches, yes."

"Then I should be able to take care of myself. I don't need Will Lewis's MPs babysitting me."

"Have you ever tried to cook a meal while standing on crutches?" Mickie asked.

He thought about that for an instant, then fell back onto the pillows again. Mickie's heart ached for him. His eyes were closed in weary defeat, but the muscles of his arms and shoulders stood out rigidly and his fists were clenched in frustration. He looked strong, perfectly able to care for himself. She knew how difficult it was for him to accept his handicap, even on a temporary basis. He wasn't a man who easily allowed anyone else to care for him, and he'd been forced into a helpless position for weeks now. He must think it would never end.

She reached out to lightly touch his arm. She had held her desire in check ever since the morning they had exercised together, but now the temptation was too strong. His skin was warm and smooth, and her fingers moved lightly on it in a barely perceptible caress. He turned with a scowl, and she quickly removed her hand.

"I'm sorry, Mark, but you can't stay alone. It's too great a risk to take with your health. Your sense of balance will be affected for a while, and a full-leg cast is big and bulky to drag around with you. If you fell, you could reinjure your leg. You might not be able to get up again, you could even throw a blood clot. It just isn't safe."

"But if someone were staying with me?"

"That would be insurance enough. You just shouldn't be alone."

Mark considered that for a moment. He hated to admit it, but she had a point. He wouldn't have Lewis's goons babysitting him, and that was final, but if he had to have a babysitter, then who...? He thought about it, an idea forming in his mind, startling in its unexpected simplicity.

"Would someone have to be with me twenty-four hours a day?" he asked carefully, and watched her face.

She shrugged. "If you stayed with a relative, they'd have to go out to the drugstore and stuff. If you were careful while they were gone, it would be all right, even if they weren't there with you every minute."

He nodded and lay back, gazing up at the ceiling. He was aware that Mickie was watching him, trying to guess his thoughts. She was going to be surprised when he shared them with her! His idea was a good one; it solved a couple of very sticky problems, but unfortunately it also created a new one. And yet, it made such good sense.

Mickie was his doctor, as she kept reminding him when he balked at doing his exercises. She should be in favor of anything which could contribute to his recovery. She was *supposed* to take care of him, Mark told himself, and glanced over at her. She was watching him, her face gentle. That gentleness, that womanliness, sometimes surprised him. She could be prickly, abrasive, tough as nails if she wanted to be, yet underneath there was a woman, soft and warm and sweet.

His body responded to the memory of her sweetness, her lips soft and yielding, her mouth warm on his, her body lithe and slim under his hands. A man could get addicted to that mouth, that body, to her touch... He willed away the response, but the memories lingered. He wasn't ready to let that sweetness go, he hadn't had his fill of her yet. He needed just a little more time to drown himself in her, sate himself with her. When he'd had his fill, he could walk away. He only had to convince her that this idea of his was as perfect as he knew it to be.

He turned his head on the pillows to look at Mickie. Her face was so carefully expressionless that he could almost see the little wheels turning in her brain. He smothered a smile.

"Mickie?"

"Yes?"

"I…" He hesitated, wondering how best to approach the subject. "Could I be discharged if I had a place to stay? A place that met all those criteria of yours?"

"Yes, of course you could. We don't want to keep you prisoner, just to keep you safe."

Mark felt a surge of triumph that he was careful to conceal. "When?" he demanded. "When could you let me out?"

"In about a week. You're healthy enough."

He nodded. "Mickie?" he asked again.

"Yes?" she asked quizzically, puzzled by his repeated questions.

He wondered how she'd react to his bombshell. He took a deep breath. "Can I live with you?"

Chapter 8

She stared blankly at him. "Wh..." Her voice emerged as a strangled squeak. For a moment neither her voice nor her brain seemed to work. "What did you say?"

"I said, could I live with you? At your house? Could I be discharged if I lived with you?" His voice began to rise with impatience.

"Live? With me?" She knew she was stammering like an idiot, but she couldn't help it. Her brain was having difficulty accepting the message her ears were sending.

"That's what I said!" He scowled, apparently annoyed with her inability to comprehend. "You said I need a place to stay and some kind of follow-up care. Your house is big enough and secluded enough. It should be a safe place for me to stay until I'm fully recovered."

"How do you know what my house is like?" It was the only question she could formulate.

"Connie told me about it," he replied impatiently. "So, can I stay with you?"

"I don't know! I need to think about it, okay?"

"What's to think about?"

"What's—There are all kinds of things to think about! My career, for one thing. I mean, I've already gotten more involved with you than I should have. Taking you home with me would look pretty fishy, wouldn't it?"

"Don't be stupid! It wouldn't look fishy; it wouldn't look any way at all, because no one would know. I'm not even supposed to be here, am I? How can I leave here and go to your house if I'm not even here in the first place?"

"I'm not being stupid!" she snapped, her own irritation breaking through. "I'm just trying to think this out, and if you'll quit barking at me and give me a minute, I will!"

Mark fell silent, but Mickie found it difficult to think with him staring at her, his impatience obvious. Angry and confused, she stared down at her hands and tried to consider. Finally she looked up.

"All right. You can stay with me."

"Well, what made up your mind for you?" he asked with harsh sarcasm. "You had to think about it long enough. Is it just that you still want my body?"

"Oh, sure, that has to be the answer." Mickie looked him up and down with icy eyes and gave a disparaging shrug. "Your body, cast and all, is a real bargain about now, isn't it? I guess it's just that I feel sorry for you," she lied. "I'd do the same for a stray dog."

Shaking with the force of her anger, she stalked out of the room before he could say anything more.

She'd given him his answer. She'd told him her reason, too, but it was a lie because she couldn't tell him the truth. Her love for him had made the decision for her. She loved him, therefore she would do anything she could to protect him from the enemies who threatened him. Her house would be his safe haven, and if her heart got a bit battered in the process, she would count it a fair exchange.

His deliberately cruel words hurt, though. She knew what he was doing, knew that the wall he built between them was his defense against the closeness that frightened him, but still the words hurt. He was more involved with her than he wanted to be, and it was the intention, not the involvement, that mattered. However strong the current of passion between them, until he admitted the truth of his feelings, they were going nowhere.

Cynical. Mark was cynical in a way she could barely imagine. His cynicism seemed to bubble up from a bottomless well, and Mickie had to wonder what had made him the way he was. He must have been a little boy once, optimistic and eager for life. What had happened to change him?

Perhaps it was involvement with men like Lewis that had killed the idealistic boy in him. Lewis, she was certain, had never been a little boy, idealistic or otherwise.

Mark winced as the door slammed closed behind her, then lay back, a satisfied half-smile curving his mouth. Perhaps his tactics had been unfair, but he'd gotten the answer he wanted. He knew he'd bullied her, but he was neither ashamed nor proud of that, just satisfied with the results.

He couldn't seem to sort out his feelings about her, but that was nothing new. Mickie Blake had gotten under his skin at their first meeting. God knows he didn't want her there!

Mark stared at the ceiling. She'd gotten into his blood, and he was honest enough with himself to admit that he wouldn't purge her from his system easily. He didn't want an involvement with her; it would be no good for her, and it was precisely the kind of thing he'd spent years avoiding. He would have avoided her, too, if he could have, but it was too late.

Now he had to rid himself of the need for her. He *needed* to touch her, kiss her, needed to make her want him. In a way he couldn't begin to explain, he needed to see the softening and the hunger in her eyes, needed to see them widen and blur with passion. Her open admission of wanting had shocked him, for it carried with it a demand he could not meet, but it was his own need that terrified him. Needing like that was insane; he couldn't allow it, yet the need to see her melt in his arms persisted.

And just once, when his leg was healed and he was strong and whole again, he had to make love to her.

Lewis was waiting in Connie's office to hear the verdict. His reaction to Mark's decision was as predictable as Mark's reaction to his offer had been.

" . . . so he'll stay at my house," Mickie concluded.

"Like hell he will!" Mickie could see the veins standing out on Lewis's forehead.

"That's bad for your blood pressure," she commented mildly.

"What the . . . ! What's bad for my . . . ?" he spluttered.

"Your blood pressure," she supplied. "It's bad for your blood pressure to get all worked up over something you can't change."

He glared at her. "I'm going to—"

"No, you're not," she interrupted him flatly. "You aren't going to change anything at all. Unless I'm very much mistaken, and Mark actually *is* in the Navy and subject to your command, there isn't a thing you can do." She watched Lewis's face, and after a moment she nodded. "That's what I thought. You can't *order* him to stay in any particular place at all. He asked if he could stay at my house, because *someone*," she looked over at Connie as she emphasized the word, "told him that there's plenty of room there. I've agreed to let him stay. It's done, Commander."

"You may think so, little lady, but have you considered that having him at your house will put you in danger, the same danger he's in?"

"That's one of the attractions of my house, as I understand it. It's out in the desert, and it isn't very easy to find."

"It's also isolated, isn't it? No near neighbors to call if there's trouble?" Lewis's meaning was clear, and it made Mickie angry.

"Don't you think you're exaggerating just a little?" she asked, mimicking his snide tone.

"Don't you think you're being awfully naive?"

"No, I don't! I think I'm doing a favor for a friend."

"A friend? Is that what you call it these days?"

He had gone too far.

"You are out of line," she said icily.

"Sorry." He looked at the floor for a moment. "Look, I'm not trying to push you around, but I don't think this is a good idea. If you do it, I want you to go in with your eyes wide open."

"My eyes! I'm not an idiot, you know."

"I know that, but you're not familiar with the kind of people we're dealing with. They'd shoot you to get to Mark and never give you a second thought. You'd be no more than a nuisance, something that got in the way of what they wanted."

"I'll keep that in mind," Mickie said dryly.

"They might not stop at shooting you. Rape, torture—those are some of their specialities."

"That's *enough*!" Mickie shouted. "I understand that Mark is in danger, but I refuse to allow you to intimidate me with lurid stories. I've agreed to help him, and you aren't going to scare me out of it. I refuse to believe that Mark would knowingly endanger me. You won't make me believe that he would put anyone but himself at risk."

"You sound pretty sure, but how well do you really know him? How much do you know about him, Doc?"

He was baiting her, and Mickie would have no part of it. She pushed past him to the office door. "I know that I agreed to let him stay at my house. That agreement stands. Goodbye, Commander."

She swept out of the room, head high. Mark wouldn't put her in danger, she was convinced of that. In spite of her confidence, though, she decided she'd keep her shotgun loaded while he stayed with her.

Not, of course, that Mark James was going to act as a magnet for every terrorist north of the Panama Canal. As the week passed Mickie recovered her sense of equilibrium and managed to put Lewis's warnings into perspective. He had been angry at being thwarted and had been trying to convince her to renege on her agreement. He didn't want Mark to stay with her, and she had no reason to assume he would be above using underhanded tactics. It wasn't difficult to figure out what he'd been trying to do in that conversation.

"Are you ready?" Connie asked.

"All set," Mickie replied, and switched on the cast-cutter. It came to life with a loud, vibrating buzz.

Mark, lying supine on a gurney, eyed it with alarm. He propped himself on one elbow to look at it. "Is that thing going to cut off the cast or cut off my leg?"

Mickie put the flat of her hand on his chest and pushed him back down. "If you don't lie still I'm not making any promises. This doesn't actually cut the cast; it just shatters it with vibration."

"That's a relief!" His voice was heavy with sarcasm. "You won't cut my leg off, you'll just shatter it with vibration."

"What a sissy!" Mickie positioned his cast. "Just hold it right there, Connie. Have you ever heard so much whining from a grown man?"

"Don't you worry your little head, Mark," Connie soothed him. "I'll be right here to hold your hand."

"All set?" Mickie held the cutter poised.

"Oh, Lord..." Mark began, gazing heavenward and clasping his hands piously. Laughing, Mickie bent over his cast and began to cut.

With great stealth she and Connie had smuggled him down to the casting room that evening. Wheeling him through the halls on a gurney, they made the trip during the dinner hour, when the evening shift was busy serving dinner to the patients and the casting room was deserted. Stan Adams had been in on the secret from the start, and he was waiting in the next room, preparing to help apply the new cast. Together the two women worked as quickly as they could to remove the old one, then rolled Mark over to Stan.

While Connie and Stan transferred Mark from the gurney to the table, Mickie tested the temperature of the water in several large buckets.

"What are you doing?" Mark was watching her curiously as Connie and Stan positioned his leg on a supporting frame so the plaster could be wrapped around it.

"Just making sure the water is the right temperature." Mickie took her hand from the last bucket and shook it dry. "Now relax, hold as still as you can, and we'll get this done."

She worked quickly, covering Mark's leg with a tube of socklike fabric, then cushioning that with fluffy padding. Carefully carved felt pads were placed over the prominent bones of his ankle and knee. Finally she was ready for the plaster and rolls of plaster-impregnated bandage were dropped into the buckets.

With gloves and a gown to help protect her from plaster splatters, Mickie took the first roll of bandage from a bucket, squeezed out the excess water and began rolling it around Mark's foot and ankle. Mark suffered the application quietly, and for a while Mickie was able to forget whose leg she was encasing in plaster. She was even able—almost—to ignore the fact that he was wearing nothing but a loose hospital gown. She could almost ignore that fact if she worked at it.

She was nearly finished when he spoke for the first time. "Is it supposed to get hot?"

"Huh?" She looked up from carefully smoothing the edge of the plaster so it wouldn't irritate the top of his thigh. "Oh, yes, it does get hot. A chemical reaction takes place as the plaster hardens, and one of the products is heat. This cast is hotter than the last one because it's heavier." She ran her fingers around the top of the cast, checking for rough spots. "That's nice and smooth. You shouldn't have any problems." She laid her hands lightly here and there on the cast, checking several spots. "It's starting to warm up, all right. Don't worry, though. We'll put fans on it in your room. They'll help it dry faster and cool it off. I won't kid you, though. It won't be very comfortable for the next few hours."

"No kidding." He reached to touch the cast himself, but Mickie caught his hand.

"Don't touch it. Not until it's set. If you press on the outside you could create a pressure point on the inside. In spite of the padding, you could end up with circulation and skin problems. Okay?"

"You're the boss." He obediently folded his arms across his chest. "What happens now?"

"Now you lie here, all propped up on the frame and ever so comfortable, while the plaster sets up a little bit." Mickie and the others stripped off their plaster-spattered gowns and gloves.

"And what do you do?"

She grinned down at him. "I think Connie and I will go get some supper while your leg hardens. You and Stan can play cards or something."

"Not Stan!" Mark protested. "He's a shark! He took me for every cent I had at gin the other day!"

Stan just grinned, but Connie hooted with laughter.

"That should make your wait more interesting." Mickie told Mark unfeelingly. "Just don't let him beat you too badly. He'll get a swelled head."

Laughing, she and Connie left.

"Do you want to eat in the snack bar, or the cafeteria?"

Connie considered the question gravely. "I don't know. I don't really feel like a dried out little snack-bar burger. What do you think they have left in the cafeteria?"

"At this hour? Probably a dead casserole and a couple of wilted salads." They walked through the double doors that led to the main corridor.

"Sad, but no doubt true. The snack bar is beginning to sound good."

"And isn't *that* a profound comment on—"

They rounded a corner, and Mickie choked on her words as she caught sight of the man who stood in the middle of the otherwise empty hallway. She recognized him immediately, of course, even though he was wearing a raincoat this time. She had to warn Connie, but of course she couldn't, because he was watching them closely. Mickie could only thank God that their conversation had been about food and not about Mark.

She had no idea how the guerrilla had found his way down here, into a non-public section of the hospital, but if he suspected something, she had to throw him off the scent. She took a slow, deep breath. They always said a good offense was the best defense.

She walked up to him, a courteous half smile on her lips. "I'm sorry, sir, but this area of the hospital isn't open to the public. You'll have to leave."

"Maybe I can help you find the area you're looking for." Bless Connie, Mickie thought. She had realized who this was and stepped into the breach, taking him by the arm and turning him around. "I can show you the way to the information desk. Just come this way, if you would, please, sir."

"Connie, I left my lab coat in the locker room and my money's in the pocket. I'll get it and meet you in the snack bar, okay?"

"Sure thing." Connie herded their unwanted visitor into the elevator. "In five minutes, all right?"

"Five minutes." Mickie watched the doors slide closed. She hoped Connie wasn't overdoing the helpful-staff-member bit. The spy had been effectively thwarted, though. When the lights above the elevator doors indicated that the car was on its way up, she darted back to warn the men and lock the doors.

Aware that they might be watched, she and Connie made a point of meeting in the snack bar. Neither of them had much appetite for the cheeseburgers they picked at, or the conversation they struggled to keep up. It was nearly midnight before they felt the coast was clear and it was safe to smuggle Mark and his new cast back to Orthopedics.

"I'll stay in the office for another hour," Connie whispered. "Stop on your way out; I'll have some charts for you to sign or something, okay?"

"Okay." Mickie nodded, then jerked her head at the man lying in the bed behind her. "I'll get him settled as quick as I can. I'm bushed, and I'm ready to get out of this madhouse and get home!"

"By the time you get all the way home, it'll be time to turn around and come back. Why don't you just spend the night here, Mickie?"

"No." She shook her head. "If I don't go home, who'll feed poor Sam?"

"That dog doesn't know how good he has it!" Connie laughed. "See you in a few, Mickie."

"Yeah." Mickie closed the door quietly and turned around. The only light in the room came from the tiny bathroom and it gleamed in Mark's dark eyes as he watched her from the shadows. As she walked across to him, she could see that his face was damp with sweat.

"Are you having any pain?"

He grunted. "Nothing unusual. The cast is hot, that's all."

"That's what these are for." She rolled a tall standing fan up to the bedside. Another already stood in place on the opposite side. "I know this is uncomfortable, but it's only for tonight," she reassured him. His cast rested in pristine splendor on a carefully constructed cushion of pillows and sandbags, covered by plastic sheeting and bath towels to protect the bedding from dampness. The plastic crackled as

Mickie wedged a pillow more firmly into place. She switched on one of the fans. "How does that feel?"

"Better, thanks." He turned his damp face into the flow of air.

Mickie took one step back, then stopped. She couldn't leave him like that, sweaty and sticky, his body and gown spattered with plaster. Any other patient would be turned over to the nursing staff at this point, but Mark was not any other patient. The nurse who cared for him wouldn't be in until seven AM. Mickie's heart lurched against her breastbone, and she took a deep breath, steadying herself for the task.

She moved briskly to the bedside and pressed the button to raise the head of the bed. "Tell me if you feel your cast is moving, okay?"

"Sure. What's going on?"

"I'm going to get you more comfortable; you'll never be able to sleep like this." To her surprise, her voice was light and steady.

"I'll say," Mark grumbled as the bed ground noisily to a new angle. "If you ever tried to—"

"Gripe, gripe, gripe." Mickie mimicked his cranky tone, aware that his ill-temper was directed at his own helplessness. When he was sitting nearly erect, she took a basin from the bedside stand.

"What're you doing?"

"I'm going to give you a bath." She escaped to the bathroom before he could reply. When she returned with warm water, washcloth and towels, she was holding herself on a tight rein. She switched off the fan.

"Can you lean forward for a moment?" He did so, and she quickly undid the ties which secured the gown he wore. She pushed it forward onto his shoulders, baring the long curve of his back. She laid a towel over the mattress, soaped the cloth and began to bathe him.

It was torture. She tried, she really tried, to ignore her feelings, tried to concentrate on cleaning the skin beneath her hands and forget whose skin it was, but it was impossible. The scent of him, musky and male and unmistakably his own, surrounded her, mixing with the clinical tang of the soap. She slid the soapy cloth in circles over his shoulders, shaping the muscles there, then moving in long strokes up and down his back. As quickly as she could, she finished washing and drying his back. She took the damp towel from behind him.

"You can lean back now."

Mickie could feel his gaze like a physical touch as she slipped the gown down his arms, carefully leaving it draped across his lap. She dampened the cloth again and reached out to touch his cheek lightly, turning his face toward her. Her hands were gentle, if not quite steady, as she washed his face, but she would never know how she managed it. It was torment to touch him this way, to feel him watching her with knowing eyes.

She couldn't hide her feelings as she touched his face, sensing the bones beneath the skin, feeling the day's growth of beard rasp against the cloth as she stroked over his jawline, watching the full, sensuous line of his lips curve into a smile of pure pleasure. She handed him a towel to dry with as she turned away to rinse the cloth and soap it again.

"Are you warm enough?" she asked as she turned back.

Mark smiled directly into her eyes, a slow smile heavy with meaning. "I'm warm enough," he said slowly. "Plenty warm enough."

Mickie felt her cheeks burn at the message beneath the words, but she couldn't deny that the same heat was beating through her veins. Slowly she began to wash his chest.

The lather caught in the mat of hair, white against his tan, and when she wiped it away, Mickie could feel the tightly puckered male nipples beneath it. She snatched her hand away as if burned, startled by this evidence of his arousal. Mark laughed low in his throat, and Mickie gritted her teeth, forcing herself to continue. Carefully, skittishly, she con-

tinued to wash him, stopping well above the gown, which lay
low on his stomach.

She knew he was laughing at her, even as her touch
aroused him, but she couldn't help that. Stoically she
washed first one arm, then the other, struggling to ignore the
exciting male beauty there, the hard bulge of muscle, the
strength of his hands, the grace of the long, straight fingers. She knew the warmth of those arms around her, the
magic those hands could work, and she felt desire curling
low in her stomach. It was all she could do to continue.

When she had dried his skin, she turned away again.

"What's next, Doc?" She knew exactly what he was
thinking and shot him a quick glare.

"Your leg," she answered curtly, eliciting another of
those low, feral chuckles. Annoyed, Mickie wasn't as gentle
as she might have been when she pulled the sheet away to
uncover his uninjured leg. She washed her way briskly from
his foot to his knee, then slowed again. She tried to keep her
touch impersonal, but the stroke of the cloth against his skin
was a caress. She knew it was crazy and dangerous but she
couldn't help herself. She was as aroused as he was, her
breathing uneven, her heartbeat jerky.

She reached Mark's upper thigh, swabbed tentatively at
his skin and stopped abruptly.

"Something wrong?"

She shot him a fulminating glance, then turned to the
basin. "I'll leave you to finish your bath," she said tightly
and walked away. His laughter followed her into the bathroom.

Why did he keep doing this to her—and why was she
doing it to herself? She was shaking with the force of her
desire for him, and she'd brought it all on herself. Mark had
made it more than plain that he wanted no emotional involvement with her, but for some reason he wanted to make
her want him, even though her admission of desire angered
him.

I'm an idiot! Mickie glared at herself in the mirror, then snatched a fresh gown from the linen cabinet and slammed the door sharply. She really was a complete idiot to let a simple bed-bath reduce her to jelly. Well, this was the end of it! Mark was baiting her, enjoying her discomfort, but she was guilty too, for letting him get away with it. It wasn't going to happen anymore. Jaw set and spine straight, she marched back into the dim room.

"Just in time." She could see the quick gleam of Mark's wolfish smile in the light that slanted through the bathroom door. "I'm clean as—"

Mickie interuppted him quickly. "Good. I have a clean gown for you."

"Then you can have this one." He started to lift the gown from his lap, and Mickie slapped his hand back down.

"Just stop it, Mark! Please? It's late, and I'm tired. I'm not in the mood."

"I think you are." His voice was low and caressing as he reached out to tug the clean gown from her hand. He caught her slack fingers and drew her to the bedside. "Quit torturing yourself, Mickie, and quit torturing me. Just come here and kiss me."

And, God help her, she went.

She moved down onto his chest, her bones melting from the heat in her blood. She had to touch him. It was warm and dark, and they were alone in that room, and she laid her palms on his chest, sliding them up with a deliberately slow, seductive touch. If he wanted to play with fire, she'd make sure he felt the heat.

He felt it. She heard the catch in his breath just before her lips found his, and then there was nothing else. His mouth was hungry, hot and eager as he parted her lips to plunder the sweetness inside, but Mickie's eagerness was a match for him. His hands moved restlessly over her back, but she simply clung to his shoulders and gave herself up to the kiss. It was an endless time of teasing and tasting, and it was Mark who regretfully, reluctantly, broke the contact at last.

Mickie pushed herself up and away from him again, a little bit shaky, feeling a chill on her skin as sanity returned.

"Here." She picked up the fresh gown and handed it to him. "Put this on and I'll tie it for you."

Mark looked at her for a long moment, his eyes dark and unreadable; then he slipped the gown on, smoothed it down and leaned forward for her to tie it. Not until he was covered again did he pull the other gown from beneath it and hand it to her. Mickie wondered if he were as shaken as she by that kiss. She hoped so.

"Mickie?"

She stopped with her hands full of damp towels. "Yes?"

"Have you thought about what happened tonight?"

"My God, can't you just give it a rest?" she flared with a burst of temper. "I can't—"

"I didn't mean *this*," he interrupted her, and she flushed. "I mean finding that guy waiting in the hallway downstairs."

Mickie shrugged. "I've thought about it. I guess it proves that all these precautions you and the Commander wanted aren't quite as nutty as I thought at first."

"They aren't nutty at all," he said grimly, "but I don't know if they're enough anymore. I've been thinking about it, and I've changed my mind. I'm going to let Will set me up on a base somewhere. I won't stay at your house and put you in danger, too."

"Don't be stupid!" Mickie dumped the towels in the hamper and came back to lower the bed and settle him comfortably. She shook a pillow out with a sharp jerk and lifted his head to slip it underneath. Her hand moved of its own volition to smooth the black waves, but she snatched it away from temptation.

"You said yourself that Lewis can't hide you; all he can do is try to guard you from people who already know where you are. At least at my house you'll be hidden."

"I won't do that if it will put you in jeopardy, though."

"I know you don't want to endanger me, and believe me, I'm such a coward that if I thought you were, I'd abandon you to the Navy. I don't think that's going to happen, though. And you're going to stay out at my house, just like we decided."

"You're sure?"

"I'm sure." She moved to the foot of the bed to aim a fan at his cast. "By the way, do you know how to use a shotgun or a rifle? If you know how to use them, I'll leave one with you during the day."

"Yeah, sure, I know how to use both of them. But what do you know about guns?"

"Don't worry about me. I'll take care of myself. Are you comfortable now?"

"I'm all right. I may even sleep."

"Good. I'll see you in the morning, Mark. Pleasant dreams."

"Yeah." His smile was slow, sensual. "I have something pleasant to dream about, don't I? You take care of yourself, Doc."

"I'll be fine." Mickie met his eyes bravely, but her color was high. "Don't worry about me."

"Famous last words," he growled. Mickie laughed and left the room.

The doctors' parking lot was dark and empty when she left the hospital a few minutes later, and the breeze was cold. Mickie hugged her suede jacket close around her, turning the collar up at her throat. She was shivering as she fitted her key into the Jeep's door lock, fumbling a little with stiff fingers. She never saw the blow coming. She noticed nothing until she felt an explosion of pain in her skull and saw a flash of brilliant light, and then darkness swallowed her up.

The concrete was cold and rough beneath her cheek. She was sprawled in an awkward tumble, stiff and chilled.

Vaguely she realized that she ought to get up, that she couldn't just lie there in the cold, but the message couldn't seem to get from her brain to her muscles. She hurt. She abandoned the effort and drifted for a time, but the chill seeping into her bones brought her back to awareness again. She moved, tried to roll a little, and her cheek, already raw, scraped against the pavement. The sharp pain brought her to full consciousness, and that brought a fuller awareness of pain.

She forced herself to roll clumsily onto her side, biting her lip against a wave of nausea. The stabbing agony in her skull merged with the pain of her torn cheek and the aches and bruises from her fall, but slowly, with exquisite care, she managed to clamber to her knees.

She huddled there, holding her head in her hands while lances of pain danced behind her eyes. When the dance slowed she reached out to the side of her Jeep, stretching up, seeking the door handle. If she could just reach it, she thought with laborious logic, she could use the handle to pull herself to her feet, and if she could stand, maybe she could walk back to the hospital.

With the careful deliberation born of confused thought processes, she took it one step at a time. First she reached up for the handle, wrapping her fingers around it, then . . .

"Hey! Who's there?"

The rough demand came from several yards away and was followed by the sound of heavy footsteps. Mickie didn't attempt to answer; the effort was beyond her.

"Who is that?" A powerful flashlight beam slanted between the cars and caught her. "I said who . . . ?" The footsteps reached her, and the security guard swore under his breath. "Dr. Blake? My God, what happened to you?"

Mickie was still concentrating on the Herculean task of standing, feeling that that was somehow important. She pulled hard on the door handle and felt a surge of triumph as she managed to lift her knees from the concrete. It was a fleeting victory, though. The effort sent a wave of pain and vertigo through her, and the security guard caught her just as her grasp loosened and she would have fallen.

Mickie let him gather her lax body into his arms, but stiffened as he began to walk away from the Jeep. "Purz..." she muttered, and he paused.

"What's that, Dr. Blake?"

"Purse," she whispered thickly.

"Oh, yeah."

He looked around, at something of a loss. He'd only been on this job for three weeks, and the most exciting thing to happen in that time had been the entrapment of a stray cat in one of the garbage dumpsters. A mugging, the mugging of a doctor, no less, was practically cataclysmic! He didn't know whether the training manual would say he should retrieve her purse or take her straight to the emergency room.

"Purse!" Mickie repeated more urgently, and he gave in.

If it meant that much to her, he'd find the damned purse and take it in with her. Women! He couldn't figure this one out, dragging around a purse that could double as an overnight bag, afraid to be without it for a minute. It was right there, though, on the pavement by the Jeep. Carefully he propped Mickie against a shiny new BMW, holding her steady with one hand while with the other he scooped the spilled contents back into her red tote. With the bag hooked over one arm, he picked Mickie up again.

"Purse?" she mumbled, her head lolling against his arm.

"Yeah, doctor, I got your purse. Okay?"

"'Kay." She relaxed, going limp in his arms, and he headed for the Emergency Room entrance, walking fast.

Mickie let events flow around her, vaguely aware of the bright lights, the familiar sounds and smells. She could hear the young security guard explaining how he'd found her, as he turned her and her purse over to the Emergency personnel. Mickie listened with abstract interest. This was some other patient's history. After all, this sort of thing didn't happen to her.

Her limp body was deposited on a gurney and wheeled into a treatment room. With interest she watched the pattern of the ceiling passing overhead. Funny how she'd never noticed it before. In the small, blue-tiled treatment room she suffered the removal of her grease-stained skirt and shredded pantyhose, then let herself be relieved of her jacket and blouse, and be covered by a warm blanket in passive acquiescence.

"What happened to her, anyway? Did the guard know anything about it?" The voice was one Mickie recognized, and she opened her eyes a fraction.

"Got hit, Jim," she whispered.

"Glad to know you're with us, Mickie." Jim Forrest grinned down at her from his great height. An emergency medicine specialist and former college football player, he ran the emergency department with an iron will concealed within a cuddly bear's jovial manner. Now he took out an ophthalmoscope and peered into Mickie's eyes, looking, she knew, for signs of brain injury.

"Don't have a concussion," she told him, her voice only slightly slurred.

"Why don't you let me be the judge of that?" He peered into one eye, then the other. "What happened to you out there?"

"Got hit." Mickie reached up to indicate the bump on her head. "Right here." She lifted her head to show him, but had to lay it quickly down again when the room began to spin.

"Just let me check..." He slid his hands carefully beneath her neck, but Mickie turned her head to one side, pointing to show him.

"Right here."

"I'll find it. And you hold your head still! I don't know if your neck is all right."

"'S okay," she insisted. "Just my head."

"And your face, and your knees, which look like the wrath of God, by the way, and I intend to check you out. Lie still."

"Jus' put something on my knees. No stitches."

"I'll take care of your knees!" Jim was becoming exasperated. "You *relax*, all right?"

"Yeah, yeah. What's the matter with my face?" She reached up to investigate, but he grabbed her hand.

"You scraped it on the pavement. It's messy, but it doesn't look very deep." He tucked her hand down beside her.

"Let me see...." She reached up again, and again Jim grabbed her wrist.

"Mickie, will you *please* shut up and lie still? *I'm* going to treat *you*, not the other way around. And if you don't cooperate, I'll have them get out the restraints."

Mickie's eyes widened.

"I'm not kidding. Mary?" he addressed the nurse standing across the gurney from him. "We're going to clean up her knees and her face—and she's going to lie very still and be very quiet. *Isn't she*?"

"She is," Mickie muttered, and they went to work over her.

"Mickie! What in heaven's name...? What on earth happened to you?" The cry came from the doorway as Connie burst in. "Oh, Mickie!" she wailed, then turned on Jim. "Is she going to be all right?"

"I'm going to be fine." Mickie, whose mind was already much clearer, answered for herself, disliking the sensation of having others talk around her. "They're just trying to clean me up. Purely cosmetic."

"Is it really? There's nothing serious?" Connie demanded of Jim and Mary.

"Basically, yes. If Dr. Busybody here will just lie still and be quiet until we get done." Mickie obediently subsided.

"She was hit on the head," Jim told Connie. "And was unconscious for an undetermined amount of time. Is that right, Mickie?"

"Yeah."

"She's becoming more alert by the minute," Jim told Connie. "Aside from the scrapes and bruises, she seems to have gotten off relatively easy."

"Well, thank goodness for that!" Connie sighed. "I'll take her home with me tonight. I'm just glad they called me."

"Who called you?" Mickie demanded as the others shifted their attention to her battered knees.

"The ER nurses. Somebody had to, after all."

"You don't have to take me home with you, Connie. I'll be fine."

"You know as well as I do that you should be observed for twenty-four hours. You're coming home with me. You have to," she concluded smugly. "I have your keys. I got them out of your purse."

"That's a sneaky trick, Connie."

"It's a pretty good one, though, isn't it?"

Given no choice, Mickie allowed herself to be painted with antiseptic and wrapped in bandages. Her skull was x-rayed, she was questioned at length by a polite but persistent policeman, and was finally delivered to Connie's car in a wheelchair.

She passively went along with the program until she saw who was waiting for her in Connie's living room. She looked up as she was pushed into the house, then dropped her head into her hands with a groan.

"Oh, no! Not *you*!"

Chapter 9

Yeah, it's me, all right," growled Commander Lewis. "It's nice to know you're so glad to see me, Doctor."

"Commander, I don't mean to be rude. I just don't feel much like arguing with you right now, okay?"

"Look, I know you don't feel good, and I don't want to make you sick or anything. I just need you to tell me everything you can about the man who attacked you."

"The trouble is, I really don't know anything," Mickie told him. Connie helped her move from the wheelchair to the sofa. "I wasn't able to tell the police much of anything, either."

"Except that you also saw our guerrilla friend hanging out where he didn't belong tonight."

Mickie carefully rested her aching head on the back of Connie's sofa. "We went over that about five zillion times. We saw him in the hallway. Connie took him upstairs to the main desk, and we went and pretended to eat dinner, just in case someone was watching us. There was no one around when we took Mark back upstairs, but we used the service elevator, just in case. That's all."

"And the guy who hit you over the head?"

"It could have been a woman who hit me over the head," Mickie shrugged. "I didn't see or hear anything at all."

"Nothing? Not a sound, a smell, a glimpse of anybody?"

"Nothing at all. I wasn't expecting to be hit over the head, and I guess I wasn't paying attention."

She hated to admit that, but mercifully the Commander declined to use her words against her. "Okay," he said, scribbling on a small note pad. "You didn't see or hear anything. How about your purse? Is anything missing?"

"No. The officer asked me that, too. My Jeep was unlocked, though. I guess it was searched."

"Your purse was, too. The security guard said the contents had spilled out. You always carry it zipped up?"

"Always."

"Think carefully now." Lewis leaned forward in his armchair, watching her face. "Was there anything in your purse or your car which referred in any way to Mark and his case? Anything at all?"

"Nothing." Mickie didn't need to think about that answer. "I never carry anything with me that refers to him. It's all locked in Connie's office."

"Do you have any notes or anything at home?"

"I write a memo each evening and file it in my office at home. I don't refer to him by name, though. I just write anecdotal notes about his treatment and progress."

"Anyway," Connie added, "it's a matter of record that Mark James was discharged. That's documented in Medical Records. Why should Mickie be carrying around information on a patient who's been discharged?"

"I hope that's what they think now." Lewis didn't sound especially hopeful. "I think that's what they're looking for. With luck, your yammering at him in the cafeteria and the innocence of your belongings tonight have put them off the track, at least for the time being."

"I thought putting them off the track was your job!" Connie protested angrily. Her protective instincts were roused by the attack on her friend, and she directed her hostility at Lewis. "Why aren't you taking care of this?"

"That's what I'm trying to do, Mrs. Ramirez." He turned back to Mickie. "I can have you guarded, if you want."

Mickie was as astonished by the offer as she was by the qualifier of, "if you want." However, unwillingly it had been made, it was generous. She was pretty sure she had been nothing but a headache to Lewis since the night they'd met. He'd probably have preferred to toss her to the sharks after all the grief she'd given him.

"You should have thought about protecting her before this happened!" Connie snapped. "Whatever your sleazy business is, you should have kept it out of the hospital!"

"I'd rather have kept it out of there, believe me, but Mark refused to go to a military hospital. Now, all I want to do is get him out of there as soon as I can."

"I don't want a guard, anyway," Mickie said. "That would only make me conspicuous. Mark will be out of the hospital in two days, three at the most. He'll be out of sight at my house. I don't want to do anything to call attention to myself. That might prompt them to follow me out there."

Lewis nodded agreement, surprising Mickie again. "That could be just about the best place for him, somewhere isolated, off the beaten path."

Mickie eyed him speculatively. "Aren't you the same one who told me all those horror stories about endangering myself by having Mark at my house?"

Lewis shrugged, ill-at-ease. "I can change my mind sometimes."

"Mm-hm," she replied noncommittally. Lewis's approval was almost enough to make Mickie reconsider her decision. If he thought it was a good idea, there had to be something wrong with it!

Nevertheless, three nights later, at eight in the evening, Mark surreptitiously left the hospital.

He was smuggled downstairs through a rarely used tunnel behind the Emergency Department and placed in an ostensibly empty ambulance.

Mickie had left the hospital over an hour earlier and eaten a solitary dinner at a fast-food hamburger stand. She'd returned some books to the library, browsed a while, and then driven to a park on the edge of town. There she sat down on a bench to wait. She threw crumbled cookies to the gulls and starlings as dusk turned to darkness and the air cooled.

The park had been deserted for almost half an hour when the ambulance pulled up. She moved quickly to help transfer Mark to her Jeep, then braced his cast with a folded blanket against the bumpy road they would travel. With a quick goodbye to the ambulance driver, they were gone.

"Were you followed?"

She shook her head. "Nope. I had a hamburger and took some books back to the library, and then I sat in the park and froze for half an hour. Nobody followed me."

"And if someone followed the ambulance?"

"We've got that covered. I'm going to take a roundabout route to my house. I braced your leg because the road is bumpy. It runs through some hills way out in the desert, and we're going to stop for a while and watch the view up there, just in case anyone else is using the same road. If they are, we'll see them, because it's impossible to drive that road without lights."

Mark chuckled. "You have it all figured out, don't you?"

"I hope so. Getting bopped over the head seems to have made me cautious."

He looked over at her. The broad swath of scraped skin on her cheek was clearly visible in the glow of the dashboard lights. His lips tightened in a hard line. "That shouldn't have happened."

"My feelings exactly." Mickie grinned at the road ahead. She could smile about it now that the headache, which had been severe two days ago, was almost gone. Her face would look battered for a week or so, but she was alive. She figured she could live with a battered face. Mark, it seemed, could not.

"Damn!" His explosive oath surprised her.

"What?"

"I never meant to cause you any harm. I shouldn't even be here with you!"

"Well, it's a little late to worry about that now, because we can't turn back. And you didn't cause me harm, you know. The guy who hit me did that."

"I put you in that position, though."

"You didn't *put* me anywhere," Mickie corrected him firmly. "I'm a big girl, Mark. I make my own decisions."

"And look where that got you—mugged in the hospital parking garage."

"It got me a bad-tempered house guest who wants to back out of coming before he's even seen my house. Don't you know that's not polite?"

Mark had to chuckle. "I've seen your 'car'... and I use the term loosely. I'm almost afraid to see your house."

"You don't like my car?" Mickie patted the dash comfortingly.

"I just didn't expect something like this. Where's the BMW, or the Mercedes, or whatever it is that doctors are supposed to drive?"

"When you see my driveway, you'll understand. I couldn't inflict it on a nice, shiny Mercedes."

"Now I'm getting nervous. Is your house a tarpaper shack at the bottom of a canyon?"

"Well, it is at the end of a canyon."

He groaned. "Just tell me one thing. Does it have indoor plumbing?"

"I think I'll wait and let you find out for yourself." Mickie grinned into the darkness ahead of them. "Here's our scenic route. Brace yourself."

She swung the Jeep onto a narrow gravel road, which soon became a narrow and deeply rutted dirt road. Mark held on to the roll bar and the door handle, protecting his leg as best he could from the bouncing of the Jeep. They drove for several miles before Mickie slowed, looking for the turnoff.

"Just past a big prickly pear," she muttered, "and . . . there it is!" She braked hard and turned off the road, hearing Mark swear as they bumped through a deep rut.

"Can we just sit quietly for a while?" he asked when she had pulled to a stop. "It's so peaceful."

"We can sit for a minute or two." She killed the engine. "There should be a pair of binoculars in the glove compartment. Would you get them for me?"

"Sure." He opened the door and produced a pair of high-powered field glasses. "Here you go."

"Thanks. You sit tight." She opened the door and slid out. "I'll be right back." She spent about five minutes scanning the hills all around them, then climbed back in.

"So what's the verdict?" Mark asked as she buckled her seat belt.

"All clear. There's nobody out there but the rattlesnakes and the coyotes. We'll be home in fifteen minutes."

"You promise it won't take any longer than that?" Mark gripped the roll bar again, grimacing.

"Cross my heart." Mickie started the engine with a roar.

Her estimate was almost exactly accurate, but Mark wasn't paying any attention to the time when they arrived. He had fallen silent when Mickie turned off a country road to pass between tall stucco gateposts capped with red clay tiles. He said nothing as she followed the gravel drive for nearly half a mile along a winding canyon and past clumps of tall eucalyptus and wind-twisted pines. They rounded the last curve, where the drive detoured around a massive boulder, and he saw Mickie's house, sitting at the head of the canyon. Mickie ran the Jeep under the portico, stopped smoothly and set the parking brake.

"Welcome home," she said as the engine grumbled into silence.

Mark looked at her, dressed in a very ordinary pink cotton dress and plain pumps, at the Jeep, dusty and battered, then looked again at the big adobe house. "This is home?"

"This is it. Come on." She climbed out and pulled his canvas bag from behind the seat. "I want to get inside, even if you don't." She walked around to open his door and take out his crutches. He slid carefully to the ground, and Mickie handed him the crutches.

She slung her tote onto her shoulder and picked up his bag again. "Come on in."

She didn't look to see if he was following as she unlocked the heavy front door and led the way inside. He wasn't acting especially pleased to find that she lived in a comfortable home and not the tarpaper shack he'd teased her about. She didn't know what the big deal was. She lived in a house, but so did most people. Closing the door behind him, she switched on the hall lights.

"That's the living room over there." She pointed to the right, then to the left. "And, my father's study over there. I use it as a combination library and TV room."

"This is your parents' house?"

"It was. I grew up here. My parents died in a plane crash ten years ago."

"I'm sorry."

"Thank you. The dining room is through there, and the kitchen's in the back." She switched on more lights as she walked through the house, Mark following in her wake. "My mother's solarium is beyond the kitchen. The house is shaped liked a 'U,' with a patio in the middle. The bedrooms are in the other wing, over here." She led him to the first of the bedrooms. "This is the guest room. You're the guest, so..."

"...this is my room." He finished the sentence as he followed her into the room. It had always seemed a large room to Mickie, but as Mark maneuvered his crutches and cast inside, he seemed to fill it with his muscular bulk. "It's very nice." He stopped and shook his head. "No, that's not good enough. After the hospital and the jungle, a room like this doesn't quite seem real."

"It's just a guest room, Mark." Mickie set his bag on the floor. "That's all."

"It's a lot more than that to me." Mark looked around him with an appreciation that approached wonder. A wide cherry bed, covered with a patchwork quilt, dominated the room. A wing chair and lamp table stood by the window, and a pottery vase of mixed flowers rested on the nightstand. "This means returning to real life." He turned to look down at her, his face grave. "Thank you."

"Don't thank me," she said with a small smile. "After all, you're the one who browbeat me into letting you come."

"You don't play fair, do you, lady?"

Mickie's smile faded as she looked up at him. "Neither do you."

"If you don't want me to stay..."

She ignored him, turning away to point to another door. "Your bathroom is through there. My room is the one next door, and my office is at the end of the hall. If you need me, you just have to call."

One dark eyebrow rose in silent comment. Mickie felt herself flush angrily at the unspoken taunt. He knew her offer to share her home was not an offer to share her bed, yet he persisted in baiting her with innuendo and implication. The walls he put up around himself were sheer and high, and topped with the broken glass of his cutting words. He was aware of her feelings for him and wasn't above using those feelings to create distance between them.

It was a defense mechanism against something he feared, and Mickie understood—too well. If she hadn't understood, his tactics might have worked. She might have been so hurt and furious that she would simply have given up on Mark. Instead, she knew what he was doing, and knowledge brought a certain tolerance. She knew, but she didn't have to like it, and she didn't have to stay here and take it.

"Dinner will be ready by the time you've cleaned up," she told him, her voice and face empty of emotion. "We'll eat in the kitchen. I'll see you there."

Her anger cooled as she changed into jeans and a loose blouse. When she stopped fuming she remembered that she hadn't put towels in the guest bath.

"Oh, rats!" Muttering in annoyance, she collected an armful of towels from the linen closet and returned to Mark's door. It was closed, and she knocked softly.

"Come in."

She shouldered the door open, walked two steps into his room and stopped short. She'd interrupted him in the process of changing his shirt, and Mickie was stopped in her tracks by the sight. Stripped to the waist, he was magnificent.

She knew she should say something, should take the towels into the bathroom, but she could only stand there, staring stupidly at the broad expanse of hard muscle, her gaze following the dusting of dark hair that disappeared into the low waistband of his jeans. He had indeed made a spectacular recovery during his weeks in the hospital. His body was strong and beautiful.

She finally managed to drag her gaze from his chest, only to meet his eyes and find that he was watching with unconcealed amusement. Mickie took just a moment too long to recover her composure, and when she spoke, her voice came out as a humiliating squeak.

"I br—" She tried again. "I brought you some towels."

"Thank you," Mark said gravely, his eyes gleaming with suppressed laughter.

Mickie hurried to arrange the towels in the bath, aware that her face was scarlet, but unable to do anything about it. He knew she was embarrassed, and he knew exactly why, and he was enjoying it, damn him! She flung the last towel over the chrome rod and fled the room with a hasty mutter about dinner in a short time. To her fury, she heard him laugh softly behind her as she made her escape.

She had herself under outward control by the time Mark joined her in the kitchen. The room was warm, inviting and filled with appetizing scents, and the gleaming copperware hanging from the beams was reflected in the black window-panes.

A lasagna casserole Mickie had prepared the night before was heating in the microwave, apple dumplings were baking in the convection oven, a salad waited in a large wooden bowl, and Mickie was blending a salad dressing in the food processor. She looked up as Mark entered.

He used his crutches well after several days of practice. He had put on a thin cotton polo shirt, and the bulge and flex of his arms and shoulders as he moved was a fascinating study; she could have watched it for hours. With an effort, she dragged her gaze away.

Luckily, he didn't notice her staring this time, because his attention had been captured by the sight of Sam, sprawled in front of the stove.

"Who's this?"

Sam heaved himself to his feet and went to greet the stranger.

"That's Sam. I hope you don't mind dogs."

"Not at all." Mark massaged Sam's ears, and the Labrador whined happily, his tail beating the air. "I like dogs." Sam took that as an invitation. He leaned companionably into Mark's legs and nearly knocked him down.

"Sam, down!" Mickie called. The dog dropped obediently to the floor. "Good boy. Have a seat," she told Mark, nodding toward the heavy, scrubbed oak table. "This will be ready in just a few minutes."

"It smells wonderful." He maneuvered his way to a chair. "This is a great room," he said, looking around him at the tiled floors and countertops, the dark beams and white-washed ceiling, the copper pots and strings of dried peppers hanging overhead. "Comfortable."

"I've always liked it. I'm glad you do." Since he seemed prepared to ignore what had passed between them earlier, Mickie was more than happy to do the same. She finished the dressing, dipped a fingertip in the bowl and tasted. "Mmm...needs salt." She added a dash and flipped the machine on, then off again. "There." She placed a cruet on the table in front of Mark. "Would you pour the dressing in here while I get the lasagna?"

"Sure. Do you mind if I ask you a question?"

"That depends on the question." If he wanted to reopen hostilities, she wasn't about to play along. Mickie set the salad bowl on the table.

"What are all these machines?" He looked at the appliances ranged around the room. "Do you cook with them, or something?"

"Or something." Mickie grinned. "Yes, I cook with them. Which one were you wondering about?"

"All of them. About all I ever cook with is a frying pan."

"That's an electric frying pan." She pointed out a large electric skillet which could also bake pizzas and deep-fry doughnuts.

"What about that?" He pointed.

"A convection oven." Mickie entered the game willingly. She much preferred this discussion to a confrontation of the thoughts and feelings they were both concealing. She demonstrated the microwave as she finished heating the lasagna.

"What's that?" He pointed to a complicated-looking machine in the corner.

"An espresso machine, and the one next to it is an ordinary coffeemaker."

"If you can call a computerized coffeepot ordinary." Mark shrugged. "Why does it have all those buttons and numbers?"

"It has a digital timer. I set it at night and coffee's ready when I get up in the morning." They were both laughing as she brought serving spoons to the table and took her seat. "I know I have a terrible weakness—" She cut a large serving of the lasagna. "Could you hold your plate up here?"

"Of course."

"Thanks." She picked up her previous line of conversation. "It's probably a fatal character flaw, but I just love gadgets. And you know," she went on quickly as Mark started to chuckle, "it's not all a waste of hard-earned money, because they do make cooking easier. I made the noodles for this lasagna with my pasta machine."

He snorted. "I didn't know there were machines for pasta. You like to cook, huh?"

"It's sort of like therapy for me. I love it."

"Do you cook like this just for yourself?"

"Myself and Sam." The dog raised his head and grinned at the sound of his name. "He disposes of lots of leftovers, and he never tells about the culinary experiments that went wrong."

"There can't be many of those." Mark tasted the lasagna. "This is great."

"Thank you." Mickie grinned. Mark returned his attention to his dinner.

The air of harmony prevailed through the meal and the espresso Mickie prepared with her gleaming chrome and enamel machine, to Mark's vast amusement.

"Isn't it good, though?"

He sipped, savored the hot, dark coffee, and nodded. "Very good. And very authentic."

"You've been to Italy?" Mickie asked, interested.

He shrugged. "Little Italy, in New York. It's the next best thing."

"I've never been to New York. I'd like to go, but now that I can afford it, I never seem to have the time."

"The curse of a busy life, I guess. Living on the West Coast, you must have been to San Francisco, though?"

"Oh, yes! I love to visit, especially in the spring—" Mickie stopped short as the wall clock caught her eye. "Good grief, look at the time!" It was past midnight. She drained her coffee cup and stood. "I had no idea it was so late! And I have surgery tomorrow at seven!" Mark started to rise, but she waved him back into his chair. "No, don't get up. You stay and finish your coffee; you're not the one who has to be up at five."

"No, it's late, and I'm tired, too." He rose and picked up his cup.

"I'll take care of that." Mickie took the cup from his hand. "You have enough to handle with your crutches."

"You're probably right." He watched as she quickly dealt with the few remaining dishes and filled the coffeemaker for morning brewing. "Is that everything?"

"That's it." Mickie closed the dishwasher and switched it on. She led the way from the kitchen, turning off lights as she went. Outside the guest room, she paused. Mark stopped close behind her, so close that the warmth of his body reached her. His scent was heady, shaving lotion and hospital soap and man, in a richly seductive combination.

"Well...good night," she said awkwardly. The easy dinnertime banter must have lulled her into a false sense of security, because suddenly she had no idea how to handle this simple good-night.

They were doctor and patient, but they were more than that. They were—or had been—friends, but they were more than that, too. They were lovers, and yet they weren't, not yet—maybe never. What should she do now? It was the moment for a good-night kiss; the sensual pull was strong between them, and yet... The timing was wrong, as wrong as it could be.

She stepped back, moving outside the circle of his spell. "Good night, Mark. I'll try to phone tomorrow, and I'll see you in the evening."

"Good night, Mickie." There was a rich undercurrent of laughter in his deep baritone.

She fled.

"Idiot!" Mickie muttered when her bedroom door had closed behind her. "You are an idiot!"

Mickie didn't want to fight with Mark; it took too much out of her. But on the other hand, she wasn't sure she was up to the strain of several weeks of dinners like tonight, followed by scenes like the one outside his door. How on earth was she going to handle this? And how was she going to handle *him*? "What have I gotten myself into?" she muttered.

Shaking her head, she kicked off her shoes and began to undress. She had shimmied out of her jeans and was unbuttoning her blouse when she heard the crash. It was followed by a flurry of angry swearing and a second, heavier crash from the guest room.

"Oh, my God, no!" Mickie sprinted out the door.

Chapter 10

Her mind whirling with visions of catastrophe, Mickie sprinted down the hall and flung Mark's door open. He lay facedown, sprawled awkwardly on the floor. She couldn't tell if he was conscious or not, and her stomach tightened into an icy knot of stark fear.

"Oh, my God!" She flung herself to her knees beside him, reaching to check for a pulse, for breathing. "Mark, are you all right? Mark!"

"Yeah, Yeah, I'm all right," he muttered as he rolled painfully onto his side to face her. He put out an arm to shove himself up.

Mickie pushed him back down. "Lie still!"

"But it's wet!" he protested.

Mickie looked at the floor around him, noticing the mess for the first time. He lay in a wet litter of pottery shards and crushed flowers, the remains of the bouquet that had decorated the nightstand. The little wicker table lay on its side in the corner of the room.

"No kidding it's wet! I don't suppose I need to ask what happened?"

"I don't suppose you do." His voice was harsh, but Mickie couldn't tell whether that was from pain or anger. "I took my shirt off, and I was trying to get out of my jeans when I lost my balance. I grabbed that table."

"But it wasn't enough to hold you up."

"Not quite. As soon as I grabbed it I could tell it was never meant to keep someone from falling."

To Mickie's relief he seemed to be more disgusted by his own clumsiness than in pain, but she was taking no chances. "I know it's not very comfortable lying there in the mess, and I'm sorry about that. I don't want you to move, though, until I know you haven't done any serious damage."

"Is that going to take long? There's something sharp under my shoulder—uh!"

Mickie reached under him and retrieved a fragment of the vase. "Here" She dropped it into his hand. "A trophy. Now don't move, please." She ran her hands over the cast, checking for cracks or weakness, then palpated his foot. "Are you having any pain in your leg?"

"Not in the broken one."

"What?"

"When I fell the cast landed on my other leg."

"Terrific! If you do that again you could have two broken legs to deal with. You don't feel any pain in the broken one, though? No sensation that the bones might have shifted?"

"No, nothing like that."

"No dizziness, or shortness of breath?"

"Nope."

"How many fingers am I holding up?"

"Three."

"Okay." She bent over him, sliding one arm beneath his shoulders, then grasped his arm with her free hand. "Let me help you sit up, slowly, and we'll get you up on the bed." Carefully, with Mickie supporting as much of his weight as she could, Mark sat upright, then levered himself up to the side of his bed. She knelt at his feet. "Lift up your foot."

"What?"

"Lift up your foot. I want to get these jeans off before they can do any more damage."

"Oh. Okay." Obediently he lifted his uninjured leg, then held very still while she eased the too-tight denim off the cast.

Tossing the jeans aside, she put a hand on his chest and pushed gently. "Lie down. I want to make certain your leg is okay."

"It feels fine."

"That's wonderful, but lie down anyway."

"Okay, boss." He did as she asked, lying back against the pillows. "But I'm telling you it feels fine."

"I'm the doctor, remember? You let me be the judge of how fine it is." It took Mickie a few minutes to make certain that neither his leg nor his cast had suffered any damage in the fall. When she'd finished she straightened and sat on the side of the bed, shaking her head. "You're a lucky man, Mark James." She smiled at him, limp with relief. "A fall like that could have been a major disaster."

"But it wasn't?" Mark answered her smile, his eyes warming as he looked at her.

Mickie could feel her cheeks heat under his gaze. Mark had apparently been watching her as she worked, watching with some appreciation. His lips curved into a small smile, and she was suddenly very conscious of the fact that he was dressed in nothing but tiny briefs, and that she wore only bikini panties and a half-opened shirt.

She looked down, away from his eyes, and saw that her shirt hung loosely away from her, its only fastening one lonely button. Her small, round breasts were bared to his appreciative gaze. She quickly straightened, tugging the blouse around her, but she could feel the swelling of her breasts and the tightening of her nipples, all too clearly revealing her response to that caressing regard.

"No, it wasn't a disaster," she managed to reply, though her voice was breathless. "Your leg seems to be fine."

"You're a good doctor, Mickie Blake. I think I owe you my thanks."

He moved quickly, taking Mickie by surprise as he caught her shoulders in his hands. Mickie was off balance, perched on the edge of the mattress, and could offer no resistance as he pulled her into his arms. She tumbled down onto his chest and into his embrace, into a kiss that was hot, demanding, almost angry. That ferocity didn't frighten her, and she met it with a fierceness of her own, with a hunger fueled by the frustration and anger of their last tense days in the hospital.

She clutched his shoulders, returning his kisses with all the love and wanting she had been holding inside. Her body was sprawled over Mark's, and his hands moved restlessly across her back, sliding the thin cotton of her shirt over her skin.

Mickie was melting against him, dissolving as the heat of his hands on her back, the heat of his body beneath her, began to burn through her body. Her hands moved, shaping the muscles of his shoulders and stroking up his neck until she tangled her fingers in his hair. It had grown long during his hospitalization, and she savored the silky texture of it as she savored the taste of his kiss.

He ran his palms down her ribs to her waist, measured its narrow span with his hands, then slipped them beneath the loose shirt to find her skin. Mickie shivered at his touch, *frissons* of delight running along her nerves. His palms were callused from exercising on the machines, and that slight roughness against her skin was almost painfully erotic. She moved instinctively, tantalizingly, against his body, as she lifted her lips from his to press little nibbling kisses along the line of his jaw and onto his throat.

The bedclothes rustled softly beneath them as Mark gathered her closer into his arms, and Mickie welcomed the warmth, the sense of safety, she found there. He didn't want her to feel safe in his arms, of course, but in spite of him, she did. He wanted her, and something primitive and feminine deep within her reveled in the power she had to make him want. He wanted her, and that wanting created a bond between them, whether he wished it or not.

Mickie was tied to him already, by her love and her desire, gossamer bonds, but stronger than steel cables. Hearts and flowers would have been nice; she would have liked him to whisper sweet words to her, to admit his need for her, but the hearts and flowers would have changed nothing. Whether he chose to admit it or not, whether he were kind or cruel, he was the man she loved. She would share her love with him, would give him the tenderness she craved for herself, and perhaps, just perhaps, it would come back to her. She loved him. The rest was just gilt for the lily.

With a little murmur of surrender, she found his lips with hers again.

Mark heard that wordless murmur and growled a response low in his throat as he took her kiss. He hadn't intended this any more than he had intended to become captivated by her in the first place, but both had been inevitable. He couldn't resist her any more than he could deny that he had wanted to make love to her for weeks now.

He moved his palms in circles over her back, delighting in the feel of her, the supple line of her back tapering in to an impossibly small waist, then flaring out again into the sweetest little... He caressed the filmy nylon of her tiny panties, toyed with the lacy waistband resting just above the gentle curve of her derriere. He felt her quiver, then sigh and melt against him as his fingertips slid beneath the lace. Her skin was smoother, sleeker, than satin, and so warm. Mark felt his heartbeat accelerate as he touched her, reveling in the answering response of her body. He stroked, feeling her skin heat beneath his fingers, then ran his hand up to lift her slightly away from him. Her breasts were round, heavy and full, the taut nipples brushing his chest. Mark weighed them gently in his palms, teasing her nipples with his thumbs until Mickie gasped and collapsed onto his chest.

Her shirt was wadded between them, and Mark pulled at it. He didn't want any barriers. He wanted her skin against his; he wanted to be close until they could get no closer. The shirt resisted his efforts to remove it, and Mickie suddenly pushed herself up. Kneeling beside him, she shrugged it off and tossed it aside; then he reached up to her and she came back into his arms, her body soft and slim and more desirable than anything he had ever known.

God, she was sweet! Her desire was pure and unembarrassed, and the knowledge of it fed Mark's own desire. He tried to roll, to take her more fully into his arms, but the heavy cast held him pinned to the bed.

He swore under his breath. "This damned cast . . ."

"You shouldn't try to move," Mickie whispered.

His arms tightened around her shoulders. He had to move; couldn't she understand that? He pulled her closer, and her legs bumped his cast. He grunted softly as he tried to shift it out of her way.

"Sorry," he muttered.

"It's all right."

"But I can't move."

She touched his cheek, and he turned to catch her fingertip between his lips. "I can," she whispered. It was the merest breath of a reply, but it was enough.

Mark lay back, and Mickie followed him, covering his body with hers, her legs sliding along his, satin-smooth against the crisp hair on his thigh. His cast was a hindrance, but in the face of their passion only a minor one, quickly forgotten.

Mickie lay above him, teasing him with her lips, her hands, the seductive movements of her supple body. Mark had longed to make love to her, but in the end it seemed it was she who made love to him, stripping the briefs from his body, then running her hands back up his good leg to stroke his chest and feather across the ridged muscles of his stomach. Mark groaned, and she relented, her caresses taking him close to insanity.

When he could bear it no longer he caught her wrists and pulled her hands up, holding them above her head as he brushed a fingertip across her lips, then traced a line down her throat, explored the small hollow above her collarbone and slid over the bone to follow the curve of her breast. He could feel the catch in her breath as he circled one pink nipple, watching it tighten in response to his touch.

He wanted to pleasure her, wanted to make her feel the things she made him feel. Mark had never been a selfish lover, but his need to please this woman went deeper. He refused to analyze the way he felt, the way she made him feel; he only knew what he needed. His fingertip followed a line down to her navel, then lower, and Mickie sagged helplessly against him. Mark touched her softly, insistently, and Mickie squirmed closer, the little undulations of her body driving them together to madness.

When they could bear it no longer, Mark wrapped his arms around her, she twined her legs with his, and they moved together easily, naturally, as the rhythm built and quickened, and then they were consumed by an explosion of whirling light and sensation.

It was only after an eternity's journey together that they finally parted. Mickie slipped off Mark's body to cuddle close by his side as he slid into an exhausted sleep. She knew he needed rest now in the same sense that he needed air to breathe, and she was determined that he would have it. He'd had a long day today, after weeks of hospitalization, and he wasn't as strong yet as he wanted to think he was.

And she hadn't exactly improved the situation, Mickie thought wryly. She should have checked Mark's leg, helped him into bed and gone quietly on her way. Instead, the long-smoldering flame had finally caught between them, burning all her good intentions to ashes in a single blinding flash.

Beside her Mark muttered something unintelligible as sleep claimed him. Mickie worked quickly to make him comfortable, slipping a pillow beneath his head and straightening the tumbled bedclothes to draw them over him. She pulled the quilt up and reached across his body to cover him warmly. With a final pat to the soft cotton, she moved carefully away. As her weight left the mattress, though, his hand suddenly shot out to catch her upper arm in a painful grip.

"What're you doing?" he asked in a thick mutter.

"Just covering you up so you won't get cold."

"You?"

"I'm going to bed, Mark."

"Stay!" His voice sharpened, and his grip tightened, pulling her down. "Here, with me." He was going to wake up if she tried to go, and Mickie hesitated for only an instant. He was exhausted; he had to sleep.

"Okay," she whispered. "I'll stay. Go to sleep. I'll stay with you, Mark."

"Mark...?" He might have chuckled, but she wasn't sure. Then he was gone, relaxing back into sleep with a deep sigh.

Cautiously she slid beneath the blankets, careful not to disturb him. He reached out and drew her to his side, tucking her into the curve of his body with her head cradled on his shoulder. Rationalization was easy. If she wanted Mark to rest quietly, she would have to sleep with him. Smiling, Mickie nestled warmly at his side and let sleep capture her as well.

She awakened very early, still smiling. There was no moment of confusion as to where she was, or why; there was instead a sweet, sure knowledge. Mark lay comfortably on his back with Mickie tucked against his body, her arm draped across his midriff. His arm was bent, cradling her head and curving around her neck so that his hand cupped her breast in an unconscious caress. He was still deeply asleep, his breathing slow and regular. From outside, she could hear a high birdcall, though only the first faint trace of dawn had begun to gray the window.

Mickie lay quietly for several moments, luxuriating in the rightness of it all. It was rather surprising to her to realize just how right this felt. Surely she should be having some second thoughts, experiencing some regrets, yet there were none. This sangfroid of hers was unexpected, and in the face of the coldly objective reasons why this relationship was a tremendous mistake she found it rather difficult to accept in herself. After all, Mark didn't return the feelings she had for him. He was hiding things from her, his feelings, his secrets, so many things he wouldn't share. He was frequently hostile, as well as wary and suspicious and cynical about women. And he was still her patient.

She should have been shuddering with horror, but instead Mickie felt a sense of peace and fulfillment she had never known. Mark might be wary and cynical, he might want her only because she was a woman and she was there, but surely the force of her love had to count for something. Something that felt so right could not be wrong.

Careful not to disturb him, Mickie pressed a featherlight kiss to Mark's shoulder and left him.

She almost tripped over Sam, who was curled up and sleeping just outside the door. He blinked blearily up at her before his face disappeared behind a vast yawn, Mickie stepped across him, and the dog heaved himself to his feet to follow her to her room, apparently undisturbed by the latest turn of events. Mickie rubbed his ears.

"You think it's right, too, don't you, boy?"

For an answer he paused just inside her bedroom door and stretched himself, one vertebra at a time, then collapsed on the rag rug by her bed. Laughing, Mickie tossed her shirt and panties in the hamper and went to shower.

When she was ready to leave for the hospital she poured the last cup of coffee out of the pot and switched off the coffeemaker. Her soft tap on Mark's door was unanswered, and she eased it open to see him sprawled on his back, arms outflung across the bed. She carried the cup in and set it on the nightstand, then tiptoed out, still smiling. The first pink glow was tinting the mountains, and it was a wonderful day.

From his chair in the living room Mark watched the last purple-orange stain of sunset fading from the mountains. The ice in his glass clinked softly as he sipped the small measure of aged Kentucky bourbon he'd poured himself. Mickie had invited him to make himself at home, and he had taken her at her word. In doing so, he found he felt at home, more so than he had expected. He had almost forgotten how comfortable a home could be, a home as distinguished from a house, or more particularly from a hospital or a filthy guerrilla camp. It was good to be back in the real world. It was good to be here.

He looked around at the comfortable chairs and sofas, the oriental rug aging into mellow elegance, the dark beams across the whitewashed ceiling, the light curtains that lifted in the evening breeze. He knew he ought to close the window, because the air was cooling rapidly as night fell, but he was too comfortable for the moment to stir himself. He swirled the amber liquor in his glass, watching the abstract movement, thinking of nothing, comfortably, curiously at peace.

The room was in near darkness when he heard the snarl of the Jeep's engine above the melody of night sounds. It was late. He wondered if she worked fifteen-hour days as a matter of routine, or if this was unusual. She didn't look strong enough for such a killing schedule, but looks could be deceiving. He smiled into his glass. Mickie Blake was a lot stronger than she looked.

She was in a hurry, too. He could hear the engine whine, the tires protest, as she took the curves of the long drive too fast. Then she rounded the last huge boulder, her headlights raking through the room as she turned toward the portico. Her brakes shrieked, the gears ground, and she jerked the Jeep to a stop, letting the engine sputter and die as she flung her door open.

From his armchair Mark couldn't see her but he could follow her progress with his ears. He gathered his crutches from the floor beside him, preparing to stand and greet her,

but he couldn't move as fast as she could. Her rapid footsteps echoed under the portico; then the front door was
flung open, banging sharply against the porch railing before it crashed closed again. Mark was still struggling to his
feet when Mickie stalked past the living room doorway,
making for the rear of the house. He couldn't be sure, but
it looked as though she had been crying.

In spite of himself, because he didn't want to feel that
way, Mark was concerned about her. Swearing under his
breath, he fumbled his crutches into place and followed her.
As he reached the kitchen the back door slammed with a
crash that echoed through the house, and by the time he
clumped out to the patio she was already in the pool. He
hurried toward her, opening his mouth to call out. The
words died in his throat when he saw what she was doing.

He stopped short in the pool of blackness beneath a
weeping fig growing in a huge tub. He knew he should
speak, knew he should let her know he was there, but he
stood frozen. The faint light of the rising moon didn't illu-
minate the scene clearly, but he saw a glimmer of light on the
water, and he saw Mickie's jerky movements as she stripped
off her clothes. She flung them to the ground around her—
shoes, blouse, skirt—then she wriggled out of a lace-
trimmed teddy and stepped to the side of the pool.

She stood there for an instant, poised, arms at her sides,
tall and slim and graceful. Silvered by moonlight, she was
unreal, a naiad from mythology. Mark didn't breathe.
Slowly she raised her arms overhead, then flexed her knees
and sprang into a graceful dive.

She entered the water with a minimal splash, and when
she surfaced she struck out for the opposite side of the pool.
She swam hard, with the same suppressed anger in her
strokes that he had heard in her footsteps. Something was
wrong; something had upset her deeply. Mark collected a
couple of big towels and clumped his way to the poolside to
wait for her to finish.

Lap after lap she swam, churning her way from one end of the pool to the other, fighting to work out whatever strong emotion she was struggling with. Long after he thought she must be collapsing from exhaustion she still swam, away and back, away and back. Mark stood patiently on the tile deck, but his worry for her grew as he waited for her to finish.

At last he could see her slowing as she neared the end of the pool, and instead of making another of the smooth racing turns she had been executing, she caught the edge of the pool. Gasping for breath, she flung one slim arm onto the deck and leaned her head against the tile, letting her legs float up behind her.

"Let me help you out." She looked up, startled to see him. Mark reached one hand down to her. "You're going to get cold," he told her, but she just stared at him.

"It doesn't matter." Her voice was flat, lifeless.

"Yes, it matters! Come on out of there before you get pneumonia or something."

"You get pneumonia from pneumococcus bacteria, not from swimming."

"Come out of the pool, Dr. Einstein, before you freeze!" Mark reached down for her again, but she waved him away.

"You're on crutches, remember? All that will happen is I'll pull you in here with me. Move over!" He didn't move quickly enough, and she flapped her hand irritably at him. "Go on, move over!"

He stepped aside, and she planted her hands on the tile to heave herself out, water streaming from her body. Unconcerned with her nakedness, or too upset to care, she scrubbed her hands over her face, wiping the water—or the tears—from her eyes. Propped on his crutches, Mark held a thick bath sheet between his outstretched hands. She stepped into it, letting him fold it around her.

"Come into the house, Mickie. Get warm, and get something to eat."

"I don't want anything." She shook her head, sprinkling him with droplets from her curls. "I couldn't eat, anyway." She tucked a corner of the towel between her breasts to form a sarong and shrugged, her shoulders drooping tiredly. She plodded across the tile to a chaise and slumped onto it.

Mark followed with the other towel. "Put this around your shoulders. You're still too wet."

"All right, all right." She took the towel and did as he told her.

He lowered himself awkwardly onto the other chaise, lifting his cast up to rest on the plastic webbing. He laid his crutches beside the chair and leaned back with a sigh. "There! I don't know if I'll ever learn how to maneuver this thing!" He watched the moonlight on the pool for a moment. "What happened today, Mickie?"

"What?" She turned sharply in her chair.

"You're upset. What's wrong?"

"You don't want to know." Her voice was a sullen mutter.

"I asked." The words hung in the still air between them until Mickie heaved a deep sigh.

"I thought the world was wonderful when I got up this morning. The sun was shining, it was a beautiful day, and everything was great—until about two this afternoon. I got called to the ER." She took a deep breath. "You know the elementary school down the street from the hospital? St. Joseph's. It's the pink stucco building in the middle of the block."

"Yeah, I know it."

"Well, there's a crossing guard on the corner by the doctors' parking lot. His name's Ernest Walker. He's seventy-four, and he has three grandchildren. Two boys and a girl. He showed me their pictures one day. He's out there every morning and every afternoon, and he always wears one of those Day-Glo orange vests—you can see them a mile away—he has a stop sign he carries and everything. You couldn't possibly miss seeing him there."

"I know."

"Well, he was taking two kids across the street today, and a drunk driver came down the hill and hit him!" The words began to tumble out, her outrage pushing them along in an angry torrent. "He pushed the kids out of the way, or they might have been killed, but he couldn't move fast enough himself. The impact broke his leg. Only it didn't just break his leg, it shattered it, completely shattered it. They brought him in and we took him right to surgery, but even though we tried to put some kind of a bone back together, tried to pin it or wire it, or something, there was nothing..."

"What did you do?"

"There was nothing we could do. He lost the leg. It was beyond saving, even with all the hundreds of thousands of dollars' worth of equipment and all the new surgical techniques we have. All those miracles of modern medicine," she said bitterly. "They just don't amount to much sometimes."

"How is he? Will he be all right?"

"He'll live." She shrugged. "I talked to him before I left this evening."

"Mmm?"

"He was joking with the nurses. He even tried to pinch one girl!" She gave a laugh that was more nearly a sob. "And he asked me to leave a catalog of prosthetic legs with him, so he can pick out the best-looking one! He wants to be back on the corner with his new 'mail-order' leg, he says, so he can show it off to the kids. It will be a while before he can do that, though. And it shouldn't have happened in the first place!" Her voice broke, and she took a slow breath, forcing back the tears that threatened to fall.

Mark searched for something, anything, to say. "The guy who hit him, the drunk, what about him?"

She laughed harshly. "What do you think? He sideswiped a car after he hit Ernie and finally ran off the street and into somebody's front yard, but there wasn't a mark on him. He was so drunk he didn't even know he'd hit a man!''

"Do the police have him?''

"They arrested him. I guess this is about his fifteenth drunk-driving offense. He lost his license over a year ago, but it didn't stop him driving. He's probably out on bail by now, and driving himself home!''

"Stop it!'' Mark said sharply. "Don't torture yourself! They've toughened the laws on drunk driving; you know that. They don't just let them go anymore."

"You'd like to think they don't! But if not, why was he driving in the first place?''

Her voice was heavy with anguish, and Mark ached to comfort her. He wasn't good at that, though; he'd never been good at emotional things. He'd always been the tough guy, more comfortable with actions than emotions. He didn't know the words to say, didn't know how to ease her pain.

"You said he was in good spirits tonight, though. It sounds like he'll be able to deal with what's happened,'' Mark offered, hoping to give some comfort.

"He was, but that's not so unusual. People's first reaction in a situation like this is usually simple relief to be alive. Only later does the loss sink in. That's when they become depressed. It's a crushing thing to have to deal with, and I don't want that to happen to Ernie." She sat for a moment, then struck the arm of the chaise with her fist. "Damn! I don't want any of this to have happened to Ernie! I should have been able to save his leg! There should have been some way, something I could have done!''

"Stop it!'' Mark pushed himself upright on the chaise. "Stop punishing yourself! You're a good doctor, a good orthopedist, and you know it! If there had been a way to save his leg you'd have found it. There was nothing you could do—you told me that yourself. You have to accept what happened and go on.''

"That's awfully easy for you to say, isn't it? Accept it and go on," Mickie parroted with biting accuracy. "Do me a favor, will you, Mark, and save the platitudes? I'm not in the mood for them." She shoved herself out of the chaise, tossing aside the towel that had covered her shoulders. Her sarong was loosening, and she tightened it with a jerk.

"Where are you going?" Mark grabbed his crutches and struggled to his feet.

"To get a drink!" she threw over her shoulder as she stalked toward the house. "I need one."

Mark watched her go, cursing his own ineptitude. Other men would know how to handle a situation like this; why didn't he? There had to be some way to help her, some words to say that would ease her pain, but what were they?

"Damn it to hell!" he muttered.

There was nothing he could do.

It might be a lot easier on both of them if he let her handle her pain in her own way. He had nothing to offer anyway, and if he tried he'd just end up with his other foot in his mouth. Since she didn't seem to want him around, the best thing he could do for either of them was just to take himself to bed and get out of her way. He was sure that would be best for them both.

Chapter 11

This was a bad idea.

He was sure it was, yet Mark shoved his crutches under his arms and followed Mickie as quickly as he could with his awkward stride. He couldn't have said why he was going to her. He didn't know what he might be able to do. For once in his life he was confused, uncertain, and he resented that. He resented the woman who was responsible for his uncertainty, too. He was sliding deeper and deeper into an involvement he didn't want and couldn't afford, but there seemed to be nothing he could do about it. He couldn't just leave her as she was, alone and hurting.

He found her in the darkened living room, sitting in the chair he'd occupied earlier. She was slumped back, half lying in the soft leather depths, with her legs stretched out before her, crossed at the ankle and propped on the ottoman. Her towel sarong had ridden dangerously high on her thighs. A vivid vision flashed into Mark's mind of Mickie as she had stood nude on the edge of the pool. It stirred him, stirred memories of her pliant and passionate body in his arms the night before, and he banished it only with an effort.

The decanter of bourbon rested on the table beside her. The short crystal glass she cradled in her hand ws half-filled with the mellow liquor he had enjoyed. She wasn't treating it with the respect it deserved.

As he entered the room she lifted the glass and took a large gulp. She shuddered as the spirits burned the back of her throat then swallowed, gasped and coughed, wiping away the tears that filled her eyes.

"Not much of a drinker, are you?"

Mark switched on a lamp he passed on his way across the room to the sofa. However bad Mickie felt, it wouldn't do her any good to sit and drink in the dark.

She shrugged. "I don't suppose I ever considered being a two-fisted drinker to be a talent I needed to cultivate. I might have been wrong about that, though. It could be a useful ability."

She raised her glass again and drained. it. She breathed deeply as the liquor went down, but this time she didn't choke. Sagging into the chair, she let her head fall back, the glass resting between her slack hands. Her eyes were closed, and she sat motionless for so long that Mark wondered if she had fallen asleep. She surprised him when she suddenly reached for the decanter again.

"Haven't you had enough?"

She glared across at him then poured, shaking her head. "Oh, no, I haven't had enough. Not nearly enough." The decanter thumped back onto the table, and she drank again. "Funny," she commented.

"What's funny?"

"After a while this stuff doesn't taste so bad."

"It still tastes the same; your brain just doesn't realize that."

"Oh." She considered that for a few moments. "There must be some interesting physiological explanation to account for that."

"No doubt."

There was another long pause, the night silence broken only by the yip of a coyote somewhere in the hills.

"Damn it!" Mickie exploded so suddenly that Mark tensed. She sat up straight in her chair, staring at him with eyes wide and dark with pain. "How can I sit here and make stupid jokes about physiology? What good did all that physiology do Ernie? What good did any of my training do him? What good did *I* do him?"

"You probably saved his life," Mark said quietly. He watched her carefully, trying to judge her mood, searching for the right words to say.

She gave her head a quick angry shake that tossed her damp curls, dismissing that idea. *"Anybody* could have done that. I'm an orthopedist; I'm the specialist they called in. I was supposed to save his *leg.* Instead, all I could offer him was a modern variation of the medieval barber's remedy. I used sophisticated drugs and instruments, but the end result was the same, wasn't it?"

"Self-pity doesn't become you, Mickie."

"Probably not." She didn't even care enough to be angered by the gibe. She lifted her glass to drink again. "I don't think a prosthetic leg is going to become Ernie, either."

Mark took a deep breath, controlling a surge of anger. He wanted to shout at her, to command her to stop this pointless self-flagellation. She was hurting herself for nothing, and he couldn't stand that. He couldn't stand to see her hurting.

"Mickie, you have to stop this—"

"Do I?" she interrupted him and swung her feet to the floor. "I don't have to stop thinking or talking or feeling . . . or drinking. That little bottle there—" she flung her hand out in a gesture that went wide and nearly knocked the decanter flying—"That little bottle," she repeated, speaking with the telltale careful enunciation of the inebriated, "may be the only thing that can do me any earthly good right now." She refilled her glass sloppily, splashing whiskey onto the polished mahogany tabletop. "And I *don't* need you preaching at me, okay?"

"No, it isn't okay, and you know it! Damn it, Mickie, I understand how you—"

"You don't understand anything, you know that, Mark?"

She tossed down the last of the bourbon without blinking and heaved herself out of the chair. Her sarong was loosened by the violent movement and nearly fell off, baring for a moment one small, high breast and a long slice of flank and thigh. Mark felt again the quick, involuntary stirring of his body, bringing with it the unwanted memory of last night, her slim body warm and eager in his arms. He willed that memory away. Last night had been a mistake, one he had to put out of his mind.

She jerked the towel close around her body again, glaring down at him as she tucked the free end between her breasts to secure it. "You don't understand *anything!* Not anything at all! And I don't want to be preached at anymore!"

She turned on her heel and swayed, lurching dizzily to one side. She grabbed the chair to steady herself, then marched stiffly out of the room.

Mark sat where he was for a moment, prisoner of a welter of strong emotions, all foreign to him. He had found that he cared about Mickie, and he was astonished at himself.

It wasn't like him, not at all. He had always been the cool one, always in control, always sure of himself. He liked it that way, but now he was out of control, floundering, at a loss to know what to do. He felt that he had to help her, and that infuriated him. He worried about her, cared that she felt pain, and that caring went far deeper than the casual concern he wanted to feel.

He'd been a fool, Mark realized, a stupid fool. He'd committed the fatal error of letting a tall, slender woman with flaming curls and a sharp tongue get under his skin. If he were smart, if he had any sense at all, he'd just forget his efforts to "help" her. He wasn't accomplishing anything beyond annoying her, anyway. He should forget *her*, too.

But he couldn't forget that she was hurting. She was alone and hurting, and he was a weak, stupid, idiot who hadn't the strength, or the cold-bloodedness, to shut her out of his mind. Cursing himself for his soft heart and soft head, he shoved himself to his feet and went after her.

He was still cursing when he paused in the hallway outside her door. The door was closed, she obviously wanted to be alone. The logical thing to do was turn around, go to his own room, go inside and shut the door. Mark had always prided himself on his logical approach to life, so he turned on his crutches to face his own door.

Then he heard the sound. It was quiet, so quiet that he almost missed it. Mickie was crying. Unwillingly Mark turned back. He took the doorknob, hesitated for an instant, then turned it and eased the door open.

The darkness in the room was broken only by a thin slice of moonlight slanting between the curtains. It fell across the bed in a band of silver, across Mickie, who huddled face-down, her shoulders shaking with the sobs she was trying to stifle in a pillow. She didn't hear him enter, didn't realize anyone was in the room with her until he gently touched her shoulder.

"Mickie?"

"What . . . ?" She started violently, rolling half onto her side to turn a tear-stained face up to him. "Go away! I said I wanted to be by myself! Go away!"

"No," he said quietly, seating himself carefully on the bedside. "I'm not going away. You shouldn't be alone now."

"Oh, what do you know about it? Go away. Just go—" Her voice broke. Mark dropped his crutches to the floor and reached out to pull her into his arms.

"I know enough to know you shouldn't be alone."

He wrapped her in his embrace, and she let the tears fall again. Holding her warm and safe as she sobbed out her frustration and pain, Mark murmured soothing nonsense into her hair. He knew it wasn't the words but the security of his arms around her that truly helped her. Mickie's resistance to his interference was at an end, and she lay slack against him, half across his lap, her arms around his neck and her face buried in the curve of his shoulder as she gave herself up to her grief.

Mark had only intended to give her comfort. He thought he had put that momentary surge of lust behind him, and yet, as Mickie's sobs slowed and then died away, his concentration began to wander. Her towel had all but slid from her body, and his hands were moving over the silken skin of her back in a caress that had begun as solace and was becoming something else entirely. A little voice whispered to Mark that what he was doing was wrong, reprehensible, and yet...

And yet, was it really so wrong? The strong, slender arms around Mark's neck tightened, and the soft pressure of her breasts against his chest sent a surge of heat through his body. He held himself rigidly still, exercising an iron control, waiting. Mickie hugged him close, then lifted her head. Her lips brushed his shoulder in a feather-light kiss that scorched his skin, then moved to his neck, the angle of his jaw and, finally, to his lips. He could feel the tears on her cheeks.

His control wavered. She kissed him again, and it collapsed utterly. He caught the back of her head in his hand, tipping her mouth to his for the kiss they both needed so badly. He searched her mouth, deep and sweet, and she met him with a hunger to equal his. She tasted of mellow old bourbon and smelled of flowers and woman and a faint tang of chlorine from the swimming pool.

Her hands moved restlessly over his back and shoulders and down to the buttons of his shirt. She tugged at them impatiently, pulling them free and pushing the shirt out of her way with an almost desperate roughness. Mark tossed it aside and drew the damp towel from under her. She aided him by arching her body up off the bed to free the towel, a sinuous movement that went to Mark's head like warm brandy. He flung the towel away and fumbled with his belt buckle.

Mickie aided him, and his last garments were quickly disposed of by hasty, shaking hands. The heat was rising around them, beating in their blood and hanging thickly in the air.

Mark wanted to be gentle, to love her slowly and tenderly, but her body was slim and silken and burning hot against him, and his wants were lost in the floodtide of their mutual needs.

Mickie twisted her body around him, seeming to cling and touch and kiss and caress him everywhere at once, until he was reeling from the assault on his senses. Her breasts were full and taut against his chest, her derriere soft and sweetly curved beneath his hands; her slim fingers were a torment and a delight upon his chest, his stomach and lower.

He caught her finally, crushing her to his chest as he rolled onto his back, taking her with him. They moved as one, and Mickie slid down his body with a sure ease that joined them and moved them into the eternal ballet. She was a witch, magical, irresistible, and the flame burned brighter and brighter between them until it consumed them in a blaze of blinding light and swirling sensation.

Mark held Mickie's spent body close as the last aftershocks of pleasure slowly died away. She felt like an armful of nothing, her bones too delicate, her body too slight, to carry the pain she knew. She had cried in his arms, and then she had cried again, but the second tears had been healing, purging the bitterness and agony. There was still pain, he knew, and out of character as it was, he wanted to take the burden of that pain for her.

Their heated bodies began to cool, and he reached down to pull the blankets over them. Mickie breathed deeply, almost a sigh, and rubbed her cheek on the warm skin of his shoulder in a catlike caress. She didn't really understand how it had happened, but she had no regrets. Their love had been a healing love. Her grief remained, but the painfully twisted knot of agony within her had eased. She could face the reality of what had happened today and begin to accept it.

Despite her vehement denials earlier, Mark's arms were the safe haven she had needed. She had drawn strength from him, had found comfort with him, had shared her grief and fury and found them eased. His arms tightened around her, and she turned into his embrace, cuddling against his side, nestling there, her cheek pillowed on his shoulder. She could feel his head turn toward her.

"How are you?" he whispered into her hair. "Are you okay?"

"I'm okay," she murmured and nodded, rubbing her face against his skin. "I'll be okay."

"You did everything you could, you know." His voice was a deep rumble beneath her ear. "You told me there was nothing else to be done, nothing that could have saved his leg."

"Mm-hm."

"You mustn't beat yourself up over something that can't be changed, Mickie. That's the road to insanity."

There was a pause. "You do understand, don't you?"

"Of course I do. We all want to think that we can fix every problem and make it better. One of the most difficult ideas to accept is that there are always going to be some things we can't change."

"Harder for some of us to accept than for others, maybe."

He chuckled softly. "You doctors are notorious for your complexes about omnipotence."

"Yeah, well, they teach us that in med school."

"Teach you what? How to have a God complex?"

"That's the course—God-complex 101." There was a bitterly self-deprecating note in her voice.

"Don't be so hard on yourself." He shook her in gentle reproof. "You don't have any kind of complex and you know it. You just have highly specialized skills that you're accustomed to using. You rely on those skills, and it's difficult to accept the fact that sometimes they aren't enough, that you can't always do everything."

Mickie squirmed sideways so she could prop herself on her elbow to look down at his face. She raked her fingers through her tumbled hair, turning the copper curls into an aureole that caught the moonlight in a golden net.

"You really do understand, don't you? That anger, the feeling that you ought to be able to *do* something, but you can't. That sense of failure."

"Except that you didn't fail. You saved a man's life, and it sounds as if he has a pretty good attitude about what's happened."

"But the depression will set in later."

"It might, or it might not. He's not a young man, with a young man's immaturity and sense of invulnerability. An older man will find it easier to put things into perspective."

"You think so?" Mickie laid her palm on his chest and rested her chin on her hand. "You think his age might help him deal with this?"

"I'm sure of it. It's not just age, but the wisdom that age brings. He's experienced a lot in seventy-odd years, gains and losses. He's probably lost family members, maybe some friends. He'll understand that there are worse things in this world than losing a leg." Mark tucked one hand behind his neck and looked up at the ceiling. "I've done a lot of thinking about the loss of a leg in the last few weeks, and I'm not saying he's going to be happy about it, but I think a man his age has a perspective on things that younger people don't have."

"I hope you're right. Oh, I *hope* you're right! I don't want Ernie to suffer any more from this than he has to."

"Have confidence in him. That's all you have to do. And in yourself."

Mickie drew a long shaky breath and closed her eyes. "How do you do it?"

"Do what?" He turned his head the fraction necessary to touch a kiss to her forehead.

"How do you understand things I don't even know myself?"

"I don't. It's just logical."

"No, it's not, it's remarkable, and it's one of the things I love you for."

Mark went very still. "What did you say?" he asked after a moment's silence. His voice was rough, harsh.

Mickie reached up to touch his hair. "I said I love you." He jerked his head sharply away from her caressing hand, his stillness beginning to communicate a message to her. "Surely you must have realized?"

"Why? Why should there be anything to realize?"

"Because we made love, that's why!" Mickie pulled back, trying to read his expression in the darkness.

"Because we made love," he mimicked with biting sarcasm. "A woman's classic line—or trap."

"What are you talking about? What could possibly be a trap?"

"Are you serious? Lying here, together in this bed, you tell me you love me, and that's not a trap? Come on, Mickie, you don't have to drag it out. Just tell me what you're getting at. What is it you want?"

"I don't want anything!" she protested. She sat up, pulling the sheet around her, no longer comfortable with his eyes on her body. She stared down at him in stunned confusion. "I don't *want* anything. I was just telling you, that's all."

"But why tell me? Why tell me now?"

"Why *not* tell you? It's true. I love you."

"Well, you shouldn't. You can't love me. It's a mistake, and you *mustn't* love me!"

"I can't imagine why not," she replied tartly. "Anyway, it's too late for all that. It's a fact. Like it or not, I love you. I realized I loved you ages ago."

"Well, it's a fact that had better change," he growled. "I don't want your love."

Mickie sat very still for a moment. Something had occurred to her. "Are you married?"

"No, I'm not married," he sneered. "And if you think you're going to lure me into that, you're nuts!"

His voice was an angry snarl, but Mickie sat quietly, looking at him with a combination of pity and sadness. He had opened himself up to her, if only in a small way. He had helped her when she needed it most, and eased her grief and given her hope. After such generosity, why did he retreat behind his wall of hostility again? "I have no intention of luring you into anything," she said softly, saddened by his withdrawal after such closeness. "I just thought you ought to know the truth. What you do with that information is up to you."

Mark heaved himself up and swung his legs off the bed, careless of his cast. He scooped up his crutches and his clothes, and pushed himself to his feet. "There are traps and there are traps," he muttered and clumped out of the room.

Mickie watched the door swing closed behind him. She didn't know whether to be sorry for him or angry but the central puzzle remained: Why was he hiding from her? And *what* was he hiding? What was the secret that was keeping them apart?

"Does it matter what he's hiding?" Connie asked over their cafeteria lunch. "What difference would that make? The fact that he *is* hiding something is what ought to worry you."

"What do I have to worry about? Except I worry about him, of course. I wish I could help him. He's not happy this way. He's hurting, he's retreating behind this wall he's built, but I don't know what I can do for him."

"You don't have to do anything for him!" Connie's voice began to rise and she stopped short, looking around to see if anyone was listening. The cafeteria's other patrons seemed more interested in the day's special than in their conversation. She leaned over the table, close enough to speak softly. "You shouldn't try to do anything, either. Mickie, if he's hiding his emotions, or some deep and dark secret, that's his problem, and his alone. You can't help someone who doesn't want your help."

"Says who?" Mickie retorted. "Psychiatrists help people who don't want help. They do it all the time."

"Are you a psychiatrist?"

"No."

Connie sat back in her chair, folding her arms across her chest in satisfaction. "I rest my case."

"Connie Ramirez, I'm surprised at you." Mickie spooned up the last of her soup and pushed the bowl aside, regarding Connie quizzically. "Aren't you the one who was pushing so hard to start a romance between me and Mark?"

Connie shrugged. "I know I did a little matchmaking, but this has gone further than I expected. You think you've fallen in love with him, and that worries me, Mickie, because you don't really know anything about the man!"

"So maybe I should ask him some questions." Mickie smiled, undisturbed.

"Oh, sure! After the way he's reacted to you so far, I'm sure he'll be just thrilled to bare his soul to you for the asking."

"Connie, you're making entirely too much out of this."

"Am I? Mickie, the man has too many secrets. He smooth-talked his way into staying at your house, possibly putting you in danger. You still don't know anything about him or this weird situation he's in, and it worries me. It may seem safe, way out there with the cactus and the rocks and the coyotes, but that guy who mugged you could find you just by looking in the phone book. Mark is putting you in danger, and he owes you an explanation."

"I haven't had any reason to ask him to explain," Mickie insisted. "I'm not doing this because of any explanation; I'm letting him stay with me because I love him."

"That's inspiring, Mickie, really it is, but it's not enough. Does he love you?"

"He says no. He says he doesn't want my love." Mickie shrugged. "That doesn't matter anyway."

"I'd say it mattered a great deal. As far as you know, he could just be using your house, and using *you* because it happens to be convenient! He might be a spy, like Lewis, but he could be anything, a revolutionary, a mercenary, even a drug smuggler, for all you really know!"

Mickie pooh-poohed those suggestions as outlandish, but Connie's words had touched a nerve. She was well aware that Mark had secrets, a lot of secrets. The sixty-four-thousand-dollar question was, of course, just what were those secrets? Even if Mark couldn't possibly be involved in anything like drugs, or the export of revolution, spying had its seamy underside. The unwelcome suspicions, once acknowledged, were difficult to dismiss.

Those suspicions reared their ugly heads again when she drove up to the house that evening and found a car sitting in the drive. A nondescript blue sedan, several years old, it was so unremarkable as to be suspect for its very blandness.

The kind of car a spy would drive. The thought leaped unbidden to her mind, and she dismissed it immediately as ridiculous. It could be just a burglar. She didn't think about the incongruity of the words, "just a burglar." What she dreaded was something much more complicated than burglary.

She parked the Jeep as quietly as she could and walked softly across the tiled porch, then stopped short. The front door was ajar. The feeling of dread deepened into a cold knot in her stomach. Mickie slipped into the house and pulled the door quietly closed behind her. It didn't make sense that a garden-variety break-in artist would leave his car standing in plain sight in the driveway. Something was very wrong; she could sense it.

The house was empty; it *felt* empty. Mickie slipped across the hall and peered around the kitchen doorjamb. The room was empty, but she could hear the sounds of men's voices, and she moved carefully across to the back door. The voices were raised in anger, and Mickie peered out to see Mark and Lewis on the patio, arguing. Mark sat in a wrought-iron chair, his cast propped in front of him, while Lewis paced to and fro like a chained bulldog.

"Cameron King can't do that!" he was shouting at Mark, punctuating his words with sharp jabs of his fist at the air between them. "Cameron King can't do something so stupid! Cameron King can't go down—"

Cameron King. She knew that name. Cameron King was a writer—one of the most successful writers currently working, in fact. She'd read several of his books, one just a few weeks ago. A non-fiction exposé of industrial espionage and international dealing in advanced technology, it had been riveting, capturing her attention as completely as his previous work, a fast-moving spy thriller. He was highly regarded but mysterious, a maverick with a low public profile and a reputation as a modern-day adventurer.

A modern-day adventurer with a broken leg and a false name. The man sitting on her patio, the man who had held her and comforted her and made sweet love to her last night, was not named Mark James at all, but Cameron King.

"I can go anywhere I damn well need to!" he insisted to Lewis, as if to confirm her conclusion. "I have to go back there, and I'm going!"

Mickie stood rigid and shocked, unashamedly listening. It might be eavesdropping, but this was her house. She had a right to know what the hell was going on.

"Oh, are you?" Lewis retorted. "Why? Why do you *have* to go back? It's idiotic, going to a place where your cover is blown, where you already failed, where you got yourself captured!"

"Damn it, Will, that's not a valid argument!" Mark turned in his chair to glare at Lewis. But he wasn't Mark, Mickie reminded herself. He wasn't the man she'd known as Mark James. He was Cameron King.

"Neither is yours! Or is all this stuff about how you *have* to go back just a smokescreen for something else? 'Cause I'll tell you, you're wasting your time. You know the rules. If you've got any damned ideas about writing some book about this job, you can stick that—"

"I have no intention of writing about it! I know the damned rules. Don't worry, no one will ever read about my little sojourn in San Miguel. I don't write about Company business."

"Then what—?"

"I have a job to do, the job I didn't finish."

"What's the point?" Lewis countered. "Your cover was blown when you were captured. It doesn't matter what name they knew you by, Cam King or Mark James, they're still gonna know your face when they see you again. I know you tried to convince them that your presence in the country was perfectly innocent, but it's obvious that they didn't buy it. They wouldn't have thrown you in prison if they'd believed you, and you know it. If you show again you're a dead mackerel. You're not useful to the Company anymore, Cam."

"That's your opinion. I'll decide for myself what I can or cannot do."

"No, you won't! This is a Company job and I have final say."

"I'm not bound by any contracts!"

"No, but you're bound by law and by regulations. This is my responsibility and I have the final say in who goes down there! Other agents have already gone in to finish this, Cam. You aren't needed anymore.!"

"You can't say that!"

The argument sounded as if it could go on for a long time, but Mickie had had enough.

She was, she realized, shaking with the force of her fury. This was her house, but it had been used—*she* had been used. She'd been used, and lied to, and she was fed up. The back door crashed open against the side of the house, and both men looked around to see her stalking across the patio.

"You!" She pointed a trembling finger at Lewis. "Get out of my house."

"Doctor Blake, I didn't know you'd be home so early—"

"I'll just bet you didn't!" she snapped. "Get out."

He looked at her set face and icy eyes, and with a muttered goodbye he went.

Mickie watched him leave the patio then slowly turned to the man seated in the white-painted chair. He had deceived her and manipulated her. She had thought him a friend and found him a stranger, and she was hurt and frightened and very, very angry. It was a struggle to keep from lashing out at him physically as well as verbally.

"Why?" she whispered. "Why didn't you at least tell me who you are?"

Chapter 12

W_{hy?}

Her voice had dropped, and the single quiet syllable stabbed through Cameron King. He reached one hand out to her as he collected his crutches and tried to stand. She ignored the gesture and he sat back down.

"Mickie, I—"

"It's not as if I can't keep a secret," she went on. "I would have kept your secrets for you. I hear privileged information about my patients all the time. I don't betray their confidence; why should you assume I'd betray yours? I hid you at the hospital and then kept you safe here, didn't I? But then, maybe that isn't it at all." She took a few agitated steps away, then wheeled around to face him, standing stiffly on the uneven tiles. "Has it been something else all along? Was this just some sick game you've been playing, *Cameron King*? Have you been having fun with me? Is my house nothing but a convenient motel with a few 'extra amenities' for you? Or are you getting material for another of your books? Is that it?''

"Mickie, it's not like that!" Mark struggled to rise, to follow her as she paced aimlessly around the patio, too agitated to stand still.

"Oh, isn't it? Well, forgive me if I don't want to hear what it *is* like, will you?"

"Mickie, let me explain—"

"You *used* me!" she spat, cutting him off. "You used me, and you didn't even have the decency to tell me your name!"

She scooped up a handful of smooth pebbles from the base of a tubbed kumquat and juggled them in her hand. Then, in a movement so violent that it startled him, she spun around to hurl them away onto the open ground by the pool.

"Has all this been instructive for you?" she demanded, turning on him. "Have you enjoyed it, Mr. King? Have you gotten a kick out of watching me fall in love with you? For all I know, all those convincing protests were just some kind of reverse psychology ploy. Did you tell me that I mustn't fall in love with you just to see if I would? Maybe you just wanted to know how far I'd go!"

The man she knew as Mark balanced awkwardly on his crutches, watching her in impassive silence. That impassivity infuriated her. She wanted to shatter his composure, to strike out and hurt him as he had hurt her.

"I guess you got your answer to that, didn't you?" she asked bitterly. "I went to bed with you! I made love with you! At least, I thought then that we were making love, but now I don't. I don't think love had anything to do with it. And maybe it doesn't matter to you at all! Maybe my love and I are as unimportant to you as the truth!" She saw him flinch at that and felt a stab of primitive satisfaction.

Her pain was naked, raw and open, and she made no attempt to disguise it. Cam felt a wrenching guilt at having deceived her. He had tried to warn her against an involvement with him, but his warnings had been weak ones, contradicted by the other messages he had been sending her. She had fascinated him from the time he'd met her, and he had allowed that fascination to overpower his better judgment. He swung himself on his crutches and took a couple of steps toward her but he said nothing.

"I don't know," she said at last, shaking her head. "I don't know why you ever insisted on coming here in the first place. I thought you probably didn't have a home to go to, but Cameron King is rich! Someone like Cameron King obviously has a home somewhere, maybe two or three of them."

"I have a home, of course," he said quietly. "It's in Connecticut. But I can't go there right now." He hesitated, looking down at the tiles beneath his feet, obviously ill at ease. When he finally spoke, it was in a rush of words.

"Mickie, I know this is an impossible, arrogant imposition, especially now, but I have to ask you. I need to stay in California, to stay here with you, if I may, for just a little while longer, until this business is finished."

Mickie stared, unable to believe what she was hearing. She couldn't even formulate an answer, could only stand there with her mouth hanging open in fury and shock.

"I'll be happy to pay you for your hospitality."

That tore it.

"My God," she breathed. "When will it end?" He opened his mouth to speak. "You shut up!" He said nothing. "Don't you *dare* insult me with your damned money! First you play me for an idiot all this time; then you con me into bringing you into my home, thinking you have nowhere else to go, no one else to help you, and then you—" She broke off, leaving the rest unsaid. "And now you tell me you need to stay on here for some sort of business! Heaven knows what that might be! *Business*! Are you running drugs, Mr. Mark James, or Cameron King, or whoever the hell you are? Or is it guns? Are you a spy, or a revolutionary, or what?" She started to laugh, a little wildly. "You want to stay? You really want to stay here?"

"Mickie, I *need* to stay here."

"You don't want to, you *need* to." She mimicked his tone with biting accuracy. "Well, how can I possibly refuse such a gracious request? And why on earth should I care? I'll probably get dragged off to jail along with you! Only don't you dare insult me with your bloody money! You may have more money than God, Mr. King, but I don't want any of it. I do just fine, thank you very much." She stared at him as if she'd never seen anything quite like him in her life— except perhaps maybe a snake or a bug. "Enjoy yourself at the Hotel Blake," she invited caustically and turned away. "I need a drink."

Cam followed her, bitterly sorry she'd had to be hurt this way. If he'd suspected things would go this far he would have made different decisions, but hindsight would do him no good now. She was in the living room, already standing before the antique liquor cabinet with a glass in her hand when he caught up with her. He paused in the doorway. About to comment on her sudden predilection for liquor, he wisely changed his mind. This was not the time.

"Mickie?"

She turned slowly to face him. "Mr. King?" she asked coolly.

"Cam."

"I beg your pardon?"

"Cam. I'm called Cam."

"I can't imagine why you should think I'd care what you're called," she said icily.

This was going to be more difficult than he'd thought. He had to try anyway. "Mickie, I'm sorry. You have to know that I never intended to hurt you in any way."

"The road to hell," she commented and took a deep swallow of her drink.

"I beg your pardon?"

"The road to hell. It's paved with good intentions. You can keep your apology, Mark—Cam. Whatever" She shrugged off the issue of his name. "I really don't want to hear anything else you have to say. Good night." Drink in hand, she brushed past him, and moments later he heard the very definite closing of her bedroom door.

Wearily Cam clumped his way across to the cabinet and extracted the bourbon. He grinned wryly when he saw the level of liquid. It had taken a beating in the last couple of days, and he was about to hurt it again. He'd have to buy her another bottle and hope she didn't throw the replacement at his head.

Mostly, he hoped she could somehow learn to forgive him. He could understand the reasons for her anger; God knows he'd given her plenty of reasons to despise him. Cam splashed a generous measure of the bourbon into his glass and took a deep swallow. Yes, she had ample reason to be furious with him, disgusted with him. He felt the guilt to prove it, but mingled with that guilt was a growing regret.

She had offered him her love, along with her trust, and his duplicity had shattered both. Only now, now that he had destroyed it, was he beginning to realize the treasure he might have had in her love. She wasn't like the many women he had known over the years, the poseurs and the users who couldn't understand the meaning of openness or honesty. She wasn't like the women who wanted him only for what they could take from him.

She wasn't like the woman who had made him love her and only then showed him the ugliness beneath her beautiful facade. She hadn't asked anything of him, but had wanted only to give, and he'd thrown her gift back in her face. She had offered him closeness and human warmth, but he had pushed her away time and again.

He could have trusted her. He saw that clearly now that it was too late. He could have trusted her with any information, with his identity, his life. He could have told her the truth from the beginning, but instead he'd lived up to all the accusations she had just leveled at him. Using, manipulating, lying, deceiving, he was guilty of them all. Worse, though, he had hurt her, and he would live with that guilt for a very long time, perhaps forever.

He was guilty, and he was afraid for her safety. The best thing he could do for her right now was to get out of her life as quickly as he could, but that wasn't possible. His departure would jeopardize any chance of finishing the job he'd started, and it would also leave her alone and in danger from the guerrilla agent who had followed him to San Diego.

If he stayed where he was and allowed the guerrilla's search for him to continue, it might be possible to lure the agent into the open, into a trap. Cam was glad that Mickie was away from the house for twelve hours every day. He almost wished she could be persuaded to stay someplace safe, away from her house entirely, until he knew that the agent, or agents, had been neutralized.

With that complication out of the way he might have a chance to apologize to her, to explain and to recapture the magic they had shared.

Cam stared into his glass, his mouth twisting into a bitter line. He was kidding himself. After what he'd done to her the magic was lost, crushed under his unfeeling bootheel. He tipped the glass up and drained it in a gulp.

"You're letting him stay?" Connie was outraged. "How can you do that? Why on earth didn't you toss him out on his behind, cast, crutches and all?"

"Don't you think I've asked myself that question a million times since yesterday?" Mickie toyed with the cold pancakes on her plate. She hadn't eaten breakfast at home, so she'd bought some in the cafeteria, only to find her appetite nonexistent.

"It's just not like you," Connie muttered, "to let someone push you around this way. You're always so strong."

"Cut it out, Connie! You make me sound like some obnoxious superwoman, with a mixing spoon in one hand and a scalpel in the other. Don't lay that burden on me, okay? I'm just me."

"Uh-huh, but 'just you' is usually a pretty strong lady."

"Well, not today. I feel like wet spaghetti today." She took a sip of coffee, burned her tongue and sighed heavily. "Oh, Connie—you know why I did it."

"Because you still love him in spite of it all."

"And that makes me feel like a fool, like an idiot! I don't have any self-respect left at all!"

"It shouldn't make you feel anything of the kind! Love isn't anything to be ashamed of. On the other hand, Mr. Cameron King has a few things to be ashamed of . . ." Connie's voice hardened. "I just wish I could get my hands on him for five minutes. He has no right to put you in a position like this, and if you still love him, then he has a responsibility not to use that love to hurt you."

"That's the problem," Mickie said helplessly. "I wish I could hate him, just be angry and not feel anything else. I don't think he really meant to hurt me. He *did* and he made me so angry that I think I'd have hit him if I hadn't gotten away from him last night, but I honestly don't think he ever meant to."

"Oh, come on, Mickie, he knew what he was doing! He knew he was taking advantage of you."

"He didn't really want to ask to stay on with me, either." Connie shook her head skeptically, but Mickie pressed on, leaning forward as she tried to make her friend understand. "He didn't want to, but for some reason he had no choice. It showed in his eyes. I kind of felt like I *had* to let him stay. I felt that it was more important than I knew."

"If you really felt that way, then I guess you have to do what seems best to you. It still makes me mad, though."

"I never said it didn't make me mad." Mickie grinned ruefully. "I'm mad as hell, even though at the same time I love him and I want to help him."

"Odd combination of emotions."

"You ought to be on this end."

"I'll bet. But don't let him put you through the wringer, Mickie. He doesn't have that right. And I think you should get a few straight answers from him, too."

"Such as?"

"Such as what Cameron King was doing getting himself captured by guerrillas in central America, and why he has to hide out at your house, for starters. He owes you that much."

She supposed he did owe her at least that consideration. The more she thought about it, the more certain Mickie became that Connie was right. She would cooperate with him, but he would tell her exactly what was going on, and he would tell her tonight, like it or not. She approached the house in a pugnacious mood that evening, prepared to do battle.

She wasn't to be given the opportunity.

Mouth-watering aromas greeted her when she entered the house, and she followed them to the kitchen, where she found Cam at the stove. Unselfconsciously, if eccentrically, dressed in jeans, a sweater and a pink ruffled apron, he was standing propped on one crutch, stirring something in a deep saucepan. Sam watched the proceedings intently from the rag rug by the back door. Another pan steamed on a back burner, and a big bowl of salad sat in the center of the scrubbed table. She stopped short in the doorway, but he'd heard her, and he turned.

"I knew you'd be tired tonight," he said, his expression guarded. "You shouldn't have to cook a meal, too." His voice was as carefully controlled as his face, the only inflection a quiet politeness, and yet Mickie thought she saw an uncertainty in his eyes, almost an apology.

Her mind working rapidly, she glanced at the table, which was already laid for a meal, at the stove, and back to Cam's face. If that was the way he wanted to play it, she would go along. For now, at least.

"It smells wonderful," she replied with a careful courtesy to equal his. "What is it?"

"Spaghetti. I have pretty limited culinary talents, but there are a couple of things I can cook."

"Spaghetti sounds good. I'm hungry."

"Why don't you go and change? This will be ready in a few minutes."

"Okay. I won't be long."

Bemused, she walked away, wondering how long this extremely polite veneer could cover the emotions boiling just beneath it. He was hiding behind another one of his walls, the wall of charm and consideration this time, but a barrier to guard his thoughts and emotions nonetheless. He was still hiding from her, and Mickie wondered what he was hiding now.

She returned to the kitchen to find the meal waiting for her and Cam opening a bottle of wine.

"Do you like Chianti?" He held the bottle up for her inspection.

"I love it, but not tonight, thank you." She reached out to stop him from pouring her a glass. "I'm on call tonight."

"So, no wine?"

"No alcohol at all. You go ahead, though."

"No need." He worked the cork back into the neck of the bottle. "I'll join you in iced tea."

"I'll get it." Mickie turned toward the refrigerator, but he headed her off.

"Sit down. This is on me."

"If you think you can walk on crutches and carry two glasses of tea..."

"I've been working on a system this afternoon. I have to make a lot of trips, but this apron is real handy."

"That apron? I don't get it."

"It has pockets, remember?" He turned, grinning with pride, the first honest emotion he'd shown her. Two tall glasses, already filled with ice cubes, rode in the deep pockets on the front of the apron. Mickie had to laugh.

"I didn't remember at all! I don't know if I've ever used that apron. I don't bother with them much."

"And you thought I just picked this one because it was cute, right?" He plucked the glasses from the apron and set them on the table, then put down the pitcher of tea that he'd carried hooked by one finger.

"Wel-l-l." Mickie poured the tea, avoiding his eyes and trying not to laugh again. How could he make her laugh after what had passed between them last night? How many men was he, this charming deceiver? Was he spy, writer, user, friend...lover?

"Hey."

"Hmm?" Mickie looked up, startled out of her reverie.

"You were a long way off. Here's your mail." He held out a fistful of envelopes and journals.

"Thank you." Mickie took them and began leafing through them as he turned away to serve the spaghetti. Bills, advertisements from drug manufacturers and medical journals were glanced at and tossed aside for later scrutiny. She opened one envelope of heavy, cream parchment and drew out the single page it contained. "Oh, no!"

"What is it?" Cam dropped the ladle back into the sauce with a splatter and spun around. She was staring in horror at the letter. "Mickie, what's wrong?"

"He's coming back!" It was nearly a wail.

"Who's coming back, for God's sake?"

"Jon is, and he'll be here—" she glanced at the calendar on the wall "—tomorrow!"

Cam couldn't decide whether this was a disaster or not. He crossed the room to the table. "Mickie, who the hell is Jon?"

"Oh, you know who he is." She flapped the letter at him. "I was at that dreadful dinner with him the night you were admitted to the hospital."

"He's the boyfriend, the reason you were wearing that dress?"

"He's not my boyfriend," she replied automatically. "But he's coming back tomorrow." There was a wealth of disgust in her voice as she frowned at the letter. "I wouldn't have minded a little more warning."

"Why do I get the feeling you aren't thrilled at the prospect?"

There was something more than casual interest in his voice, and Mickie suddenly remembered who she was talking to. "I'll deal with it," she said, dismissing the topic of Jon. She reached for the salad bowl. "It doesn't matter. Would you pass me the dressing, please?"

To her relief, he let the subject drop, passed her the cruet of dressing and served himself with salad.

Mickie concentrated on her meal, seething inside. She had managed to completely forget that Jon's return from Europe was imminent, but apparently Jon hadn't forgotten anything. She had wounded him deeply, he had informed her, by neglecting to write to him in Switzerland, but he was coming to see her as soon as he arrived in San Diego. He was probably going to be magnanimous and give her a chance to apologize, Mickie thought, scowling at her salad plate.

"How was your day?"

"Huh?" Jerked out of her reverie, Mickie looked up to see Cam watching her.

"How was your day?"

She shrugged. "Nothing out of the ordinary. It was really pretty quiet."

"How's your friend who lost his leg? Ernie?"

"He's pretty good, actually." Mickie tasted her spaghetti, savoring the tangy sauce. "This is very good. You're a better cook than you let on."

"Like I said, I only cook a couple of things, but I do them pretty well. It's easier to be good when you specialize."

"I guess so." She took another hungry bite. "To answer your question about Ernie, he's doing really well. He's surprising me. Usually the euphoria wears off after twenty-four hours or so, and the patient will become depressed, but he isn't reacting in the usual way. The euphoria's gone, so he's not on top of the world, but he's not depressed, either."

"Is he still planning to show off his artificial leg?"

"Oh, yeah. The kids from the school can't wait to see it. They can't come up to the unit to visit him, but he's getting lots of cards and pictures from them."

"I'll bet that helps him."

"It does, but he's simply handling it well. He's realistic about the rehabilitation process, and he's anxious to get started." She looked across the table at Cam. "You were right about him."

"It wasn't anything special. It just seemed logical, that's all."

"It was perceptive, nevertheless. I meant to tell you about him last night, but—" She fell suddenly silent as she realized she had stepped onto treacherous ground.

"But something else came up, didn't it?" He was watching her from beneath half-lowered lids, his eyes revealing nothing.

"You could say that." Mickie looked at her plate. "You know, Mar—I mean Cam. I'm sorry, but I have trouble remembering that your name's not Mark. Cam, I have to have some answers. I was going to wait until after dinner to get into this, but since it's come up..."

"Since it's come up, can I tell you the whole story now?"

Mickie looked up, her eyes grave, and held his gaze across the table. "I think you owe me that much."

His eyes were very dark as he studied her. Slowly he nodded. "I think you're probably right."

He looked down at his hands, which were loosely clasped on the tabletop. Mickie had a sudden vivid vision of those strong hands moving over her body, seeking, tempting, exciting, delighting. She shook her head, trying to banish the tantalizing image, but she could feel the heat in her cheeks.

"Mickie?"

She looked up to find Cam watching her curiously. "What?"

"Are you okay?"

"Yes, I'm fine. I'm sorry."

"Yeah. Well, to start at the beginning, Connie Ramirez was right."

"Right about what?"

"When she guessed that Will Lewis is a spy. He is, though I think you already knew that. I can't tell you what agency he works for, or what his job is. Suffice it to say that at one time he was my boss."

"Your boss?" Mickie stared. "You worked for him? As a spy?"

"I did. Is it such a disillusionment?" Cam watched her intently. "I'm sure you must have guessed something like this."

"I don't know." Mickie shook her head helplessly. "It just seemed so farfetched."

"Well, it's true. I was an agent until three years ago."

"But you were writing then. I have some of your books."

"The writing made an excellent cover. I had a reputation as a loner, traveling the world while I gathered material and then disappearing for months on end while I was writing. It all fit together very neatly."

"I can see that it would." She hesitated a moment. "But how did you start?"

"I was recruited. I enlisted in the service after high school and did some intelligence work, but when I got out I wanted to put all that behind me. I went to college and then held a lot of different jobs while I worked on my first book, bartending and construction, stuff like that. The book was published, and I started researching the second. I had to travel to Europe and the Middle East for that one—it was on the international drug trade—and while I was in France I was approached by an agent. They're very careful about recruitment; they sound out your opinions on all kinds of things, and they investigate your background very thoroughly before they actually come right out and ask you if you're interested."

"And you were interested?"

"I'm a patriot. I don't always agree with the president who's in office at any given time, I don't always agree with government policy, but I love my country, and I was given an opportunity to do something useful. I continued writing, doing the work I wanted to do, but some of the trips I made had a dual purpose. I was with them for eight years."

"What happened?"

"Nothing. There was no dramatic disillusionment or anything like that. I was getting older, and I felt I was ready for a different kind of life. I was debriefed, and I resigned."

"But that was three years ago. Why were you in San Miguel?"

"The inscrutable hand of fate." He shook his head. "I had been out of the agency for nearly two years, and then just over a year ago I got a phone call from San Miguel. The connection was terrible, and the call was cut off before it was finished, but it was from an agent I had worked with in central America shortly before I quit. He was involved in something that we had worked on together, and he was in trouble. He called me for help. There was no way I could turn him down."

"So you went to San Miguel."

"Well, first I went to the agency and waded through about nine miles of red tape. Then I went to San Miguel in a sort of unofficial-official capacity to help my friend. And promptly got myself captured! God, that was stupid!"

"You can hardly blame yourself for—"

"Can't I? I knew what to do. I'd been trained for it, and I had plenty of experience, God knows. But when I got there I got sloppy, and I ended up spending a year as the guest of some gentlemen I'd rather have avoided."

"What…" Mickie hesitated. "What were they doing? If you can tell me, that is. I don't want you to give away any government secrets, or anything."

"I can't give you any details, but I can give you the general overview. As you so eloquently told me last night, I can trust you. To put it simply, they're running a pipeline that's smuggling drugs into the US and then using the money from that to foment revolution in their country and neighboring ones. They have to be stopped."

"Good Lord, yes," Mickie breathed. "I had no idea something like that was going on."

"Few people do. It's part of the agency's job to discover that kind of thing and put a stop to it. It's important." He leaned back in his chair, gazing out the window at the darkening sky. He seemed to be searching for the right words to say. "It's important, Mickie, but maybe I've let it become too important."

"I'm not sure you could make something like that *too* important."

"I did." he replied grimly and shook his head. "I was trying to minimize the damage that my capture did to the whole project. I was trying to flush out the man who followed me here, and you became part of that. I made a lot of mistakes, bad ones, and you can never know how much I regret hurting you." He looked up to find her watching him impassively.

"Mickie, I'm sorry you got involved in this at all. I've put you in danger, you know, whether you've realized that or not. The only reason I haven't insisted that you leave town for a while is because that might give them the idea you do know something useful. I never meant to make you a target, Mickie." He looked across at her, his eyes dark with pain. "God, I'm sorry I dragged you into this mess!"

"You didn't drag me into anything. I could have refused to go along with it at any time and turned you over to Commander Lewis." She managed a wan grin, but Cam wasn't amused.

"Maybe you should have. Even if that would have been an admission of a sort, at least I'd have been surrounded by Marines with guns, and the guerrillas would leave you alone."

"As far as we know they *are* leaving me alone. Nothing has happened out here, has it?"

"Not out here, not yet. You were mugged, though, and I think we can assume we know who did it," Cam replied darkly. "It's what we don't know that worries me. I don't suppose you'd consider staying with Connie until this is over, would you?"

"No," she said simply. "Anyway, you said that would just call attention to me."

"I hate to admit it, but it probably would."

"So I'll stay here, and come and go just as I normally do. Why did..." Mickie paused, then asked "Why did you want to stay on here?"

"Because he, or they, will have a hard time finding me here. While they're looking, they may give themselves away to Lewis's men. With luck this will break soon, and then I can get out of here and out of your life and let you get back to normal. That's what we're hoping for."

"Except you're still hoping to go back to San Miguel."

He looked up and met her gaze with a calm certainty that sent an icy dread running through her veins. "I still have a job to do. If there's a chance that I can accomplish something, I'll go back."

Chapter 13

He meant to go back.

Mickie played with the rest of her meal, her appetite nonexistent. Could he really return to San Miguel and deliberately put himself again in the line of fire? He could, of course. She knew that, just as she knew he was telling her the truth at last, holding nothing back. It was ironic that even though he was at last willing to trust her and tell her the whole truth, he was also hoping to leave her as soon as possible. One wall had been torn down, but another had been erected in its place. They were farther apart than ever now.

It was better that way, though. It had to be. After all, Mark James, the man she had thought she was in love with, didn't even exist. Cameron King was a stranger.

"Mickie?"

"Huh?" She looked up, startled, and found him watching her with open curiosity.

"Are you okay? You looked like you were a long way off."

She shook her head. "I'm fine. I was just wandering."

"Do you want any more?"

He indicated her plate, and Mickie looked down to see that her nervous fingers had reduced a slice of crusty sourdough bread to a pile of crumbs. She wasn't doing a very good job of hiding her feelings.

"No, thank you. It was wonderful, but I think I've had about all I can eat." She started to rise, plate in hand, but Cam reached across the table to forestall her.

"Don't get up. You're tired. I'll clear, and you just relax there. Would you like coffee?"

"Thank you." She stood in spite of his protest. "I guess I am kind of tired. If you don't mind being left with the dishes, I'll take my coffee to my room."

"Of course. I'm going to clean up."

She didn't argue. If he offered to play housemaid, who was she to quibble with him? Her immediate need was for privacy, for time to think about Cameron King, and about Mickie Blake.

"Think, think, think!" she muttered as the Jeep bumped around the last curve of her driveway. "All I do is think, and I still can't come up with any answers!" She was in a rotten mood, and she didn't feel like pretending otherwise. Her fruitless thinking had kept her awake nearly until dawn, and a string of aggravating little problems at the hospital had done nothing to improve her attitude. She was glad the day was over, and she looked forward to microwaving the leftovers of yesterday's spaghetti dinner. She was too tired for any concerted culinary effort.

"Mar—" She caught herself. "Cam? Where are you?"

"In the kitchen," came the reply.

Mickie's eyebrows lifted in surprise, and she went to investigate. She stopped short in the kitchen doorway. "Are you at it again?"

Cam turned from the stove to grin at her. "I have to earn my keep somehow. Dinner will be ready whenever you are."

Mickie peered around him at the stove. "I thought you'd exhausted your recipe collection with the spaghetti last night."

"I said I could cook two things. Steak is the second. How do you like yours?"

"I beg your pardon?"

"Your steak. How would you like it?"

"Oh! Medium. Medium is fine."

"Coming right up." She didn't move, and he looked pointedly at the doorway. "Whenever you're ready?"

"Uh, sure. I'll only be a few minutes." Obediently Mickie made for her room, with Sam in close attendance. She stopped so abruptly in her doorway that the dog nudged her thigh to urge her on. She reached down to stroke his silky ears gently as she stood staring into her bedroom, astonished.

It gleamed. Mickie was neither particularly sloppy nor compulsively neat, so her room was usually tidy. It was not usually immaculate, not like this. She remembered leaving her thin cotton nightgown tossed over the bedside chair that morning, and a messy stack of medical journals had decorated the nightstand. She had overslept, and had pulled the sheets and quilt roughly up, not really making the bed.

The nightgown had vanished—into her closet, she assumed. The bed was freshly made, with knife-edge hospital corners, and the journals were neatly stacked on the writing table, beside a bouquet of pinks and violas collected from her garden. Every surface was shining, the ever-present California desert dust vanquished. The air held the sharp tang of lemon oil, mixed with the clove perfume of the pinks. The carpet still bore the faint tracks of the vacuum, and Mickie tiptoed almost hesitantly across it to peek into her bathroom. It was the same there. All the surfaces gleamed from energetic polishing, and the mixed aromas of cleaning solutions lingered.

"Good grief!" She backed out, pulling the door closed behind her, and stood stock-still in the center of her bedroom. He must have worked like a galley slave to get all this accomplished today, hampered as he was by crutches and a cast. A faint clank of metal on metal from the kitchen caught her ear, and she listened for a moment, wondering. Why? Why had he cleaned all day, then gone to work in the kitchen tonight?

When she rejoined him after a quick shower and change of clothes she hesitated to ask and Cam didn't volunteer his reasons. She had the feeling it would be awfully easy to become accustomed to coming home each evening to an immaculate house and a good meal. Finally she told him so.

"This is terrific." She forked up the last bite of her steak. "You underrated your cooking talents yesterday."

"I was telling you the truth." He rose on his crutches with practiced ease and took Mickie's plate.

"Well, I still think you're a lot better than you give yourself credit for." Mickie smiled. "You're not a bad housemaid, either. My room is beautiful. Thank you."

"You're welcome, but I feel like I should be thanking you. It feels good to have something constructive to do after so much wasted time."

"I suppose so. I suspect I could get used to a clean house and a delicious meal every night, though." She grinned. "I mustn't let you spoil me."

Cam looked up, one corner of his firm, sexy mouth rising in a half smile. There was a light deep in his midnight-dark eyes that Mickie couldn't read.

"Not to worry." He shook his head briefly. "You won't get spoiled. You're not the type, and I won't be here long enough to spoil you. This mess has to be finished soon, and then I can get out of here and let you get back to normal."

"Mm-hm." Mickie managed to nod and smile and feign concentration on her salad. But beneath the calm surface she was in turmoil.

She should have been glad he was going. She should have been relieved, should have been grateful for his tact and discretion. Instead she felt a growing anger that was no less powerful for its unreasonableness.

The change in him had been so abrupt, and so complete, that she found it difficult to accept. It was difficult, as well, to maintain the courteous facade. They had been friends, and then lovers, but since that traumatic evening when she'd learned the truth about him, everything was different. No longer lover, or even friend, he might have been a casual acquaintance, a near stranger.

He scrupulously avoided touching her now. He avoided being near her, he hardly even looked at her anymore. Once again he politely but firmly insisted on doing the dishes and banished Mickie to the living room with a cup of coffee.

Mickie tried to tell herself she should enjoy this lady-of-leisure situation, but it wouldn't wash. She didn't feel pampered; she just felt isolated.

"Rats!" She gulped her coffee, burned her tongue and swore, feeling like a fool.

She should be glad, she told herself again, glad that he was polite rather than hostile, glad that he was throwing himself into the housekeeping with such enthusiasm. She wouldn't have thought to suggest it, but housework was probably as good for him as formal therapy. She should be glad, and she was. She *was*! He was treating her politely; he was making a remarkable recovery and he would be well enough to leave soon. And she wasn't glad at all.

It hurt. Had the closeness and the passion they had shared meant so little to him? Was she really so easily dismissed from his mind? He certainly wasn't easily dismissed from her mind. The humiliating truth was that she still loved him.

Whoever he was, wealthy writer and former spy Cameron King, or man of mystery Mark James, she still loved him. In spite of his deceit, his lack of trust, his cruel accusations, she still loved him. It had been a foolish love from the start, but it was now a love without hope or future. Mark James might have needed her, but Cameron King had everything. Once he was finished with her treatment and her house, he would have no need of Mickie Blake.

"Would you like a refill?"

Mickie twisted around to see Cam standing in the doorway, a thermal carafe and another cup in the pockets of the pink apron. "No." She shook her head. "No, thank you. I haven't finished this yet."

"Mmph." He stood by the leather armchair that had been her father's favorite and divested himself of the apron and its cargo before sitting down. "I think I'm getting a pretty good system worked out."

"It looks that way. I'll have to suggest aprons with pockets to the OT Department. They could be useful in a lot of situations."

"It's been useful to me." He poured his coffee and sipped. "What's OT?"

"The Occupational Therapy Department." Mickie began to explain further, but her mind wandered.

He was being as polite and circumspect and discreet as she could possibly have wished. But perversely she *didn't* wish. She watched him from beneath lowered lashes and she remembered. She looked at his mouth and remembered his kiss, hot and sweet as the coffee he drank, remembered the taste of him as he drank the honey of her lips. She watched him pour from the heavy carafe and remembered the touch of his hands on her body, seeking and finding and delighting. She watched the play of muscle beneath his thin sweatshirt and the one-legged jeans they had cut off to make room for his cast, and she remembered the power and the gentleness of that body, entwined with hers.

A hunger began to grow, burning inside her, a hunger she was forbidden to appease. She wanted him, wanted him desperately, but there were new barriers between them now, which only made that wanting more powerful. It hurt to know that he felt none of the tension she did. He seemed immune to it, immune to her, and Mickie found that maddening.

The doorbell interrupted both her reverie and her absent-minded discourse on occupational therapy. She glanced at her watch as she rose.

"It's kind of late for somebody to come all the way out here."

"Mickie!"

Cam's sharp call stopped her on her way to the door. "Yes?"

"Make sure you know who it is before you open the door."

Her eyes widened. "You think it might be that guy...?"

"It's possible."

"Should I get the gun?"

"Just check to see who it is first," he suggested with a hint of a smile. Mickie flushed, embarrassed, and went to see.

From his chair Cam couldn't see the front door, but he heard Mickie swear under her breath when she looked outside, then the rattle of the chain and the shooting of the bolt.

"Mickie, darling!" The voice was a man's, a clear, clipped tenor.

"Hello, Jon." Mickie's reply was cool. "What are you doing out here at this hour?"

"Didn't you get my letter? I sent it from Lucerne last week. I came straight from the airport to see you."

"Well, you shouldn't have," she said, and backed away from the door, into Cam's line of sight.

"Of course I should have!" Jon protested, following her into the hall. He reached out to take her in his arms, but Mickie evaded him. "I've been gone for ages, Mick. I've been looking forward to our lovers' reunion all that time."

"We're not lovers, Jon." Mickie folded her arms across her chest.

"Oh, come on, Mick, don't be that way," Jon wheedled, but Mickie was firm.

"I've tried to tell you this, Jon. We never had much of a relationship anyway, and it's time to stop pretending."

"I was never pre—" Jon broke off as he looked into the living room.

He stared at Cam. Cam stared back, studying the man who was acting as if he owned Mickie. Smooth. That was the word that came to mind. Sleek, blond hair; soft, manicured hands; polished clothes...smooth. And bland. Cam couldn't imagine what Mickie, with her fire and spice, could want with *him*.

"Good evening." With the minimum of awkwardness Cam levered himself out of his chair to stand supported on his crutches.

Jon stared, looking from Cam to Mickie and back again. His smooth face hardened into lines of petulance and umbrage. "I guess I know why you've been avoiding me, don't I?"

Cam felt a surge of anger at the man's tone and moved forward. "You don't know—" he began, but Mickie interrupted him.

"It's all right, Cam." She stepped past Jon to stand between the men. "Jon, I've been trying to tell you that we have nothing between us. If you won't listen to me, that's not my responsibility, but you have no reason to be angry."

"Don't I? You've been carrying on while I've been out of the country, and I have no reason to get mad?"

"Jon, I don't want to fight with you. And, for your information, the question of whether I have been 'carrying on,' as you so graciously put it, is none of your concern. You have no claim on me. I tried to tell you that before you went. You refused to listen, but that doesn't mean I never said it. All we've ever been is friends, Jon. Let's leave it at that."

"Leave it at what?" Jon demanded, his face red with fury. "Leave it that you don't want to see me anymore?"

"Look, Jon," she said tiredly, "I never wanted to hurt your feelings. You wanted things from the relationship we had that I didn't—I *don't*—want. I could see that even before the Association dinner. There's no point in going on with this. I'm sorry."

"I'll just bet you are!" His face twisted into a mask of jealous fury. He glanced past her at Cam. "I'll bet *he* fits into it somewhere, too! What's he doing here, anyway?"

"He's staying here." She offered no explanation.

The ruddy color of Jon's face deepened with his anger. "He's staying here? In the house? With you?"

"Well, he's not staying in the garage, if that's what you mean!" she snapped. "Don't be an idiot, Jon! Of course he's staying in the house. It is my house, after all."

"Yeah, it's your house, and *I* never stayed here!"

"You were never invited." Her voice was quiet and cold. "You weren't invited tonight, either. I think it's time you went home, Jon."

"I hope you think she's worth the trouble," Jon spat over his shoulder as Mickie herded him toward the door. "She's a cold fish, but maybe the big money she makes sounds good to you."

Barely able to control his fury, Cam moved toward them, but Mickie waved him back. She didn't need his assistance. She could handle Jon herself.

"Shut up and go home, Jon," she said wearily. "Just go home."

"And leave you in your little love nest, huh? Sure!" he sneered.

She slammed the door behind him with a force that echoed through the house and marched back into the living room. Her face was set and furious.

"I'm sorry you had to listen to that." She walked back into the living room and stopped while she was still some distance away from Cam. "Damn! I apologize. That had nothing to do with you, and you shouldn't have been subjected to it."

"Don't worry about it. I'd thought I might be able to help, but you handled the boyfriend very nicely yourself."

"Terrific," she muttered. "A talent I've always wanted, the ability to handle obnoxious stockbrokers well! And he's *not* my boyfriend!"

Cam took a couple of steps toward her. "There's a bottle of white wine in the refrigerator," he offered. "Would you like a glass?"

"Yes." She nodded. "Yes, that sounds good. In the refrigerator, you say?"

"Top shelf." He followed her to the kitchen. "Would you like to take it to the living room?"

"No, I don't think so. If I go back in there I'll probably throw a lamp or something. It's warm tonight; let's go out on the patio."

When they were settled on loungers by the pool Cam gave her a considering look. "I heard from Will today."

"What did he have to say?"

"They had a lead on the guy, but it faded out again. He was spotted, but they couldn't track him down. It mostly amounts to the fact that they know he's still in the country, so he's apparently still looking for me—or for us."

"So what do we do now?"

Mickie sipped her wine and felt herself begin to relax. She liked talking to him this way, as equals. He was treating her as a partner in this last attempt to uncover the agent; he was talking freely to her. She enjoyed that, and yet she found it was not enough. Too little, too late, she supposed.

She glanced at him, her eyes tracing the strong lines of his good leg, stretched out beside the injured one, and lingering on his hand resting loosely on his thigh. Square and brown and strong, with long straight fingers, fingers that could make such magic... She looked away, but though she stared blindly out at the stony hills behind her house, she saw his hands, saw him.

No, fickle creature that she was, it wasn't enough for her to be treated as a partner, as an equal. It wasn't enough that he talked freely with her, now that he trusted her. It wasn't enough because, more than anything else, she wanted him to love her.

Never satisfied, are you Mickie? She took a long drink of her wine and yanked her attention back to Cam's words.

"We don't do anything," he was saying. "I hide out here and teach myself to be a gourmet cook, and you go to the hospital in the morning and come home in the evening, just like always. There's one thing I want you to do, though."

"What's that?"

"Pay attention when you're driving home, okay? If anyone follows you, or if you even *think* anyone is following you, *don't come here.*"

"Well, okay, but where do I go?"

"To a police station, or a fire station, or even a military base. Just someplace where there's official help and where the guerrilla won't be willing to follow you."

"What do I say to these official people, though? I can just see myself trying to explain that I'm being followed by a guerrilla agent from San Miguel who's after a famous author who's staying incognito at my house. I'd get *myself* arrested, instead of the agent!"

"Very probably, if you told them all that!" Cam laughed. "No, all you have to do is tell them that you think you were being followed, try to describe the vehicle, and call Will Lewis. He'll clear up any problems with the authorities. Just make sure you don't lead anyone back here. I don't want them to know where you live."

"You're assuming they don't already know. It would have been easy enough for them to find out. That night when they searched my purse, for instance."

"Don't even say that!" he snapped, his vehemence surprising her. "If I thought they knew where you were, I'd take you a long way from here, like it or not. And I'd see that you were kept away for a long time."

"Don't be melodramatic! It's you they want, not me."

"Let's hope it stays that way. It's bad enough that I let you get dragged into this damned mess!"

Mickie had no reply to that. She drained her wine and set the glass aside. The moon was rising, silvering the hills around them and painting a shimmering ribbon across the surface of the pool. A light breeze ruffled the water and broke the glimmer of moonlight into a million sparkling shards. The night breeze was light but cool, and Mickie shivered, rubbing her arms.

"Are you cold?"

She shrugged. "Just a little. I'm okay."

"No, you're not. You'll freeze sitting still." He was peeling his sweatshirt over his head as he spoke. "Here. Put this on." He tossed it into her lap.

"No, thank you."

"Put it on. I read an article in one of your medical journals about the cold. Apparently women feel cold more than men. Take the shirt. You need it. I don't."

"Okay, okay, if you're going to quote one of my own journals at me, I'll put it on! Anything but that!" She pulled it over her head, trying to ignore the warmth and scent of his body on the soft cotton. It was impossible, but at least she tried.

"I'm glad to see you can be sensible." Cam sat back in his chair, folding his arms across his chest. There was silence for a time. Then in the distance, on the other side of the hill perhaps, they heard a coyote bark, and a still more distant answer. "Who do you suppose he was calling? His mate?"

"Hard to say," Mickie replied laconically. "He might just be defending his territory, or something."

"Or something," Cam agreed. "Can I ask you a question?"

"Hmm?"

"Did you mean it—when you said you loved me?"

Mickie stiffened in her chair. What right did he have to ask that? After what had passed between them, how could he put her in a position like this? The surge of anger warmed her, blotting out the pain, momentarily at least. Her lips pressed together in a tight line.

"I meant what I said, but you'll recall that I said I was in love with Mark James. I didn't even know Cameron King," she replied coldly, and stood. "I still don't know him. And whatever I felt for Mark James died the night I learned that he never really existed." She turned on her heel and walked quickly into the house, biting her lip hard.

Her anger had dissipated by the next morning, replaced by a bleak sense of imminent loss. Cam didn't help. He was in the kitchen waiting for the coffee to finish dripping when she walked in. She halted in the doorway when she saw him there and almost turned away.

"Come in, please." He waved her in when she would have turned and gone. "I'm just waiting for this to finish. I'll get out of your way in a minute, but there's one thing I want to say."

"I'm not sure I want to hear it," Mickie replied dully.

"Maybe you don't," he told her grimly, "but I want to say it. I had no right to ask you that question last night. It hurt you, and I'm sorry. I just want you to know that I won't impose on you any longer than necessary. All I want is for this thing to be over, so I can get out of here and leave you alone."

She mumbled some acknowledgment of his "reassurance," but it was bitter medicine to accept. He thought he was making her feel better, of course. He had no way of knowing just how empty life was going to feel without him. How soon would he be gone? she wondered. How many more evenings would she be able to talk with him, to simply gaze at him, storing away memories for the lonely evenings ahead?

Somehow she made it through that day despite her unhappy thoughts, her anticipation of the loneliness to come. It was late when she drove up the long drive, and her mood was as dark as the night sky. How on earth had she managed to get herself into a crazy situation like this, anyway? Her life had always been fairly uncomplicated, fairly normal. All it had taken was one simple call from the hospital, though, one new patient to be admitted, and suddenly her life was a mess!

"Sheesh!" She swung into the garage with a squeal of brakes and climbed out of the Jeep. She pulled her briefcase and tote bag out, started to slam the door, then stopped, reaching back in for her black bag. The batteries in her ophthalmoscope needed recharging.

"*My* batteries need recharging," she muttered and kicked the door closed, then staggered out into the yard.

A flagstone path wound from the garage to the house, but the stones were uneven, and in the darkness Mickie favored the direct route across the lawn. Light from the back door spilled across the grass, but it didn't quite reach her. The ground wasn't level. Small bumps and tussocks of grass looked dangerously similar, and she walked carefully, because Sam's penchant for digging frequently left booby traps for the unwary.

But it wasn't one of Sam's excavations that brought her down.

Chapter 14

Coming silently and viciously out of the darkness behind her, the attack caught Mickie completely off guard.

A blow that must have been meant for her head went wide and struck her shoulder with enough force to knock her to her knees. Her bags flew from her hands as she landed heavily on the uneven ground, catching herself on her outstretched palms and skinning them badly.

Crouched there on the ground she was utterly vulnerable to her attacker, and before she could regain her balance her right arm was seized and jerked behind her. She twisted involuntarily away from her captor. Her back arched into a bow as her arm was wrenched savagely up between her shoulder blades, and pain knifed through her shoulder.

Mickie had taken a self-defense course in college. She exercised regularly and did physically demanding work. She'd always liked to think that she would be able to make use of that strength and training if the need arose. To her fury, now that she was in real danger, she couldn't even get out a good, solid scream for help. The best she could manage was a pit-ifully thin squeak before a sweat-slick hand was clamped over her mouth.

Her attacker was hissing some sort of orders in her ear, but his Spanish was too fast and too colloquial for her to understand. When she didn't obey him quickly enough he hauled her to her feet by her twisted arm, every movement sending waves of white-hot pain flooding through her.

Mickie had an expert's understanding of bones and joints, but this was her first experience of the kinds of stress that could be applied to them. She was lightheaded with pain and felt a growing conviction that her arm would be ripped from its socket any minute. She hated to make this so easy for her attacker. She knew she had to stop him, but how? He was thwarting her struggles with a humiliating lack of difficulty as he forced her toward the house.

Toward the house—where Cam was waiting for her. Mickie saw with a sudden, horrible clarity what the guer-rilla intended. She herself was of no importance to him, but he meant to use her. By threatening her, he would force Cam to give himself up, to allow himself to be captured—or worse.

She began to fight again, jerking in his hold with the adrenaline-fueled strength of desperation. She would not—she *could* not—let this stupid animal use her to get to Cam. Cam was just foolishly gallant enough to make a sacrifice of himself for her sake!

Again she bucked in her captor's grasp, clawing with her free hand at his wrist, at the fingers clamped over her mouth. She raked his skin and heard an angry mutter, but his grip didn't loosen. Using a half-remembered bit of self-defense lore, she grabbed his little finger, supposedly the most vulnerable, and twisted it back with all her strength. He grunted something explosive in her ear, but his hand came away from her mouth for an instant. It wasn't much, but it was enough for her to scream to Cam.

"Cam!" she shrieked. "Cam, call—"

The hand slapped across her mouth again, and she promptly buckled at the knees, forcing her captor to carry her limp weight. She ignored the flash of agony from her twisted arm. She *would not* just walk meekly up to the door. If he wanted to get her there he'd have to drag her. And it would cost him.

Mickie refused to count the cost to herself. She had to see that Cam was kept safe; nothing else mattered. She clawed at the man's hand again, striving to uncover her mouth. She had to call to Cam, but more than that, she had to breathe, or she'd pass out and her efforts would be for nothing. Kicking out, she dug her heels into the grass, trying to use her weight to slow him down, even knock him off balance if she could. Fighting back, he snarled something in her ear, jerking hard on her arm.

The pain was a palpable thing, heat and nausea and lights that danced before her eyes until the dizziness passed. They were so near now, only ten yards from the house. Mickie had to do something, anything, to alert Cam. She opened her mouth as wide as she could and managed to bite the guerilla's hand, hard.

"Aiee!" The hand was jerked away and Mickie fell forward, all her weight on her twisted arm, which seemed to be past the point of simple pain.

"Cam!" she screamed again. "Stay in—"

She was too late.

The back door crashed open to reveal Cam, braced on his crutches, holding her rifle leveled at the guerrilla. The agent halted, keeping Mickie in front of him as a shield.

"Get back!" she yelled at him, half hysterical. "Go back inside!"

"Are you okay?" he bellowed. "Has he hurt you?"

"I'm okay, but you—"

"*Silencio*!" barked the guerrilla, then added a string of commands directed at Cam.

"Cam, I can't underst—" Mickie yelled, then broke off with an anguished gasp as the guerrilla jerked harder at her arm.

"Shut up! He just wants you to shut up!"

The guerrilla shouted something else, and Cam replied in an exchange too fast and colloquial for Mickie to translate. The gist was easy enough to grasp, however. The man would kill Mickie unless Cam surrendered. That was unthinkable. Cam couldn't surrender. She would not *allow* him to surrender.

The incongruity of that thought didn't occur to her, nor did the realization that she didn't have a great deal of control over the situation. She had to protect Cam; there was room for no other thought in her mind.

The guerrilla hadn't covered her mouth again, but now he held both her arms tightly. Apparently he considered her mouth less dangerous than her uncontrolled hand. She lifted her head, not so quickly that she would arouse the guerrilla's suspicions, but in a smooth movement that she hoped would catch Cam's attention. The night breeze ruffled her hair and she shook her head, as if shaking it out of her eyes.

She didn't know if Cam could read her face across the thirty feet or so that separated them. She could see nothing of his expression. Silhouetted against the outdoor light behind him, he was a powerful shadow, his face no more than an indistinct blur. She stared at him, unblinking, praying, willing him to read her thoughts, to understand what she was going to do. The rifle was trained unwaveringly on the guerrilla, but Mickie knew rifles as well as he did. At that range he couldn't fire without taking the risk of striking her.

She ignored the dead eye of the gun barrel and stared at his face. He and the guerrilla shouted another harsh exchange across the yard. As they argued she could feel a barely perceptible loosening of the crippling grasp of her arms. His attention on Cam, the man wasn't so concerned with her. She widened her eyes, watching Cam intently.

He understood. In the middle of a harangue from the guerrilla, Cam gave a barely perceptible nod. Mickie responded instantly, flinging herself sideways and down, tearing out of the man's grasp to sprawl on her face as the roar of the rifle blast split the night once, then again. A scattering of dust was thrown over her as a bullet dug into the ground, and behind her she heard the guerrilla yell in pain and fury.

He had been struck in the leg, above the knee, but he still had his pistol. Mickie rolled quickly to her knees. As she looked back at him, she saw that he was trying to get into position to aim at Cam.

She scrambled across the grass and grabbed for the pistol. The man spat something at her and swung the gun in her direction. With no sense of fear for herself and with a savagery she hadn't known she possessed, Mickie attacked him, kicking the gun out of his hand. With a bullet in his leg he couldn't move quickly enough to get to the gun before her. She seized it and trained it on him as she rose slowly to her feet, her hands unnaturally steady.

Later she would realize with a sort of fascinated horror that if there had been any further threat to Cam, she would have shot the man without hesitation.

Now Cam hobbled across to them, a crutch in one hand and the rifle in the other. "Are you all right?" He put his free arm around her, and Mickie leaned into his body, beginning to tremble.

"I'm okay." Her voice only wobbled a little. "B—but he needs some first aid . . . on his leg."

Together they looked down at the guerrilla, who was lying a few feet away, clutching his leg and glaring at them. He spat something in Spanish, and Cam laughed. His rejoinder brought another muttered epithet from the man.

"Are you sure you want to bother with his leg? It would be easier just to leave him there."

"No!" Mickie gave him a shocked look. "I can splint it and bandage it with the stuff I have in my bag. I can't leave him like that."

"You would if you knew what he just called you," Cam said dryly.

"What was that?"

"You don't want to know."

"I've probably been called worse." Mickie giggled shakily. "To my face, too. Here," she put the pistol into his hand and took the rifle, "this is loaded. I've got some splints in the car." Cam turned the gun on their prisoner, and she ran toward the garage.

"Watch him," Cam said when she returned with her medical supplies. "To say he's hostile is to understate the case."

"I'll watch out." With bandage scissors she bent to cut the man's trouser leg away, and he kicked her. "Ow!" The scissors flew from her bruised hand.

Cam barked something at the guerrilla, then turned to Mickie, exasperated. "I thought you were going to be careful."

"So what am I supposed to do—tie him up?"

"I think we'd better. That is, if you still insist on patching him up."

"I have to. You know that." He muttered something that could have been assent, and Mickie nodded, satisfied. "There's some rope in the garage; I'll go get it."

Trussed like a chicken, the guerrilla was finally persuaded to part with the information that his name was Morales. After his wound was splinted and bandaged Mickie repacked the last of her tape and gauze and straightened.

"Okay. Let's get him up to the house."

"How?"

She looked at Cam and then back to Mr. Morales. "I don't know, but we can't leave him sitting out here, can we?"

"Why not?"

"For one thing, because someone will have to sit out here and hold a gun on him, and *I* don't want to."

Cam considered that for a moment. "Neither do I; he's not worth the inconvenience. Do you really think we can get him inside?"

"If he'll cooperate. What do you think?"

"I'll convince him to cooperate." Cam directed a barrage of rapid-fire Spanish at Morales, who argued, swore and then bad temperedly allowed himself to be assisted, or dragged, into the kitchen. They more or less dumped him into a chair, with Cam sitting opposite him, holding the pistol on him.

Mickie went directly to the telephone. "What's Lewis's number?"

Cam told her, and she punched the numbers in rapid succession, eager to reach Commander Lewis and deliver the man and the problem into his hands.

"Yeah?"

"Your telephone manners could use some work, Commander."

"Who's this?" His bored tone had sharpened at the sound of her voice. "Blake? Is that you?"

"Of course it's me, and it's *Doctor* Blake, thank you very much."

"Yeah, yeah, what's going on? Why are you calling?"

"I've got a present for you. Something you've been waiting for."

"He's there." It was a statement, not a question.

"Right the first time."

"You and Cam—are you all right?"

In spite of herself, Mickie was touched that he'd asked. "We're fine. It was kind of hairy for a few minutes, but we're all right. He was—"

"Wait a minute, Dr. Blake!" Lewis interrupted hastily. "Don't tell me about it over the phone, okay? I'll be out there with some of the guys as quick as I can. Can you two handle things until we get there?"

"Yeah." She looked over at Cam who still held the gun. "We can handle things."

"Forty minutes," he barked and slammed the receiver down.

He was true to his word. It couldn't have been more than forty-one minutes later that she heard what sounded like a convoy of vehicles roaring up her drive. As promised, Lewis had brought a veritable battalion of agents, cold-eyed men with guns and hand-held spotlights who spilled out of the cars to stand waiting in her drive. Lewis was one of the last to emerge, stumping through the loose cluster of taller, younger men who awaited his orders.

He marched up to Mickie, who was standing at the door, her rifle in her hand. He glanced at the rifle, then nodded a brief greeting. "Dr. Blake."

"Commander."

"Where is he?"

"In the kitchen. Cam's holding his own gun on him."

Lewis's teeth showed briefly in a rather grim smile. "Sounds like Cam." He signaled to the agents, two of them joined him, while the rest trotted out of sight around the house. "Let's go see what we can find out." With Mickie and the two agents in tow he marched inside. "Do you think we could have some coffee, Dr. Blake?"

"Of course."

Making coffee seemed to be the only thing Mickie was needed for. The troop of agents spent the better part of the night alternately combing the hills around the house, drinking the gallons of coffee Mickie made and attempting to interrogate the uncooperative Señor Morales. It should have been very dramatic, the police scouring the hills, searching for spies, but to Mickie it all seemed like an anticlimax.

By dawn they had found his car, hidden in a small canyon about half a mile away, and followed his trail from that canyon to her house. Having determined that he'd had no other weapons and that he had come alone, they had taken statements from Mickie and Cam.

Morales could not be persuaded to say much, but as Mickie had observed in a weary joke to Cam at about three AM, they couldn't use the rubber hoses while she was there to witness it. She was too tired to care about any of that. She just wanted them to go home.

At around five AM they finally did, taking Morales with them and promising Mickie and Cam a full report on their findings in a few hours.

"Make that a few days!" Mickie groaned as the last of them drove away. She shut the door firmly, shot the bolt home and drooped back against the oak panels. "Yeesh! I didn't think they'd *ever* go!"

"I didn't think this would ever end!" Cam muttered and took her arm to urge her toward the kitchen. "Come and have some of the coffee you've been making for everyone else."

Obediently Mickie followed him to the kitchen and allowed herself to be seated at the table. Cam set a cup of steaming coffee before her, but she just stared rather stupidly at it for several moments before she could summon the energy to lift it. Cam reached out to add a heaping spoonful of sugar and stir it in, then a second.

"No more, please, or I won't be able to drink this!" She caught his hand before he could add a third spoonful. "I don't usually have any sugar at all!" She sipped and shuddered.

"Don't complain so much," Cam told her with a grin. "You need that sugar and caffeine about now."

"Sugar and caffeine are bad for you."

"Not that bad." He indicated the cup. "Drink up. One cup won't kill you."

He watched with a smile as she drank. Mickie studied him, in turn. There was something different about him tonight, and after a moment's consideration she identified it. He was relaxed. For the first time since she'd seen him unconscious on that gurney he was completely relaxed.

She drank again and found that the too-sweet coffee did make her feel better, however unhealthy it might be. "You're right about this. Thanks. I think it's waking me up a little."

"I probably should have looked for some champagne instead." he grinned. "It's more appropriate to a celebration."

"Appropriate, maybe, but not mandatory." Mickie held out her mug. "To the capture of our friend Morales!"

"Hear, hear!" Cam tapped his mug against hers, and they drank. "And to the end of the waiting and hiding and looking over my shoulder!"

"Hear, hear!" Mickie echoed the toast, then leaned back in her chair. Her empty mug was cradled in her hands, her fingers cupping the warm stoneware. She studied Cam from beneath the shield of her lashes for a moment, then looked directly at him. "You're different."

"Don't tell me!" He looked across the table at her, wide-eyed in mock horror. "I've grown one big eye in the middle of my forehead! The shame of it all!"

Mickie gave an inelegant snort of laughter, astonished at the change in him. "That's what I mean. You're relaxed. I never knew that relaxation would turn you into a nut, though!''

"I've always been a nut. It's a requirement for being a writer, didn't you know?''

"Well, strange as it is, it becomes you.''

"You're too kind.'' He fluttered his eyelashes at her, and she laughed aloud in spite of herself. "You're right, though. I do feel relaxed, maybe for the first time since I made the decision to go to San Miguel last year. I'd forgotten how good relaxation feels.'' He stretched his arms over his head, then spread them wide, as if to fill the room with his presence. "I can go out in public; I can show my face without being afraid of who might see me. I'm free!'' He swung his hands down to slap the tabletop. "Do you realize that, Mickie? I'm free!''

"I know it.'' She smiled. "I know how good that must feel. Are they absolutely certain that this is it? Was there anyone else working with Morales?''

"They're about as sure as they can be that he's been working alone.''

"So this is really the end of it?''

"This is the end. The end of a nightmare.''

"I'm glad. I find it kind of hard to believe, though, after so long.''

"Well, you can believe it. From what little Morales said, they were never certain that I was really a threat to them. Apparently he came on his own, and now that he's been caught he's sure they're just going to write him off as the *estupido* who went off on a wild-goose chase and got himself caught by the INS police.''

"The INS? What does Immigration have to do with this?''

"That will be the story they release—that he was arrested by the immigration people for being in the country illegally and carrying a weapon.''

"Will the other guerrillas believe that?"

"It'll work. The INS has a pretty formidable reputation in Latin America. It will verify my cover as nothing more than a dumb tourist, too. Someone who was in the wrong place at the wrong time."

"So they won't try to come after you anymore? I'm so glad! I was worried that they might try again."

"Yeah, that thought had occurred to me, too. I know something else you'll be glad to hear."

"What's that?" It was unreasonable, but Mickie felt a cold, formless dread descend on her.

"I'll be out of your hair soon. Lewis is making travel arrangements for me. I'll be out of here as soon as my reservations are set."

"Oh." The formless dread congealed into a heavy knot. "Uh . . . when will that be?"

"Tomorrow." He confirmed her worst fears with a smile. "Tomorrow night at the latest."

Mickie managed to smile back and make some unconcerned comment about his plans, while all the time something inside her was shattering, leaving only a numb emptiness behind.

"He told me he'd be gone as soon as possible."

"And he did just as he promised, didn't he?"

"Oh, yes. He was gone before noon."

"Efficient man."

"Hmm."

Connie propped her elbows on the cafeteria table, rested her chin on her linked hands and gazed across the green Formica at Mickie, exasperated. "Would you like to know what your problem is, Dr. Blake?"

Mickie shrugged apathetically. "I've either repressed a deep trauma from my childhood, or my shoes are too tight. You tell me."

Connie leaned over and looked under the table, subjecting Mickie's worn running shoes to a critical scrutiny. "It's not your shoes—not *those* shoes, at any rate."

"So, Dr. Freud?"

"Your problem is that you got what you wanted."

"Huh?"

"More than once you told me you wished he would just get out of your life and leave you alone. Haven't you ever heard that you should be careful what you wish for, because you just might get it?"

"Cute, Connie. Very droll. The trouble with that theory is that half the time I wanted him to go, and half the time I wanted him to stay, and half the time I didn't know *what* I wanted!"

"You have too many halves in there," Connie pointed out, but Mickie only shrugged.

Connie watched her carefully. She had insisted that they share Monday morning coffee because she was worried by the dull apathy that had gripped Mickie in the week since Cam had left. Mickie had occasional down moods just like anyone else, and in the years that they'd been friends Connie had tried to help her through them. She had grieved with Mickie when her parents were killed, but she had never seen her so lifeless, so lost. It was as if Cam had taken the center of her with him when he left, leaving behind only an empty shell.

"Mickie?" she said quietly.

"Yes?"

"Why did you let him go?"

Mickie shifted in her chair and shook her head angrily. "What kind of question is that?" she demanded. "What was I supposed to do? Lock him in the closet and keep him prisoner? I didn't *let* him go, Connie. He went."

"He went because he thought that was what you wanted him to do. There's a difference."

"Well, if there *is* a difference I can't see it!" Mickie snapped. "He only stayed as long as he did because he wanted to finish this job and tie up the loose ends."

"The loose ends being Morales and whoever might have been working with him?"

"Exactly. That's the only reason he stayed after—"

"After you asked him to leave," Connie interrupted. "After you found out who he really was and ordered him out of your house."

"*And* after he had accused me of trying to trap him like some kind of prize! After he implied that I was using sinister feminine wiles to force him into a commitment he didn't want to make! It's not like I booted him out into the cold when he was dying to stay, you know. He wanted to go."

"You're so sure of that, aren't you?"

"Connie, he said those things to me! Of course I'm sure."

"Well, I'm not. I'm not sure at all. I have to admit that everything about this situation has me pretty confused right now. I think that man cares about you, though, Mickie. I think he cares an awful lot about you."

"Oh, do you really?" Mickie asked with heavy sarcasm. "I thought you didn't even like him, Connie! Why are you so concerned about his leaving all of a sudden?"

"Because you're hurting. All right, I was suspicious of his motives. I still am, a little. I thought you ought to find out enough about him to know what you would be getting into if you asked him to stay. I never meant that you ought to make yourself a human sacrifice to your pride."

"Is *that* what you think I'm doing?" Mickie was offended by the idea, but Connie was certain.

She nodded firmly. "I do. You wish that he'd stayed. You didn't want him to go; you want to be with him. The only reason I can see for you to make yourself miserable like this is pride. Think about it. If you could go after him, if you could ask him to come back and know that he'd jump at the chance, you would, wouldn't you?''

"Of course not!" Mickie's response was quick and vehement. "I couldn't go after him and *beg* him to come back!"

"Because you're afraid he'd turn you down and then your *pride* would be dented." Connie laid an exasperated emphasis on the word. "Oh, that's sensible, all right. That's a great reason for making both of you miserable, Mick."

"Always assuming that he's miserable." Mickie was willing to concede that *she* was miserable. There wasn't much point in denying it.

"Mickie, he cares about you," Connie repeated. "I've seen the two of you together, seen the way he looks at you. He cares about you."

"Then why did he leave? If he cares about me so much, why was he in such a hurry to get away from me?"

"Because you told him to go," Connie replied quietly. "He did what he thought you wanted him to do."

Chapter 15

Mickie leaned her elbows on the kitchen table, a forgotten cup of cooling coffee clasped between her hands. What Connie had said was true. She had told him to leave, and he had gone. She had told him that her love for Mark James had died when she learned that Mark James didn't exist, and he had believed her.

Now she had to tell him the truth.

She looked across the room at the telephone. It would be easy enough. All she had to do was lift the receiver and dial eleven numbers. His card was right there, in the little teakwood file box, where he had left it. Why? Had he wanted her to call? It would be easy enough to make the call, so easy. The telephone crouched balefully by her answering machine, waiting to see if she had the courage to tell him the truth.

She did. Mickie set her cup sharply down on the table, slopping cold coffee onto the scrubbed surface. She walked

over to the telephone table, then stopped. Could she really
do this?

The clock on the wall ticked loudly. Mickie looked up at
it and groaned aloud. She had forgotten about the time difference between the coasts. It was early evening in California, but if she waited any longer it would be too late to call
Connecticut.

She could stall just a little, a cowardly imp inside reminded her. She could wait, just fifteen minutes or so, and
then it would be too late, and the call would be postponed.
And she might never work up the nerve to make it.

For a cowardly moment she wondered if that would really
be so horrible. Could it be any more painful to let Cam go
without ever telling him the truth? Would that hurt more
than to tell him that she loved him and have that love thrown
back in her face?

She didn't know the answer to that. She knew, though,
that she couldn't just hide away like a terrified child, protecting her emotions so well that they eventually atrophied,
leaving her no more than an empty shell of a woman. She
took a deep breath, staring at the phone. It stared back at
her, impassive and unhelpful.

Her hand trembled a little with the heavy pounding of her
heart as she reached out. The receiver clattered against the
instrument until she lifted it free. Carefully, reading them
under her breath, Mickie punched out the numbers. The
phone rang once, twice, three times....

"Hello?" The voice was a woman's, and Mickie nearly
hung up before the voice added, "Mr. King's residence."

"Uh...hello." Mickie fervently wished that she didn't
sound so breathless and confused. "I'd like to...speak to
Ca—to Mr. King, please."

"I'm sorry, miss." The voice was blandly polite and could
have been any age, from young to old. "Mr. King is not in
at this time."

"Oh." Mickie had never considered the fact that he might not be at home. And where was he, anyway, at almost eleven o'clock at night? Out? With a woman? "Oh. Well, when do you expect him?"

"I couldn't say, miss." Young or old, the woman wasn't particularly helpful.

"May I leave a message?" Mickie asked carefully.

"Mr. King has been out of town for several days. He didn't say when he planned to return. If you would like to leave a number, I will see that he gets it."

"Thank you," Mickie replied tightly. "This is Dr. Blake, in San Diego. My number is 619-555-9049. Would you have him contact me when he returns?"

"Of course, Doctor!" The mention of her title had wrought a marvelous change in the woman's manner. "I'll make certain he gets the message. There's nothing wrong with Mr. King, is there?"

"Not that I know of. If you would give him my number, I would appreciate it."

"Of course!" Her cooperative agreement was almost too enthusiastic. They finished the conversation in a flurry of mutual courtesies.

When Mickie finally extricated herself from the conversation she hung up carefully, laid her hands on the desktop and sat immobile, staring at the telephone for several seconds. She'd done it. She had gathered up all the scraps of her courage and telephoned Cam, prepared to make the most difficult admission and apology of her life. She'd done it, and for what?

For nothing. She had tried and failed. And she couldn't even console herself with the thought that she could try again tomorrow, because the odds were he would not be at home then, either. He'd described the way he worked to her, traveling to remote areas of the world to do his research, then sequestering himself in an anonymous little hotel, or living like a hermit in a Canadian cabin while he wrote. He might be away from home for weeks, even months. It could be months before she had a chance to tell him the truth. It could be too late.

She shook her head tiredly and dropped it onto her hands. The tears started slowly, with a sniffle, then a sob. Beside her, Sam whined, pawing at her leg and nudging her arm in concern as she cried as if her heart would break.

Mickie awakened grudgingly, reluctant to face the day. Her throat was raw, her eyes gritty from tears. She rolled slowly onto her back, aching in every bone, pulling a tangle of crumpled sheets with her. Sleep, such as it was, had come to her very late, and it had been restless and disturbed by vivid nightmares of seeking and loss. She squinted her eyes to peer at the window, then shut them tight against the glare. The sun was already high, so it must be very late.

It was. A few minutes later she tried again, rolling over to peer at her clock, and discovered that it was nearly eleven.

"Oh, boy," she groaned and rolled back, draping an arm over her eyes. "Thank God this is my day off."

It was just as well, she decided, when she greeted her reflection in the bathroom mirror. She had to wince and look away. The way she looked this morning, she'd probably have scared the patients to death! The blotchy-faced, red-eyed apparition in the mirror was not a pretty sight.

A splash of cold water helped her swollen eyes, a touch of makeup helped her blotchy face, a long shower and a shampoo helped generally, but nothing could ease the ache inside her. She knew she couldn't have dealt with patients and co-workers today, but twenty-four hours of idleness loomed emptily before her.

She dragged on a pair of jeans and a T-shirt Connie had given her, emblazoned with an enormous syringe. It was too tight, but it was the first thing she found in her drawer. Sam followed her as she plodded to the kitchen, watching with large liquid eyes as she filled the coffeemaker. Mickie pushed the basket into place and reached down to pat his head.

"Thanks for worrying, pal, but there's nothing you can do about this." Sam whined and licked her hand, and Mickie gave his ears a quick rub.

Force of habit moved her mechanically through her morning routine, and it sent her to bring in the paper, though she wasn't especially interested in the day's news. She had to squint against the brilliant noonday glare, which almost blinded her as she opened the door.

To her dismay the breeze had gotten to the paper first, scattering sections of it around the porch. Mickie bent from the waist and moved around the porch in that odd posture, shuffling the pages and sections back together. She captured the entertainment section by stepping on it when a stray puff of wind threatened to send it flying.

"Gotcha!" She folded it together again and added it to the stack. "That's all of it, then."

She pushed the paper into a messy pile and picked it up. As she straightened she looked out at the yard and drive for the first time. The newspaper dropped from her nerveless hands and the wind caught the sheets, sending them fluttering unheeded across the yard. Mickie stood and stared at the apparition in front of her.

It wasn't real, of course. It was obviously just the product of an overactive imagination and unfulfilled longings, combined with a night of abbreviated and restless sleep. She closed her eyes, shook her head to clear it and looked at the hallucination again.

It was still there.

An extremely dirty Mercedes sedan was parked under her portico. It had Connecticut license plates. There was a man in the car, slumped over the steering wheel, asleep. Mickie stared, but the apparition didn't waver or disappear. The only movement was the flapping of a sheet of newspaper caught on a hibiscus in the yard. After several moments Mickie stepped carefully down to the drive.

She walked around the car to the driver's side, trailing a fingertip across the hood. It was real, all right; her finger got dirty. She rubbed the dust off on the seat of her jeans as she stood looking in the driver's window.

Cam was deeply asleep. His arms were crossed on the steering wheel, forming a pillow for his head. His breathing was slow and regular. She bent to look more closely at his face and could see that he had gone beyond tired to exhaustion. His face was gray beneath a light coat of road dust, and his body slumped awkwardly in the seat, as if he'd fallen asleep the moment he stopped the car.

How far had he driven? she wondered, and then realized that she already knew the answer. He'd driven from Connecticut, some three thousand miles away. How long had he taken for the trip? Six days, or five, or three? He must have pushed himself beyond the point of fatigue. Beyond the point of prudence, too, she thought with a spurt of anger. He had no right to endanger his health this way, to drive cross-country alone, with a full-leg cast wedged into the car.

But he'd done it. Her anger began to fade into a sense of wonder. Cam was actually sitting there, in her driveway. For long seconds she drank in the sight of him as a thirsty man drinks cool water. It was difficult to absorb the realization that he was actually there, in that car, so wonderfully real.

He shifted in his sleep, mumbling, and his head rolled sideways into what looked like an acutely uncomfortable position. If he slept like that he'd never be able to hold his head erect again.

"Cam?" She reached in to touch his shoulder. He was definitely real. She could feel the strength of firm muscle, the warmth of his skin through the thin cotton shirt. He sighed, but slept on. She shook his shoulder gently. "Cam?"

"Huh?"

He came awake with a jerk, starting violently and staring up at her with sleep-blurred eyes. He blinked and his eyes cleared, widening and then narrowing on her, focused on her face. Carefully he reached up to touch her cheek, her hair, with a butterfly-light caress. His hand slipped over her hair and around her nape, and with the lightest pressure he drew her face down to his.

Their lips met in a kiss that convinced her of Cam's reality as nothing else could. It went on and on, warm and sweet and vitally alive. He tasted her lips, sampling delicately, tracing their outline with the tip of his tongue until she hungered for more. Mickie whispered an incoherent plea, and he gave in, increasing the pressure on her nape to crush her mouth against his as he drank greedily of her. Mickie had been dying for that kiss, starving for it, and she lost herself for endless moments in the only reality she knew or needed. When it ended and their lips parted at last she was too breathless to speak.

"Can you—can you help me out of here?" Cam asked, his voice oddly husky. Mickie nodded mute acquiescence, opening the door for him and helping him lever himself out of the car. "The crutches are in the back."

"Oh . . . yeah." Mickie's voice was a croak of sound, but at least she had spoken. She pulled the crutches and a battered canvas flight bag from the back seat and closed the door with a swing of her hip.

Cam followed the movement with appreciative eyes, and Mickie caught him watching when she turned to hand him the crutches. His gaze lifted from her lips, lingering on the front of the too-snug T-shirt, then moved to her face. She felt her cheeks warm.

"Here." She shoved the crutches at him.

"Thanks." He stuck them under his arms and then hesitated. "Uh... I didn't ask. Can I come in for a minute? For a cup of coffee, maybe?"

"Yes, of course."

Carrying his bag, Mickie led him up the steps and into the house. Her mind was a blank. She didn't understand why he was there; she didn't know what she was going to say or do, or what was about to happen. She could deal only with the banalities of inviting a guest into her home, serving him coffee, offering him breakfast.

He declined that. "I'm not really hungry, thank you. Coffee sounds good, though."

"Okay." Mickie looked at him; he was sagging on his crutches as he waited for her to close the door. He shifted his weight and winced when his leg hurt him. "Why don't you go into the living room?" she offered. "You'll be more comfortable in there. You can prop your leg up. It's swollen, isn't it?"

"Must be. I guess all that sitting in the car made it swell."

"It will do that. Sit down and keep the leg elevated. The swelling should go down in a few hours. I'll bring the coffee in."

"Thank you. That sounds great."

When Mickie saw that he could slide the ottoman over to the sofa without her assistance, she went to pour their coffee. She took two minutes to thaw some frozen bagels in the microwave. He was probably hungrier than he realized, and the sight of food might pique his appetite. She added butter, jam and cream cheese to the breakfast try, lifted it carefully and returned to the living room.

Once again she was too late. Cam had settled himself comfortably on the sofa, his legs propped on the fat leather ottoman, a soft pillow behind his head...and fallen asleep. Mickie looked down at him and smiled in spite of herself.

She didn't have the heart to wake him. The questions and answers could wait until he had rested.

She set the tray aside and carefully lifted his legs to the sofa, bracing the cast securely with some pillows before adjusting the one under his head. He muttered in his sleep, and she paused until he relaxed again, then covered him with a light afghan, and adjusted the blinds to shut out the brilliant sun. Then she quietly left him.

He might need sleep more than food, but her appetite had been reborn. She applied herself to the bagels, sharing them with an appreciative Sam, whose eclectic tastes encompassed just about everything from Alpo to zucchini.

Why on earth had Cam driven cross-country in order to come back? Certainly it would have been easier, to say nothing of safer, to travel by air. But why had he come at all? What was he going to say to her when he finally awakened? And what on earth was she going to say to him?

And why had he kissed her?

At six o'clock that evening Mickie still had no answers.

What she had were some strong suspicions, too wonderful, perhaps, to be true, and a bubbling sense of excited anticipation. There was one obvious reason for Cam to come back, of course, but she couldn't allow herself even to think it, because it would be too terrible if she were wrong.

Rather than give herself time to think, Mickie had expended a surplus of nervous energy by cleaning the kitchen until it sparkled and using nearly every one of her myriad appliances to create a sumptuous dinner.

Sam let her know that Cam was finally waking. He had taken up a position by the sofa shortly after Cam fell asleep and had remained there, patiently watchful, all afternoon. When he padded into the kitchen, panting happily, Mickie knew what the message was.

"He's up, is he?"

Sam wagged his whole rear half, grinning up at her. She stroked his ears and went to see Cam. He was sitting up, rubbing the heavy growth of stubble on his chin. He grimaced when he saw her.

"I haven't exactly been an Emily Post kind of guest today, have I?"

"I don't know," Mickie said with a grin and a shrug. "I'm not sure Emily Post covers flaking out on the couch. Maybe there aren't any rules against it."

"There should be." He took his crutches and pushed himself to his feet. The room seemed to shrink around them, dominated by his presence. "I didn't mean to do that, you know."

"Don't worry about it. You were tired, and you needed to rest."

"I still shouldn't have done it on your couch." He sniffed the air appreciatively. "What's that fabulous smell?"

"Dinner. Are you hungry?"

"Starving. I feel pretty grubby, though. Is there time for me to shower and shave before we eat?"

"Of course. I put your bag in your room." Only after she said it did Mickie realize how that sounded. "I'll be in the kitchen," she added awkwardly, and turned away.

"Mickie?"

"Yes?" She paused, her back to him.

"Do you want me to go?" There was a moment of silence. "If you do, just say so, and I will."

"No, that's all right." She turned to face him again, but she couldn't meet his eyes. "You need to eat. Just go get cleaned up. Dinner will be ready when you are."

He went without further protest and rejoined her sooner than she'd expected. "Whatever that is, it still smells great."

Mickie turned from the sink, where she was cleaning mushrooms for the salad. He was beautiful, and she wanted nothing more than to gaze at him, to feast her eyes on him.

His skin was a healthy color, now that he'd slept, his face freshly shaved, his eyes alert. His hair was still damp from the shower, neatly combed and glossy black, and everything about him was vital and alive and male. The muscles of his arms and shoulders rippled beneath the white knit polo shirt he had put on, flexing with the effort of maneuvering his crutches.

"It's just roast chicken," she replied after a moment's pause. "Nothing very fancy. I knew you liked it."

"I love it. Is there anything I can do?"

"Just sit down and eat."

Cam sat, watching Mickie move around the room. She had changed into linen slacks and a wide-shouldered, short-sleeved silk blouse which gave her a forties, Kate Hepburn look. The slacks were cream colored, the blouse a shimmering jewel green against which her skin glowed with a peachy radiance. He could have watched her for hours, enjoying the deft movements of her hands as she assembled the salad, the grace of her slim, strong body, the gentle, unconscious swing of her hips as she moved to the beat of the kitchen radio.

He felt the familiar warming of his body, the beginnings of the ache that had accompanied every thought of her since the day he'd left this house. The hardest thing he had ever done was to leave her that day, but he'd had no choice. She had told him that she wanted him to leave on the evening she'd learned his true identity, and she had never said anything to contradict that demand. And so he'd left.

He had allowed Lewis to make the plans, flying him in solitary and anonymous splendor from San Diego to Fort Knox on a military transport. He had purchased a ticket in his own name from Louisville to the Hartford-Springfield airport. If asked, he'd been instructed to say he'd been in Kentucky and Tennessee researching a new book. Cam had no idea what he had supposedly spent a year studying in

Kentucky and Tennessee, but he was perfectly willing to go along with the program Lewis had laid out. He didn't care.

He didn't care about anything if that lovely, exciting, infuriating woman wasn't a part of it. And so he had come back. With no idea of the reception she'd given him, he had driven up to her house in the dead of night and then fallen asleep in the car because he hadn't the gall to awaken her at five AM. He smothered a groan. He'd wanted to present himself in a good light, not have her discover him slouched over his steering wheel like a vagrant.

"Here you are." She set a plate of chicken in front of him, and a basket of bread in the center of the table. "Would you pour the wine?" Cam filled their glasses with the wine she had uncorked, while Mickie served herself and took a chair opposite him.

"This is great," he mumbled around his first mouthful. "Really good." *And aren't you the sparkling conversationalist, Mr. King?* he asked in silent self-disgust. *Good God, he couldn't even talk to the woman! She must think he was a total idiot.*

Her reply was a simple, "Thank you," so he couldn't tell if she considered him idiotic or not. He could think of nothing more to say, and Mickie seemed equally disinclined to make conversation. They ate in an awkward silence, broken only by "More bread?" and "Thank you," and the like.

"Would you like some ice cream? I don't really have anything else for dessert." Mickie rose and carried their empty plates to the sink.

"No, thanks. Coffee is fine." Cam handed her the rest of the dishes as she reached for them. She poured coffee into a server and brought it to the table.

"Thank you. The meal was very good. I've had too much junk food in the last few days."

"I imagine you have." Mickie's voice was quiet as she poured coffee and added cream to her own, but her eyes were angry, the first emotion she'd shown him. "Where have you been for the last few days, Cam?"

Here it is, he thought, watching the anger flicker across her face. "I've been traveling."

"Mm-hm. I gather you drove all the way from Connecticut?"

"Yes, I did."

"How is your leg?" Mickie asked, controlling her voice with an effort. The physician in her was outraged at the risk he had taken. "You've had some swelling. Have you had any numbness, any pain?"

"It feels fine. I didn't have any problems making the drive. The doctor I saw in Connecticut thought you did a great job, by the way."

"Terrific," Mickie clipped out, losing the battle with her anger. "And did your doctor in Connecticut also tell you that you should try to drive over three thousand miles with one leg in a cast?" Her voice began to rise. "Did he tell you anything about blood clots from sitting too long in one position, or about the strain of making a drive like that when you aren't fully recovered? What on earth possessed you to pull a stupid stunt like that, anyway? Don't you have any sense at all?"

Cam just smiled. "I guess I managed to break the ice." His placid observation was just enough to deflate the balloon of her righteous indignation.

She stared at him for a moment, then began to giggle. "You're nuts, do you know that?"

"So I've been told," he replied equably. "It never worried me much."

"Maybe it should have," Mickie replied tartly. "You took an awfully big risk doing this."

"Possibly. It was something I had to do, though."

"But *why*?"

"I had to see you."

Mickie's eyebrows lifted, but she kept her voice level. "The last time I checked there were still planes flying from Connecticut to California."

"I assume there still are, but I had something to prove to myself."

Mickie said nothing, but the unspoken question hung in the air between them. He nodded.

"I had to prove to myself that I'm not an invalid any longer. Sure, I still have a cast, and I know I'll have a cane after the cast is gone, but I had to see."

"See what?" Mickie was confused.

"I had to see if I was still an invalid. I'm not an invalid if I can take care of myself."

"I doubt that you really had to drive cross-country to prove you can take care of yourself. There must be a less extreme test than that. You could clean a bathroom or something, you know."

"It isn't the same, Mickie." Cam was amused.

"I suppose not, but it's safer," she replied dryly. "Anyway, you're only an invalid if you let yourself be one." Mickie smiled. "By that criterion you weren't an invalid even when you were dopey from pain pills and tied to a traction frame. I was never sure that you wouldn't just decide to quit listening to my 'doctor's orders' one day, unhook your traction weights and take off."

"Oh, no, I wouldn't have done that." He grinned. "I was too scared of you."

"Fat chance! You've never been scared of anything in your life."

His grin faded. "Yes, I have been," he said quietly, gravely. "I thought I'd die of fright when I saw that gun pointed at your head. I never want to feel that way again."

Mickie gazed across the table at him. "Oh." Her voice was a tiny thread of sound.

"I've spent the last week terrified, too."

"Terrified of what?" Mickie stiffened in her chair as an awful thought occurred to her. "Oh, my God, is it the guerrillas? Are they still trying to get to you? Are you still in danger?"

"No, no, that's not it!" He reached across the table to capture her hands in his. "The threat to me is over now. Lewis believes that, too, and he's as suspicious and paranoid as they come. My friend is out of San Miguel and I'm in no danger."

"Are you sure?" Mickie clutched tightly at his fingers. "They found you here once, they could find you—"

"It's over, Mickie; it really is. I promise you that."

"You're certain?" Her eyes were wide and fearful.

"I'm sure. Really."

His reassurance was firm, his eyes clear and candid. After a moment Mickie nodded in acceptance. She carefully extracted her hands from his and folded them on the table before her.

Her eyes were level and steady, fixed on his face. "Then what is it, Cam? You aren't a man to be easily terrified. What are you so afraid of?"

Chapter 16

He met her eyes for a few seconds; then his gaze slid away. He seemed ill at lease, oddly so, as if searching for the words to say. He shrugged, his heavy shoulders stretching the thin fabric of his shirt.

"Maybe 'terrified' is the wrong word," he said after a moment. "I meant—"

"You meant 'terrified,'" Mickie interrupted him. "You used that word. You didn't pick it out of the air, Cam; you meant it. Why?"

He shot her a quick glance. His uneasiness was evident, and contagious. It was obvious that he was uncomfortable, but Mickie had to press him. She had to hear him say it.

"I did use the word, but I don't know if it really applies. I may be making too big a thing out of this, and I don't know if I can make you understand, now that..."

"Cam, wait a minute! You aren't making any sense!"

"Don't you think I know that?" He shoved himself to his feet, tried to pace, and found it impossible while he was dragging the burden of his cast. "Damn it, I wanted to make sense!" He slammed his fist on the tabletop. "I wanted to make sense. I wanted to tell you everything logically and sensibly, and instead I'm babbling like a bloody idiot!"

"I don't want to make you babble, Cam. I just want to understand!" Mickie was standing, too, facing him across the table, her palms planted flat on the scrubbed oak. "I just want to understand," she finished quietly.

"I just want to..." He looked into her eyes, and his voice trailed away. He lifted one hand to touch her cheek very lightly, then slid his fingers into the curls at the nape of her neck, cupping her skull in his palm. His lips tightened.

"I want *this*!" he growled low in his throat as he pulled her toward him, crushing his mouth onto hers.

Caught by surprise, off balance, Mickie was barely able to stand, but she didn't care. She had been waiting for this all afternoon. She grasped his wrist with one hand, kept the other planted on the tabletop, and gave herself up to the kiss. It went on and on, warm and searching, teasing and tasting, and somehow, without conscious effort, Mickie moved around the table and into Cam's arms.

He propped himself back against the heavy table and pulled Mickie in to stand between his legs. She wrapped her arms around his neck and let herself melt into the protective curve of his body, savoring the bulk and strength and warmth of him, the hard muscles of his good thigh against her leg, the heavy planes of his chest against her breasts.

His hands moved tentatively at first, tracing warm circles over her back, then sliding down to tug her shirttail free of her slacks. His palms were warm and slightly rough against the satin skin of her back, and Mickie shivered a little at the sweetly erotic sensation. With a little wriggle she snuggled even closer to Cam and felt a deep, feminine thrill at his quickly indrawn breath. Her hands sought and found the open neck of his shirt, and she slipped her fingers inside to caress his throat and brush over the crisp hair that curled on his chest.

He tensed, and she laughed softly against his mouth, then slid her lips along his jawline to nip at his ear. He bore it for a moment, then took her chin in a hard grasp and brought her mouth back to his.

This time it was Mickie who gasped at the barely controlled violence, the passion and hunger and near fury, of the kiss. He devoured her, held her imprisoned within the steel bands of his arms as he took his fill of her mouth.

"Oh, God!" he groaned as he tore his lips from hers at last. He tucked her head into the curve of his shoulder, wrapped his arms around her and held her close, rocking her gently in his arms. "I'm sorry, Mickie," he murmured against her hair. "I'm so sorry."

She shook her head, a small smile curving her lips. "Don't apologize. I told you once before, that's not necessary."

He loosened his arms and set her slightly away from him. When Mickie would have clung to his shoulders he took her hands in his and brought them down in front of her. He looked at them, then turned her palms up and stroked the balls of his thumbs over the soft skin.

"I think it is necessary this time. I didn't mean to do that, not now." He looked up into her face, her eyes. "You're very beautiful."

She gave a snort. "Don't try that on me, Cam. I know better."

"You are."

"No, I'm not. Not with red hair and freckles! If anything, I look like a tall elf. All I need is a pointed hat and little green shoes."

He laughed at that in spite of himself. "Believe what you wish, Mickie Blake. I know the truth."

Mickie's smile faded as she looked into his eyes. "That's more than I know right now," she said quietly.

"Yeah." Cam shook his head. "I know." He looked down, studying her hands, avoiding her eyes.

"Tell me why you came back."

He shrugged.

"I have to know, Cam. Tell me why you came back."

"Don't you know?" He raised his head, looking into her eyes again.

Mickie shook her head. "You have to tell me."

"I came back because I had no choice. I couldn't say goodbye to you for the last time without telling you that I love you."

For a moment Mickie couldn't breathe. Her lips trembled as she gazed up at him, free at last to let the love show in her eyes. Carefully she took her hands from his and reached up to caress his face. "You love me?" The question was a breathless whisper.

"For so long." He slid his arms around her, linking his hands behind her waist. "Much longer than I was willing to admit to myself."

"Me too," she whispered.

"You too what?"

She tipped her head back to look in to his eyes. "I love you, Cameron King. Even when I said I didn't, I still did."

"I love you, Michael Blake." He laughed softly. "I never thought I'd be saying, 'I love you, Michael.'"

"Does it bother you? My name?" She toyed with the hair that waved over his collar, and smiled up at him from beneath her lashes.

His arms tightened to bring her more closely against him. "Any name that had you for an owner would be the most beautiful name in the world."

Mickie felt herself blush and dropped her head to rest her forehead on his chest. "You're embarrassing me."

"I won't say I'm sorry. I intend to embarrass you with compliments all the time. And now I intend to kiss you." Which he did. Mickie clung to him like a rock in a stormy sea, returning his kiss with all the love and passion she had kept hidden for so long. She protested with a little wordless mutter when he finally set her away from him.

"We have to talk, Mickie."

His expression was sober, but she pouted up at him. "I don't want to talk. I want to kiss some more."

He gave a smothered laugh. "So do I, but we have to talk first." He gave her a little push toward her chair. "Sit down Mickie."

"But, Cam—"

"Please, Mickie. Sit down."

"Okay." She was watching his face, watching the emotions there, tightly controlled, but not quite hidden. She sat.

"I have to explain something to you, but I don't—" He broke off, flinging one hand out in an oddly helpless gesture. Cam, composed, self-assured Cam, struggled with what he had to say. "I don't know where to start, Mickie. I don't know how—"

"Why don't you just do it the easy way?" she suggested. "Hmm?"

"Start at the beginning, wherever that might be."

"Yeah." He shrugged, avoiding her eyes. "Makes sense. Start at the beginning." He folded his hands loosely on the table before him. "The beginning." He looked quickly up at her, something that might have been pleading in his eyes, then looked down at his hands again.

"I was always a loner, in a way. Always alone. There were people around, and my parents loved me, in their own way, but it was a detached sort of love. They were older than most parents when I was born, and I was...unexpected. They were busy with their lives and their friends, and they really didn't know what to do with a child. We were well-off—wealthy, I guess you'd say—and I had all the *things* I ever wanted, but for company I mostly had myself, myself and my imagination.''

Mickie sat very still. She could see what it cost him to tell her these things, things he had probably never said to anyone else. She didn't yet know why, but it was important to him that she hear them.

"I went to a boarding school, a good one. I was only a fair student, but I did well in sports. It was the same there, though, and later, at college. I wasn't accustomed to closeness, and it seemed like no one could get close to me anyway. It seemed like that was just the way things were for me. I had decided that I just wasn't capable of intimacy with people, or with one particular person. Not the kind of intimacy most people share with a friend, or a lover.'' He looked at her, quickly, then away. "Women always... God, I feel like a jerk saying this, Mickie!'' He took a deep breath before he continued, staring at his half-empty cup.

"Women always... wanted me. Maybe it was for my money, maybe for my looks, or later, when I began to have a certain amount of fame as a writer, maybe it was because of that, but they wanted me. Or, more accurately, they wanted what they thought I was. They never seemed to see below the surface, though, never seemed to see through me, into me. There was no closeness, no intimacy. I never missed it.'' He shook his head in weary self-deprecation. "I actually felt pretty smug about that, if you can believe it, because I was spared all the trauma. I never knew the pain of the betrayed friend, the rejected lover, and that made me feel just a bit superior.'' His lip curled in a self-directed sneer. "I was above the petty traumas of lesser mortals.''

He fell silent, and stayed that way for so long that Mickie wondered if he would go on. She held herself motionless, waiting, scarcely daring to breathe. When he suddenly broke the silence, he startled her.

"God, that was a stupid attitude to take!" he said harshly. "Stupid and conceited. I set myself up as somehow different from ordinary people, and for 'different' you can read 'better.' *I* wasn't dependent on anyone. *I* didn't need anyone. And I guess when you take a fall for a conceit like that, it's bound to be a hard one."

"And you took a fall?" Mickie whispered.

"Oh, yes. I took a fall, all right." He looked steadily across at Mickie. "I met a woman who seemed different from the rest. She was very beautiful, and she said she loved me, and I fell in love with her. I fell in love with love, too, with the idea that I could actually feel so much for another person. And then I learned the truth. I had opened doors to her that I had never opened to anyone, and when I found that it was the fame and the money that appealed to her, that she found me rather 'boring and immature,' I was devastated.

"I promised myself that I would never let another woman do that to me. I set up barriers so high and so strong that no woman would ever get past them again and make me dependent on her. I prided myself on that, and when I took another fall my first reaction was anger, at the woman and at myself."

Mickie waited, watching his averted face, his tensely folded hands. She hated to see him hurt this way, but it seemed he had to say these things, to make her understand.

"I took another fall, harder than the first, and I found out just how dependent I could be." He looked up into her eyes. "I had never needed anyone in my life, but I needed you. I needed a doctor with the skill and training to fix my leg, and I needed someone who would stand up to me in spite of my bad attitude and bad temper, someone I couldn't intimidate. I needed someone to care about me when I didn't care about myself. You were all those things.

"I have to apologize to you," he went on. "I was a rotten patient. I took my bad temper out on you in ways I can never justify, and then I imposed on you by staying here. I'm sorry I came to you under false pretenses, and I'm sorry I caused you pain. You have to know that I never wanted to hurt you."

"Not even when you were mad at me for using my deadly feminine wiles on you?"

"Oh, God!" He dropped his head into his hands. "I really said that, didn't I?"

"I'm afraid so," she said, her voice warmed by a smile. "Don't feel too bad, though. I wasn't exactly blameless, you know. Doctors aren't supposed to fall in love with their patients. You did warn me, do you remember? You tried to tell me not to get involved with you. I refused to listen."

"That was more than I deserved." Cam shook his head in weary self-disgust. "I didn't understand what a precious gift you gave when you told me you loved me. Instead of treating it with the care it deserved, I was defensive and afraid and I threw it back in your face. That was unforgivably cruel. I didn't recognize the treasure I might have had in your love until I had destroyed it. I swore to myself that if there were such a thing as a second chance—" he spoke slowly, not meeting her eyes—"I wouldn't make the same mistake. I would cherish that love as it deserved to be cherished. I was very wrong, Mickie."

"You weren't the only one who was wrong, Cam." She rose and walked around the table to him. He stood and took her in his arms. "Do you remember when I told you that I loved you?"

"Of course I do! How could I forget the cruel things I said to you then?"

"And do you remember when I told you that my love had died?"

He stood very still, gazing down into her eyes. "I remember," he replied quietly.

"I lied to you, Cam. I was hurt, my pride was hurt, and I wanted to hurt you in return." She took a deep breath, slightly shaky, and forced herself to go on. "Maybe I even believed it myself for a while; I don't know. I just struck back at you in the only way I could. I'm not proud of myself, Cam; it was a cruel and childish thing to do. I lied to you when I told you I had only loved Mark James. I loved the man, Cam. I love him, whatever his name."

The effervescent happiness singing in her veins was reflected in Mark's eyes. Like a million bottles of champagne it bubbled and fizzed and sparkled, lifting her onto her toes as she reached for his lips. He met the kiss almost shyly, with a tenderness that seemed to melt Mickie from the inside out. She had wanted him before, but there had always been a thread of insecurity to mar the beauty of their loving.

They had shared passion, but this time they would share love. And they would share it now. She was on fire, burning for him, and she knew she would explode if she had to wait another minute. She pulled his head down to her, pressing kisses to his chin, his cheekbone, the corner of his mouth.

"Cam?" she breathed as she nipped his earlobe. "Make love to me now? Please?"

He groaned, and his arms tightened around her. "Mickie, there are so many things we have to straighten out first."

"No." Her mouth moved to his throat, sweet and searching, laying a trail of temptation down to the collar of his shirt. She pushed that aside and touched her tongue-tip to the hollow of his collarbone. He caught his breath sharply, and she smiled against his skin. "That can wait. I can't."

Deliberately she leaned into him, brushing his body with hers, teasing, promising. She could feel his response, the tensing of his body, the sharp acceleration of his heartbeat. His hands began to move with a will of their own, stroking, sensing, remembering and rediscovering the curves and hollows of her body, the blood beating hot beneath her skin.

"Mickie, we really need to talk." The words were a strained whisper.

"Later." She slid her hands beneath the hem of his shirt and over the hard muscles of his abdomen. They contracted under her touch. "Make love to me now, Cam."

"Yes," he breathed raggedly. "Oh, God, yes!" He tightened his arms around her in a hungry embrace and lost his balance.

Mickie grabbed him around the waist, bracing him until he was steady again. "Come to the bedroom. Come with me."

It was warm there, and dimly lit, the air lightly scented by a bouquet of lemon blossoms on the dressing table. As before, the moonlight fell in a silver trail across the bed, and as before, they were silent, needing no words when a touch or a kiss could speak volumes.

They moved together to the bed, then stopped, standing beside it. Mickie reached up to touch Cam's face. She drew her finger lightly across his lips and sucked in a sharp breath when he caught her fingertip in his teeth. He braced himself against the side of the bed and drew her into his arms to press hot kisses over her face and along the slender column of her throat.

"I want to carry you in my arms," he murmured against her neck. "I want to carry you into this room and lay you on the bed." Mickie felt the world begin to whirl away from her and clutched Cam's shoulders for support. "I want to see you in the moonlight." He eased the collar of her blouse open, freeing one button and then another until he could slide the silk off her shoulders. "I want to undress you bit by bit." The blouse slipped off her arms and he tossed it aside. "And kiss every inch of you."

Mickie's hands were working quickly, pulling his shirt over his head, fumbling with the buckle of his belt until he helped her open it. She pushed him down onto the bed and knelt to ease the jeans over his cast. When she had pulled them free he caught her hands.

"Mickie." She looked up at him. "Come to me. Now."

Like a moth to a flame she went, sliding sinuously up his body to be wrapped in his embrace as he fell backward onto the mattress, taking her with him. She braced herself above him, dropping her head to kiss his mouth as he tugged at her peach silk teddy, lowering the straps and pushing the thin fabric down to her waist.

"You're beautiful," he whispered, gazing at her body. This time she didn't contradict him. He drew the backs of his fingers over the thin skin of her breasts, then shaped the soft globes with his palms, feeling her nipples tighten into taut buds. The passion and the wanting were growing in Mickie, building to a pleasure and a tension that were almost unbearable. She tormented him in turn, sliding her body over his in an invitation that was as old as time. Her breasts brushed his chest in a teasing caress; her legs slipped across his, smooth skin against crisp hair, and her body waited for him, warm and pliant and welcoming.

He caught her to him, closing his arms around her and ending the teasing. He grasped her waist in his hands and brought her to him to take her suddenly in an explosion of the need that had been building in them both for so many days, freeing all the passion and love they had been forced to hide. Mickie knew nothing but taste and touch and sensation, winding in an ever-tightening spiral that finally burst into light and color and sweet release.

They slept for a a time, exhausted, twined together in a tangle of bedclothes as the band of moonlight moved across them, marking the passage of time. Mickie opened her eyes to see Cam's, warm and dark and very near, gazing down at her. She tipped her chin up and kissed his lips.

"I love you, Cameron King. I tried to telephone you yesterday to tell you that."

"You tried to call?"

Mickie nodded, snuggling close against him. His hand slid up over her hip, and he curved his arm around her waist. "I called in the evening. A woman answered."

"Mrs. Crawford. The housekeeper."

"She said you'd been gone for several days. She didn't know where you were."

"I didn't tell her where I was going. Lots of times I don't. That way she doesn't have to lie for me."

"Oh. I wondered if she really didn't know, or if she was covering for you. I wondered who she was, too. When a woman answered I almost hung up."

She could feel him smile against her hair. "Were you jealous?"

"Mm-hm. I know I didn't have any right to be, but . . ."

"There are no rights you don't have where I'm concerned. You can be as jealous as you want."

"Maybe I won't want to be." Mickie leaned her head back to smile up at him.

"You won't?" Cam was comically dismayed.

"I won't have to be." She tapped his cheek lightly with her fingertip. "Because I trust you." She hesitated. "I can, can't I?"

He shook her lightly in mock-reproof. "To hell and back. Now that I've found you, I'm not going to risk losing you, Dr. Blake."

He tightened his embrace, seeking her lips for the kiss that would seal their future together. Their mouths met, parted for an instant, and then met again to cling in a kiss that seemed as if it would go on forever. It might have done that if Cam hadn't tried to hold Mickie even closer, tangling one hand in her hair and wrapping the other around her waist. He turned his body over hers, and his cast rolled painfully onto her leg.

"Ow!" Mickie pulled her mouth away from his and sat up to ease the heavy plaster off her leg.

"I'm sorry, Mickie! Are you okay?"

She nodded. "I'm all right now. That thing is heavier than I remembered, though." She came back into his arms, adjusting her position to his cast.

"Is it heavy enough for my doctor to consider taking it off? I don't think it would break my heart to be without it."

"You don't think you'd miss it if it was gone?"

He laughed against her hair. "Somehow I think I could get along without it. And just think how much easier certain things would be."

"Certain things?" Mickie asked in a flirtatious tone, and he laughed again.

"Don't play coy with me, Mickie. Certain things, like making love with you for hours and hours—"

"Stop it!" She covered his mouth with her hand. "You'll be tempting me to take it off too soon!"

"There's no such thing as 'too soon.'"

"Oh, yes, there is, and you'd better remember that! Your leg is going to get the best treatment I can provide, and if that means keeping the cast on, so be it."

"Yes, doctor!" He saluted, and Mickie poked him in the ribs.

"I'm not really such a drill sergeant, am I?"

"You told me yourself that you're a tough lady, but I wouldn't have you any other way." He pulled her close. "I love you, Mickie." He laughed. "I love you, and I never thought I would say that to another woman. I never thought I'd be capable of it."

"You're capable of anything, and you know it."

"I hope so. I hope I'm capable of marriage, because I want to marry you, Mickie."

She grinned. "Of course you do!"

"Then you'll marry me?"

"Yes."

He seemed surprised by her quick assent, and Mickie wondered if he'd planned some elaborate strategy to persuade her. There was no need. This was what she'd hardly allowed herself to hope for ever since she opened the front door to find him sleeping in her driveway.

"Of course I'll marry you." She didn't have it in her to pretend coyness or reluctance. "If you can stand to live with a doctor, I'll marry you tomorrow!"

"I can stand it. I won't mind living with this doctor at all." He nuzzled her neck and stroked her breast, and she gasped as her heartbeat quickened. "You might not like living with a writer, though," he murmured against her skin.

"I'm going to love living with this writer." Mickie pressed a kiss to the corner of his mouth. "I can't think of anything I'd like more."

"I can." Cam took her face in his hands, and with tenderness and sweetness and a passion that took her breath away, he began to love her again.

Mickie watched his face from beneath half-lowered lids. The open love she saw there was the promise of a future shared together. She smiled as her eyes fell closed, and she gave herself up to his lovemaking. She knew that the masquerade was ended at last.

AMERICAN TRIBUTE

Where a man's dreams count for more than his parentage...

Look for these upcoming titles under the Special Edition American Tribute banner.

LOVE'S HAUNTING REFRAIN
Ada Steward #289—February 1986
For thirty years a deep dark secret kept them apart—King Stockton made his millions while his wife, Amelia, held everything together. Now could they tell their secret, could they admit their love?

THIS LONG WINTER PAST
Jeanne Stephens #295—March 1986
Detective Cody Wakefield checked out Assistant District Attorney Liann McDowell, but only in his leisure time. For it was the danger of Cody's job that caused Liann to shy away.

AM-TRIB-1

Silhouette Special Edition

AMERICAN TRIBUTE

AMERICAN
TRIBUTE

RIGHT BEHIND THE RAIN
Elaine Camp #301—April 1986
The difficulty of coping with her brother's
death brought reporter Raleigh Torrence
to the office of Evan Younger, a police
psychologist. He helped her to deal with
her feelings and emotions, including love.

CHEROKEE FIRE
Gena Dalton #307—May 1986
It was Sabrina Dante's silver spoon that
Cherokee cowboy Jarod Redfeather couldn't
trust. The two lovers came from opposite
worlds, but Jarod's Indian heritage taught
them to overcome their differences.

NOBODY'S FOOL
Renee Roszel #313—June 1986
Everyone bet that Martin Dante and Cara
Torrence would get together. But Martin
wasn't putting any money down, and Cara
was out to prove that she was nobody's fool.

MISTY MORNINGS, MAGIC NIGHTS
Ada Steward #319—July 1986
The last thing Carole Stockton wanted was to
fall in love with another politician, especially
Donnelly Wakefield. But under a blanket of
secrecy, far from the campaign spotlights,
their love became a powerful force.

Silhouette Intimate Moments

COMING NEXT MONTH

MIDNIGHT RAINBOW
Linda Howard

Traipsing through the jungle one step ahead of terrorists was a strange situation for a confirmed cynic and an eternal optimist to fall in love, but Grant and Jane fought the odds and won each other.

PRICE ABOVE RUBIES
Mary Lynn Baxter

McKenzie Moore had learned to live a comfortable albeit unhappy life without Jeb Langley. But he was back now, and his presence shattered McKenzie's hard won calm as he strove to reclaim her heart.

THE ART OF DECEPTION
Nora Roberts

Adam was cool, calm and very discreet, an excellent spy. But he had never encountered anyone as beautiful or as eccentric as Kirby, and he soon found himself losing his cool—and his heart.

THE DI MEDICI BRIDE
Heather Graham Pozzessere

For Chris, the beauty of Venice began to fade when circumstances conspired and she found herself a permanent resident of the city, a target for murder—and married to a man she hardly knew.

AVAILABLE NOW:

CUTTER'S LADY
Kristin James

AGENT PROVOCATEUR
Lucy Hamilton

WHISPERS ON THE WIND
Jeanne Stephens

SEQUEL
Elizabeth Lowell